The Love in Art

RAYNA L. JOHNSON

NEWMAN SPRINGS PUBLISHING
320 Broad Street
Red Bank, NJ 07701

First originally published by Newman Springs Publishing 2020

ISBN 978-1-64801-446-8 (Paperback)
ISBN 978-1-64801-447-5 (Digital)

Printed in the United States of America

This is a story about a young woman! How she learns the true meaning of love and how to stand strong.

In the city of New York, young Krysta is in her last few minutes of high school. She's ready to graduate with both of her parents watching her walk across the stage. She smiles at them, they smile and wave at her. Krysta's life was smooth and happy, full of joy, till she meets her father's boss's son!

Chapter 1

Krysta has just finished her two years of college. Her parents died in a car accident, not that long after she finished high school. Krysta is 5'3" tall, slim body, smooth tan skin, long light-brown hair down her back but always up in a hair clip. With greenish-brown eyes. She works at a small coffee shop part-time. She is living with her boyfriend that her parents introduced her to before they died. His name is Ford, he's 6'3" tall, light skin, short black hair, and dark-brown eyes. He works for his father's company. But he is taking care of one of the companies in New York. Ford and Krysta have known each other for four years but been together for two years, she stayed with after her parents passing. She has no one else in her family alive; both of her parents were only children.

Even though she's with Ford, she has never been kissed nor touched. He has respected that, but Krysta doesn't think that. Something in her is telling her that something is off about his respect for her decision. In her mind, Ford is loyal but he's not. Every night, after her shift at the coffee shop, Krysta goes home and cooks. Krysta thinks her life is a good one, but at the same time, she can feel that something is missing from her life. Even though she has been with a man for two years, still there's something she's missing.

It comes to her one night at the shop she works at. A group of guys come into the shop late; one of the guys slowly walks to the back to the bathroom. As he's walking to the back, he and Krysta come face-to-face. They look at each other with a slight shock as they walk past each other. He's six feet and three inches tall, with tan smooth skin, slightly buff body, brown eyes, dark-brown hair. Slightly long, almost to his shoulders enough to have it in a ponytail. They walk past each other, still looking at each other, then their heads slowly turn.

Krysta's night shift goes on and the guy, with his friends, are still hanging around, laughing and still eating. After about two hours of hanging around and eating, they finally leave. Krysta goes over to clean the table off. She looks up and the same guy looks at her as he's walking out the door. Their eyes meet again; he smiles at her as he nods his head, saying thank you, then continues walking with his friends who start messing with him. Krysta gets a glowing full smile, then she slightly shakes her head ad goes back to work. As Krysta brings the plate to the back to get them cleaned, one of the work girls tells her that those guys work at the art building across the street from the shop and they come over to the shop whenever they work long hours.

A few nights later, as Krysta is just walking out the door from work, she comes face-to-face with that guy again from a few nights ago. They stop in front of each other.

"Okay… I know I don't know you very well… Well, I don't know you at all. But can I ask you a question?"

"Umm…okay," Krysta softly replies.

"I work across the street at the art building. And I was wondering if you could help me with one of the paintings I'm working on."

"I…um… I don't do—" Krysta slowly replies.

"It's not like that… I just need to paint your face. If it doesn't sound too weird."

Krysta stares at him for a minute, then she slightly smiles.

"Only if you at least tell me your name."

He slightly grins back at her.

"Okay, the name's Ty."

"Krysta."

They both slightly smile at each other, then Krysta agrees to help Ty. Even though she doesn't know him, she does have a soft spot for art.

"Okay, can you also show me some of the art?" Krysta softly asks.

"Yeah, sure," Ty replies.

"Okay…um…what time," asks Krysta.

"Um, how about Friday? Is 8:00 p.m. okay?" asks Ty.

"Yeah, my shift ends at 7:30 p.m.," Krysta answers.

"Okay, great. So I'll meet you at front of the shop," Ty says.

Krysta nods her head and smiles at him with a slight glow. Ty grins at her, then they say their good nights to one another and walk their opposite ways. Krysta walks home; as she walks into her apartment, the lights are out. But before she can turn, they go on and she quickly turns around. And there she sees Ford! Sitting on a chair.

"Ford," Krysta says in a slight panic.

"You're late! Where the hell have you been!" Ford slightly yells.

"I…was at work," Krysta softly replies.

Ford slowly stands up and walks over to her. He stands right in front of her, looking down at her.

"You are to walk through that door at 7:45 p.m., not 8:00–8:05 p.m. Do you hear me!" Ford slightly yells.

Krysta looks down and nods her head slowly.

"Now hurry up and cook dinner, I'm hungry," Ford demands.

Krysta walks over to the kitchen and begins to cook dinner. As she takes out the pans to cook dinner, she sees that her hands are shaking.

After Krysta finishes cooking, she and Ford are sitting at the table, eating. Not talking or saying anything to each other, not even looking at each other. The second Ford was done with his food, Krysta gets up quickly and takes his plate, even if she's not done with her food. She doesn't sit back down to finish her food. She just puts it all away and starts cleaning everything, the leftovers, she puts in Ford's lunch container. The rest of the night, Krysta just cleans the apartment while Ford just sits around on the phone or watch TV. Ford doesn't pay Krysta much mind but he doesn't like it when other people talk to her or pull her away from his side. As the night goes on, it's like always, it's quiet.

The next day at work, Krysta comes into work and one of her friends come running over to her. She's 5'4" tall, light skinned, dirty-blond hair down her back, light-brown eyes.

"Krysta."

"Sam, morning. Why are you running at me?" Krysta asks.

"So…what did you and that cute guy talk about at the end of your shift last night?" Sam asks.

Krysta looks at her, trying not to laugh at her face, but then Krysta tells Sam about the guy last night.

"Wow, so are you going to model for him?" Sam asks in excitement.

"I guess but—" Krysta says.

"What do you mean but? Krysta, this is great for you. You have a beautiful face and body. Why not use it…for a little something?" Sam says.

"But I said yes. But I didn't make sure that Ford was okay with it," Krysta says.

Sam stares at her for a minute,

"Are you kidding me?" Sam says.

"What?" Krysta softly says.

Sam looks at Krysta like she can't believe that Krysta needs permission to do things. She slowly shakes her head at her. Sam takes a breath, then she looks back at Krysta.

"Krysta, you are twenty-two years old. What the hell do you need to have his permission for?"

"Sam, he's my boyfriend. I need to make sure he's okay with it," Krysta replies.

"Krysta, he's not your husband. He doesn't even treat you like you're his girlfriend," Sam slightly yells.

"Yeah, he…does," Krysta softly says.

"Krysta, no, he doesn't. He treats you not like a girlfriend but a servant. You're his obsession, a picture that no one can see or touch. Krysta, he doesn't like that you are not always by his side. You can't be with any of your friends unless you are at work. Even then, you don't have any freedom. You have to go straight home after work. He does not need to know your every move, Krysta," Sam says.

Krysta just looks at her with guilt and sadness.

"You are going to model for that guy on Friday. And you are going to do it because you want to. So you tell him you have to work the night shift and go do something for yourself for once, okay, girl?" Sam says.

Krysta sheds a tear and nods her head at her with a small smile, then their boss tells them to get to work. They look at each other and slightly laugh, then they slowly get up and head over to the sections that they are working in.

*****

The days go by and Krysta thinks about what Sam said to her, about Ford and not doing things for herself. Those days Ty didn't come to the shop, Krysta was a little nervous, but she just keeps working. After her shift, Krysta goes home. Like always, Ford is not home so she goes right to making dinner. Ford comes home and sees that Krysta is cooking. He nods his head, then he goes to change his clothes for dinner. After about ten minutes, Ford comes out of his room and sees Krysta setting up the table. He walks to the table and Krysta pulls out his chair. Then she walks over to her chair and slowly sits down. They, like always, don't look at each other or talk to each other. But then, Krysta breaks the ice.

"Um… Ford."

Ford slowly lifts his head and looks at her.

"Um…this Friday. They want me to…work the night shift. But I can home an hour early to cook dinner and everything…before I go back," Krysta explains slowly.

Ford stares at her for a minute with a plain look on his face. He takes a deep breath.

"If dinner isn't ready by the time I get home," Ford pauses, "you can forget this little job of yours, understand?"

Krysta slowly nods her head, then slowly puts her head down. As she slowly puts her head down, she slightly smiles.

The next couple of days, Krysta has a little more energy than she usually has. Then comes Friday. Even though Ty still hasn't come to the shop, Krysta gets ready for their meeting time. She brought a change of clothes for after work, even though she will be going home early at first; she doesn't want to risk running into Ford. She works her shift, but an hour before her shift is over, Sam let Krysta use her car to get home to cook dinner and everything else she has to do before Ford gets home.

Krysta gets home thirty-five minutes before Ford. She cooks a garlic stir-fry chicken dinner quickly and easy to warm up after it's cooked. She looks at the time and smiles for Ford will not be home for another twenty minutes. She quickly sets the table for just him and writes a note, then she leaves. She gets back to the shop just in time—she has seven minutes before her meeting time with Ty. Sam sees her come back into the shop and she tells her to hurry up and change. Krysta gives her back her car keys and runs to the back to change. She comes out of the locker room and she's wearing skinny jeans with a black and white off-the-shoulder shirt, white Nike sneakers, her hair rolled up in a clip. She walks out of the shop and stands out front with an excited but nervous look on her face. But her face slowly begins to change to disappointment for she is still waiting for Ty after eight minutes. Sam sees her waiting for him and feels bad; she sees that she's about to walk away. Krysta is about to walk away, but then as she turns to her right, there is Ty. Ty is leaning against the pole with his hands in his pockets, grinning at her. She looks at him with shock.

"You didn't think that I forgot, did you?"

She slowly shakes her head no, making Ty slightly laugh under his breath.

He leans off the pole and walks over to her. They look at each other.

"You are so lying." Ty grins.

She slightly smiles, then they slowly walk across the street to the art building with Sam smiling as she watches Krysta walk across the street smiling. After they walk out of the elevator, Krysta gets a shocked look on her face, for she sees all this beautiful art everywhere. Ty turns and looks at her with slight shock to see that she has a little tears in her eyes.

"Are you okay?" Ty asks.

"I just never got to see such beautiful art before," Krysta replies.

He grins at her, then he watches her look at the art around the floor they are on. She looks at Ty who is grinning at her, making her get a slight shock on her face.

"Do you still want to look?" Ty asks.

"Can I?" Krysta asks with joy.

Ty looks at her with a grin but slight confusion.

"Yeah, go ahead."

She smiles with glowing joy, then she looks at the rest of the art with amazement, almost as if she's in a different world.

Meanwhile back at Krysta's apartment, Ford walks in later than he usually does and sees that dinner is on the table but no Krysta. He slightly glares at the room, then he walks over to the table.

Back at the art building, Ty and Krysta are walking down the hall to Ty's studio. They walk into the studio and Ty puts the lights on. Krysta looks at his paintings and seeing them makes her smiles at them, then she looks at him. He begins to set up his station so he can sketch Krysta. Then he sets up the area where he wants to sketch Krysta. He puts flowers all behind the seat and beside it. All the flowers are different; he looks at her for a minute. He walks over to her and gently puts his hand on her face. He just stares at her, then after a minute, he grins.

"Okay, come here," Ty says.

He takes Krysta's hand and gently pulls her over to the seat.

"Okay, sit here. Slightly tilt your head, put one hand slightly on the side of your face and your other arm across your lap. Okay, good. Stay like that," Ty says.

He walks over to his canvas and sits on the chair. He looks at Krysta for a minute before he does anything. He then takes his black charcoal Lyra Graphite Crayon Pencil, he slightly sharpens it then he slowly begins to sketch Krysta's face. Ty sketches her eyes and lips with glowing and deep passion; her face has a shine to it. But before he gets to her hair, he stops and looks at her for a second, causing

Krysta to look at him with slight confusion. He gently puts his tool down, then he gets up and walks over to Krysta. As he gets closer to her, she looks at him nervously and a little shy. He walks over to her and puts his hands behind her head, he takes her hair clip out, causing her hair to slowly fall out. Her long soft thick light-brown hair falls, making Ty look at her with even more shock. He moves her hair so it lies on the side of her face, over her left shoulder. He stares at her for a minute, then he grins.

"Okay, don't move."

Ty goes back over to his sketch and continues to draw Krysta. He tells her to tilt her head a little more to her hand. Time goes by and Krysta completely forgets about the time, just staring at Ty as he sketches her. After about four hours, Ty finally calls in a night. Krysta smiles at him, then she looks at the time. Her face turns to complete fear and panic.

"Is it really that late?" Krysta asks.

Ty looks at her then at the clock. He nods his head yes as he looks back at Krysta. Krysta's eyes widen, then she quickly gets off the chair.

"Oh my god, I have to go. I'm sorry." Krysta panics.

"Krysta, it's okay. We won't get in trouble for staying late. Plus I work here," Ty says.

"No, you don't understand… My boyfriend is going to kill me. I have to go." Krysta panics.

Then she runs off out of the studio as she puts her hair back up in her hair clip, heading right home. Ty watches her run off, then he continues to clean up his studio then he sees the sketch he has of Krysta.

Krysta is running home as fast as she can. She arrives to the apartment and sees that the lights are the same as she left them. She runs right into the apartment, and there is Ford, sitting on the chair, glaring at her. He slowly stands up and walks over to her; she looks at him with fear as she breathes heavy. He stares at her for a minute, then he slaps her across her face, making her face turn. She puts her hand to her face where he slapped her and slowly looks at him.

"If you're late again, you won't get off so easy," Ford says.

He walks away into the bedroom and Krysta stands in the same spot, holding her face for a long two minutes after she hears Ford close the bedroom door. Then she looks at the couch and sees that she's going to be sleeping on the couch. She slowly walks over to the couch and, very slowly, sits down, holding the side of her face still. Krysta slowly leans down to lay on the couch, she slowly turns her head into the pillow and starts to cry.

The next morning, after Ford has left for work, Krysta gets up and walks into the bathroom. She looks at her face and sees that her left side cheek is red, also swollen. That day, Krysta doesn't go into work; she stays at home, cleaning and holding ice packs to her face. As time goes by, Krysta sees the sun going down, causing her to stop what she's cleaning and goes to start dinner. Ford comes home and sees that Krysta is working on dinner. He goes to change his clothes, with a grin and a nod of his head, then after about five minutes, he comes out to eat dinner. Krysta puts his plate right on the table, in front of his seat, before she pulls out his chair. She goes to sit at her side of the table, and like always, no words are spoken to each other. She just keeps her head down at her plate. Ford looks up at her.

"Do you have something that you wish to say to me?" Ford says.

Krysta slowly lifts her head and looks at him, but she doesn't say a word to him.

"I've been nice to you, haven't I?" Ford says.

Krysta still doesn't say anything to him, she just looks at him.

"I've left your womanhood to yourself. Let you live in my home and have that stupid part-time job," Ford says.

But Krysta still doesn't say anything. She slowly puts her head down, looking back at her plate.

"I have to do some shopping for food tomorrow," Krysta says.

Ford stares at her for a minute, then he continues eating. Krysta waits for Ford to finish his food before she gets up and puts the plates into the sink. She gets up and takes his plate, but their eyes never meet. The rest of the night, Ford is in his office, talking on the phone while Krysta is doing the dishes and cleaning the table. As the night goes on, the hour gets late and Ford goes to the bedroom. Leaving Krysta to once again sleep on the couch.

The next day, Ford goes to work and Krysta goes to work. As Krysta is working, she looks out the window and sees Ty walking by with some friends. She quickly puts her plates and cleaning tools down, then she slowly runs out to him.

"Ty," Krysta softly yells. "Ty."

Ty stops and slowly turns around and sees Krysta is the one who is calling his name.

"You guys go on ahead. I'll catch up."

Ty's friends nod their heads and continue walking. Ty turns his head back to Krysta and grins at her as he walks over to her.

"What's wrong? You look like you haven't slept in a couple of days," Ty asks.

She slightly puts her head down with a guilty look on her face. He looks at her with slight confusion but still a grin on his face.

"What's wrong?" Ty gently asks.

Krysta pauses for a minute,

"I'm sorry…for the other night. I just ran out without saying anything to you."

Ty slightly laughs, Krysta looks up at him.

"It's okay." Ty smiles.

She looks at him with slight shock.

"Um…can I still—"

"Yeah." Ty cuts Krysta off. "I can't pick another girl now. I already have your face. By the way, are you okay? Your face is red."

Krysta doesn't say anything at first, she just looks down.

"Um…when I was running home I…like a knucklehead, I fell and hit my face."

Ty looks at her as if he can tell she's not telling the truth.

"Okay, but next time, let me know what time you have to leave. So you're not in a panic again, okay?" Ty smiles.

Krysta slightly smiles and nods her head. Ty then slowly begins to walk away, but before he could get too far, Krysta calls him again. He turns around and looks at her.

"Um—" Krysta is cut off.

"Friday same time." Ty grins.

She nods her head, then they wave at each other. Krysta watches Ty walk away and watching from the window is Sam with a smile on her face. Not long after, Krysta gets off work early to do her food shopping. After about an hour, Krysta finishes her shopping and she decides to take a walk through the park. As she's walking through the park, she gets a shocked look on her face, for there she sees Ty. She stares at him for a minute, then she sees that he's staring at the things happening in the park. She walks over to him. but she doesn't get too close to him. But then Ty turns his head and looks at her.

"Hey, what are you doing here?"

Krysta doesn't say anything. Ty stares at her for a second, then he sees that she's holding some bags in her hands.

"Food shopping," Ty says.

Krysta nods her head. Ty looks at her, trying not to laugh, making Krysta look at him with a little confusion.

"What?"

"Are you afraid to talk about stuff or something?" Ty asks.

Krysta stares at him for a minute, then she slowly shakes her head. Ty slightly smiles at her, making her give him a shy smile.

"Um…what…what are you doing?" Krysta gently asks.

"Oh, my friends and I were taking pictures for some ideas for an art show," Ty replies.

Krysta looks at him with confusion.

"But I thought that you are a painter?"

Ty looks at her.

"Yeah, I'm also a photographer for the building I work in."

Krysta slightly tilts her head.

"Come here, I'll show you," Ty says.

Krysta gently puts her bags down and walks over to Ty. Ty takes off his camera from around his neck. He gently moves behind Krysta and puts the camera in front of her. He slightly leans to help her work his camera. Then for the next hour, Krysta and Ty keep taking pictures. Ty takes some pictures and Krysta is walking under a tree. Birds come flying, wind blows, making some of the leaves fall from the tree. The leaves fall slowly with the wind, and Krysta starts laughing. Ty turns around and gets a shock look on his face, for Krysta has such a beautiful laugh and smile that it's breathtaking. He takes his camera and slowly starts to takes pictures of her. But then a dog comes running and gently jumps on Krysta, causing her to softly fall and start laughing even more while petting the dog that looks like a German shepherd. Ty keeps taking pictures of Krysta and smiles at her. But after he takes a few pictures, he just stares at her with gentle amazement. Krysta looks at him, then she gently put her head down with a shy look and smiles. Ty gently grins at her, then he takes her picture. He smiles at her then he looks at his watch and sees that he has to leave. He slowly stands up and Krysta completely looks at him, still petting the dog.

"I got to get going. I have to get my studio ready," Ty says.

Krysta slowly nods her head, then she smiles at the dog. Then the owner calls the dog and it goes running. They watch the dog run to its owner and Ty walks over to Krysta; he reaches his hand down to her to help her up. She slowly puts her hand in his and he gently pulls her up, they look at each other. Still hand in hand, Krysta looks at her and Ty's hands and how gentle he is holding her hand. Then she looks at Ty who is just smiling at her.

"I'll see you Friday." Ty grins.

Then he slowly lets go of Krysta's hand. Krysta watches him with a smile. She then grabs her bags and heads home.

As she walks into the apartment, before she can close the door, a beautiful tall, light skin, blue-eyed blond woman comes out of Ford's office, laughing. Ford looks at Krysta, and she just stares at him for a minute, then she looks at the woman. The woman just laughs at Krysta as she walks by her to the door. The woman closes the door and Krysta looks back at Ford. He just looks at her, then he goes back into his office and closes the door. Krysta looks down at the floor away and makes dinner.

The days go by and every time Krysta comes home from work, a different woman keeps leaving the apartment. Ford doesn't say a word and Krysta doesn't either; but then came Friday, and Krysta is waiting for Ty to come and get her from the shop. Ty comes and gets Krysta but he sees that something is off about her. He doesn't say anything to her, he just walks over to her and gives her a small smile.

She looks at him with small joy in her eyes and also gives him a small smile. Then they walk across the street to the art building.

As they walk in, Krysta sees some of the new art on the walls. They go to Ty's studio, and as Krysta walks in, she sees that the studio is different. Ty made his studio look like the rain forest and there are a few girls and a few other people in his studio. Ty looks at Krysta then at the girls; they walk over to Krysta and take her hand. They bring her into the changing room in the back of Ty's studio, she looks at Ty and he just grins at her, then he walks over to his tools. As Ty gets his things ready, he tells everyone that they are all set after they got everything all set for Ty to sketch. He waits for Krysta to be done changing for about fifteen minutes. Then the girls come out first and tell Ty that she's all done. Ty says his thanks, then he waits for Krysta to come out from the changing room. After about two minutes, Krysta still doesn't come out. He gets up and walks over to the changing room door.

"Krysta, what are you doing?"

"I can't come out," Krysta softly yells.

"Why?" Ty calmly says.

"I just can't, I thought you were painting my face," Krysta softly yells back.

"I'll come in and get you," Ty calmly says back.

"Okay," Krysta gently says.

Ty slightly laughs, then he turns and looks at the studio. Krysta slowly opens the door and walks out even slower.

"Don't laugh," Krysta softly says.

Ty slowly turns his head and gets a shocked look on his face. Krysta is wearing a green camouflage one-shoulder dress down to her knees. Her hair is braided to one side, hanging over her left shoulder. Ty's shock slowly turns to a gentle smile. Krysta slowly puts her head down with a shy smile.

Ty gently takes her hand and they walk over to the spot Ty wants her to be at. He puts her next to one of the small trees in the studio. She stands next to it, gently putting her hands to it. He tells her to tilt her head onto the tree and has her put her hands on it, like the first time he sketched her face. He walks over to his sketching board and looks at Krysta. He has Krysta look as if she's listening to the tree. He sees that she's slightly smiling, almost like she's in the real rain forest. Seeing how beautiful it is with the birds, the smell, the gentle breeze, sound, and color, Ty stares at her for a minute, then he slowly begins to sketch her. Krysta stays that way, thinking that she's really there, forgetting everything in the world, causing her face to be in a place of peace. She then turns her head and looks at Ty who is smiling at her. She slowly tilts her head even more to the small tree and just stares at Ty with small pieces of her hair going into her face, for Ty has a fan going. Even though they are staring at each other, Ty is still sketching her. After Ty finishes his rain forest sketch of Krysta, he looks at his watch.

"Sorry, time's up," Ty says.

Krysta looks at him, then nods her head. Krysta goes to the changing room slowly while Ty covers his sketch. Krysta walks up to the changing room door then turns her head to Ty who is putting away his things. Then she walks into the changing room; she comes out after about five minutes. Krysta comes out of the room and sees Ty waiting for her by his studio room doorway, looking at his phone. He looks at her and grins, causing her to give him a small smile, then they both leave his studio as Ty shuts down his studio. They both head down to the last floor of the building. They come out the back building door and Krysta sees that Ty has a black and green motorcycle.

"You need a ride?" Ty asks.

Krysta slowly shakes her head.

"No, it's probably best I don't."

"Are you sure? It's going to rain soon," Ty says.

"My…" Krysta pauses.

"I know but me dropping off a friend so she doesn't get sick from the rain. Not that bad," Ty says.

"You don't know him," Krysta says.

Ty looks at her.

"So I'll drop you around the corner."

Krysta gently smiles, then she nods her head.

"Okay."

"Come on," Ty says.

Ty gets on his bike, then he reaches his hand out to Krysta to help her get on his bike. Then he takes her arms and puts them around his waist.

"Hold on, okay?" Ty says.

"Okay," Krysta softly replies.

Then Ty drives off, and Krysta holds on even tighter but starts laughing. They come to a stoplight and Ty asks Krysta where she lives. Krysta gives him the address.

"I know where that is," Ty says.

They come up to Krysta's apartment and like Ty told her, he drops her off around the corner.

"Thank you," Krysta softly says.

"Anytime," Ty replies.

Then he takes off. Krysta watches him go down the street then she walks to the apartment. As she walks to the front door, before she can open it, the door opens. She gets a slight shocked look on her face, for another woman is walking out of the apartment. She slowly walks into the apartment and sees Ford clothes are not fully on. She looks around the living room and sees that some of the things are a mess. She looks at Ford and he looks at her with a plain look.

"Clean this up," Ford demands.

Krysta takes a deep breath.

"What happened?" Krysta asks.

Ford turns his head and looks at her with a little shock and anger, but Krysta just stares at him. Ford sees the way she is looking at him. Ford walks over to her and stands in front of her, and she looks up at him. Then he backhand slaps her across the face, causing her face to turn.

"Clean it up," Ford says.

Krysta puts her hand on her face then, she kneels down and slowly starts to clean the mess.

The next day, at Krysta's work, no one can see that the side of her face is red. Ty comes in and looks for her. Krysta comes out from the back and sees Ty. She smiles, then she looks around to make sure that no one is around. She then walks over to him.

"Hey, what are you doing here?" Krysta smiles.

"Oh, nothing much. I just want to let you know I won't be around for a little while. I have an art show for a couple of weeks. I wanted to ask you to come but I don't think you can," Ty explains.

"Yeah, but thanks for thinking about it." Krysta softly pouts.

Ty grins at her.

"Tell you what, I'll take pictures for you," Ty says.

"Really? Thank you." Krysta smiles.

Ty smiles at her, but then Ty sees the side of her face but he doesn't say anything.

"Okay, I'll see you."

Ty and Krysta wave bye to each other, then Ty slowly begins to leaves. Krysta watches him leave, then she goes back to work.

After work, Krysta goes home and sees another girl leaving the apartment. She walks into the apartment, and she sees Ford putting his clothes back on and she sees a few kiss marks around his neck. Ford just looks at her.

"Clean this up."

Krysta takes a deep breath, then she puts her things down and slowly starts cleaning up the mess. As she cleans the mess, her right hand starts to hurt. She shakes her hand then she gets up and goes to start dinner.

Time goes by and two weeks has come to an end and so has Krysta's tolerance. Krysta is making dinner and Ford walks in from work. She gives him a small look then she goes back to cooking. He walks over to her and stands next to her but she doesn't look at him.

"I think we should take our relationship to the next level," Ford says.

Krysta stops chopping the carrots and slightly looks up but still doesn't look at Ford. Her face shows that she's tired yet aggravated. She doesn't say anything for a minute, then she slightly tilts her head to Ford.

"Why? You get in everywhere else?" Krysta says.

Ford quickly looks at her, then he grabs her by the arm and turns her to him. He slaps her across the face hard! Krysta moves back, almost losing her balance and her face turns; but then, she looks back at Ford. She looks at him for a second, then she slaps him across the face, making his face to slightly turn. Ford is in shock.

"I'm sick of this. We are done—I'm out of here," Krysta says.

Krysta then walks to the front door. Ford slowly turns his head to her. But before Krysta can open the door, Ford grabs her by the back of her hair. She slightly screams.

"So you think you can fight now. Let's see how well," Ford says.

Then he throws Krysta to the floor, hard, looks down at her and Krysta turns and looks at him with fear.

Chapter 2

Ty is back from his trip and he's walking on the streets. As he's walking, he passes an alley. He hears a noise, making him look for a minute. But the noise doesn't sound like a cat jumping off trash cans. It sounds like a person crying, making him go see if his hearing is right. As he slightly walks down the way, he sees two pair of legs lying out from behind a trash can. He looks around the trash can and he slowly gets a shocked look on his face. For the pair of legs belong to Krysta!

"Krysta...who...what the hell happened to you?" Ty asks.

He kneels down in front of her, then he slightly turns her head to him and sees that her right eye is shut and she can't really see out of her left.

"I'm fine," is all Krysta says.

Ty looks at her with disbelief.

"Really...how many fingers am I holding up?" Ty asks.

Ty puts up two fingers up but Krysta very slightly shakes her head, for she can't see them.

"Thought so. I'm taking you to the hospital," Ty says.

"No!" Krysta yells in fear.

Ty looks at her.

"Krysta!"

"Please don't take me there. Please...please...they'll look there first," Krysta cries.

Ty stares at her for a minute with confusion, then he slowly nods his head.

"Okay."

Ty then takes off his jacket and gently puts it around her. Ty slowly helps her up but sees that she can't really stand. He brings her out from the alley and looks around to make sure she can come out. He sees the bus stop and the bench with no one sitting there; he looks at Krysta, then he slowly takes her over to the bus bench. Ty gently puts his sunglasses that were in his pocket over her eyes after he helps her sit on the bench.

"Okay, you stay right here, okay? I'll be right back," Ty says.

Krysta slowly nods her head. Ty looks around, then he runs off. Krysta stays on the bench, waiting for Ty to come back. But she gets nervous when she hears men walking by her. Five minutes pass and Ty still hasn't come back. She slowly begins to shake, then she feels a gentle touch on her hands.

"Okay, come," says a voice.

"Ty," Krysta softly says.

"Yeah, it's me. Come on…nice and easy," Ty replies.

Ty went to get a car that one of his friends is letting him use that was only a few blocks away. He slowly and gently helps Krysta off the bench. Ty helps her get into the car.

"Okay, you get in first," Ty says.

Krysta grips his hand.

"It's okay… I'm right here, okay?" Ty says.

Krysta gets in the car and Ty slowly closes the door then runs to the other side and gets in. Ty then slowly drives off with Krysta gently holding Ty's hand and leaning back against the chair. After about ten to twenty minutes, they arrive at Ty's apartment that is on the other side of town from Krysta's. Ty has a nice apartment, not high up like Krysta's but it would get four stars; it has two bedrooms and two bathrooms. A kitchen with a built-in table, living room connected to the kitchen. Ty opens the parking garage, then he slowly drives in. He parks in his regular spot. He slowly gets out of the car and looks around. He then slowly runs over to Krysta's side of the car and helps her out so she doesn't fall. He helps her stand up by putting one hand on her side and holding her other hand. They stand there for a minute till she can get the strength to move then they walk over to the elevator and take it up to the third floor, Ty's floor. But before he takes Krysta out of the elevator, he looks around to make sure no one is around in the halls.

"Okay, we're good. Come on," Ty gently says.

They walk to his apartment, then he slowly opens the door.

"Are you sure this is okay?" Krysta softly asks.

Ty looks at her,

"Yeah, there's only me and one other person living on this floor. But he's a party guy, that's why I looked before I took you out of the elevator. And my roommate is never here, always at his girlfriend's."

Ty then guides Krysta into his apartment. He closes the door behind her with his foot, then he turns the lights on.

"Okay let's go over to the couch," Ty says.

Ty gently takes off his jacket from Krysta as they go over to the couch. He goes to hang it up, but when he turns around to Krysta, he gets a shocked look on his face.

"Krysta…what the hell happened to your back?" Ty asks.

Krysta's back looks horrible, for her shirt that slightly shows her back is showing what looks like her back has been whipped. He slowly walks over to her and gently puts his hand on the side of her back. With a slight touch, it makes her jump from slight pain; Ty looks at her as he slowly moves his hand from her back.

"Okay, just sit here," Ty says.

Ty helps Krysta sit on the couch, then he walks into his bedroom that's connected to the living room where his bathroom is and starts the bathwater. After about five minutes, Ty comes into the living room to get Krysta. He gently helps her up and guides her to the bathroom. Ty gently closes the door and guides Krysta closer to the tub.

"Okay, you're going to get into the tub. So you can clean up a little bit, okay?" Ty says.

Krysta nods her head.

"Only if you want me to, I'll help you okay?" Ty says.

"Okay," Krysta softly says.

Ty gently lets go of Krysta, but before he leaves the bathroom, he sees Krysta can't really get her clothes off. Even more, she can't truly stand on her feet without shaking from loss of balance. Ty looks at her and sees that she's slowly starting to cry. Ty looks at her with pain on his face, then he walks over to her. He gently holds her.

"It's okay. I got you, just trust me, okay?"

Krysta slowly nods her head.

"Okay, lean on me," Ty says.

Krysta leans against Ty, then he slowly begins to help her out of her clothes. First he takes off her shirt and sees that she has black and blue marks all over her arms and sides; her back is covered with slashes as if someone whipped her. He slowly shakes his head, then he slowly starts to kneel down. Krysta keeps her hands on his shoulders so she doesn't fall while Ty helps her take off her shoes. He slowly then helps her takes off her jeans that have rips all over them. He gets a shocked look on his face for the reason she can't stand right was not just her back but her legs are covered in black and blue marks plus her inner thighs. Ty slowly stands up, and Krysta completely leans on him again. Ty gently puts his hands on her hips.

"Okay, now take a few steps back to the tub," Ty says.

Krysta slowly moves back as Ty guides her to the tub, making sure she doesn't fall. They come to the tub and Ty helps Krysta get in.

"Okay, gently go down. That a girl," Ty gently says.

Krysta slowly gets down into the tub with Ty holding her outside of the tub. But as the water gets closer to her thighs, she grips tighter to Ty's arms. Ty is kneeling outside of the tub, holding Krysta. Krysta's breathing is heavy and shaking as she gets deeper into the water, holding onto Ty's arms, shaking. Ty looks at her, then gently puts his hand on the side of her face; her face is cold and nervous.

"Okay, this is going to hurt. But I have to clean out your back, okay?" Ty gently says.

Krysta slowly lifts her head up to him and slowly nods her head. Ty takes a slight deep breath, then he moves closer to Krysta. Krysta slowly puts her head onto Ty's chest, then Ty takes a small container that's in the bathroom and fills it with water. Before he pours it on Krysta's back, he looks at her.

"Okay," Ty softly says.

Then he gently and slowly pours the water onto Krysta's back. She quickly holds onto Ty even harder and she begins to scream in pain.

"I know. I'm sorry," Ty says gently.

Krysta begins to finally cry. Ty gently puts his other hand on her head, slowly rubbing her head. Ty then, with his other hand, puts the container down and grabs a facecloth. He gently puts it on Krysta's back to clean it a little more.

After about a half hour to forty-five minutes, Ty sees that her body is clean.

"Okay, stay right there," Ty says.

Ty then gets up and goes over to the bathroom closet to get Krysta a towel. He walks back over to Krysta who's still sitting in the tub. Ty kneels in front of her.

"Okay, ready," Ty says as he puts the towel in front of her.

Krysta slowly puts her arms up best she can and Ty gently wraps it around her. He helps her stand up slowly, then he grabs his bathrobe that's hanging next to the tub. He puts it on Krysta and helps her put her arms in the sleeves. He doesn't tie it, for he doesn't wish to hurt her back; then he gently picks her up so she doesn't have to walk. He brings her into his bedroom and gently sits her on the bed. Ty slowly takes off his bathrobe from Krysta, still wearing the towel. Ty takes out one of his button-up shirts for Krysta to put on. But he puts it on backward so the back is in front of her and the buttons are in the back. Ty doesn't button the back.

"Okay, I need you to lie on your stomach. I'm going to put some medicine on your back, okay?" Ty explains.

Krysta slowly nods her head then she tries to move back on the bed. Ty helps her then she slowly turns around to lie on her stomach. Ty puts the bedcovers up to her waist, then he slowly moves the shirt opening of her back. Then he slowly and gently begins to rub the medicine onto Krysta's back. Then he takes a warm steamed towel and slowly puts it on her back making her slightly jump. Ty then kneels down next to the bed, in front of Krysta, he gently puts his hand on her head and she gives him a small smile. Then tears slowly fall from her eyes; she then takes her hand and holds his. As Krysta holds Ty's hand, she slowly begins to fall asleep with Ty watching over her all night, holding her hand, hoping that it will help her sleep.

The next morning, Krysta wakes up hoping that everything was just a bad dream. But then she gets a shocked look on her face, for there is Ty, sleeping on a chair. Right next to the bed in the bedroom, near the window. Krysta tries to get up but her body is in huge pain with the smallest move she makes. She sees the black and blue spots on her arms. She slowly and very slightly turns her head to her back and sees that there's a towel on her back. She slowly turns her head back to Ty who is still sleeping. But then Ty's eyes slowly begin to open and looks at Krysta. He sees that she's awake, he gets up out of the chair and over to her.

"Hey, how you feeling?"

Ty kneels down in front of Krysta beside the bed.

"It wasn't a dream. It really happened. I should have realized it since I can't see out my right eye," Krysta cries.

Ty doesn't say anything, he just gently puts his hand on the side of her face as he puts his head down next to her on the bed.

That day, Ty stays home with Krysta who has been in his bed all day, resting. Ty is sitting on his chair, sketching as Krysta sleeps. Krysta then wakes up from a bang she hears. She looks at Ty who's still sketching. He looks up at her and sees that she's a little scared. He grins at her.

"It's okay, it's just the garbage truck outside," Ty explains.

Krysta slightly smiles, then she puts her head back down. Ty then goes back to his sketching. The sun goes down, and Krysta wakes up from the smell of smoke. Ty then walks into the bedroom and sees that Krysta is awake.

"Oh, hey there. I didn't know that you were up yet," Ty gently says.

"What's that smell?" Krysta softly asks.

Ty looks at her, then he looks around and starts to laugh.

"Sorry, I'm cooking. I came in here to open the window so it doesn't get too hot in here."

Krysta looks at him for a minute, then she softly starts laughing. Ty grins at her then he opens the window. Krysta smiles at him. Then he walks back over to the bedroom door and looks back at Krysta.

"I'll be right back, okay?" Ty says.

Krysta nods her head, then Ty walks out of the room. After about another few minutes, Ty comes back into the bedroom to get Krysta. He gently takes the covers off of her, then he helps her out of the bed. Ty leans her up. Krysta slowly puts her arms around his neck. Ty then gently picks her up and brings her into the kitchen so she can eat. Ty gently puts her on the chair with a pillow leaning against the back of the chair for her. Krysta slowly leans back, then Ty walks over to the other side of the table.

"Okay, I should have asked you but you were sleeping. And I didn't want to wake you. Do you eat meat?" Ty asks.

Krysta looks at him for a minute with a look on her face like she's trying not to laugh. Ty stares at her for a minute.

"That's messed up."

Krysta then starts laughing.

"I'm sorry. It's just really nice of you to think of me like that."

Ty slowly shakes his head at her, then they start to eat. As they eat, Ty looks at Krysta but then he looks back down at his plate. They are both a little nervous, not much is said; really nothing is said. But after they are done eating, Ty gently picks up Krysta and brings her over to the couch so she can lie down. Because of Krysta's back, she can't put any pressure on it, plus her legs are still badly sore. Cause of heat, she has to lie on her stomach. Ty lays her down, then he puts the TV on for her. He hands her the remote, then he goes to clean up the table and kitchen. After Ty cleans up everything and puts the leftover food away, he goes over to Krysta. She looks up at him and smiles. Ty kneels down next to her and Krysta then takes a breath.

"You know, you haven't asked me much about what happened to me," Krysta says.

Ty looks at her and doesn't say anything for a minute. He stares at her with a calm look on his face.

"When you're ready to tell me, I'll listen. But for now, just let me take care of you," Ty replies.

Krysta stares at him for a second. Ty then slowly gets up.

"I am going to start your bathwater. I'll be right back," Ty says.

Ty then walks into his bedroom while Krysta stays on the couch. She hears the bathwater running. After about a few minutes, Ty comes back into the living room and Krysta looks up at him. She slightly leans herself up with just her arms, then Ty helps her up even more, enough so she can sit up enough to get off her stomach. Ty gently picks her up and brings her into his bedroom to the bathroom. He closes the door, then he slowly puts Krysta down. She looks at the bathwater.

"Do I really have to take another bath? I just took one yesterday," Krysta softly says.

Ty slightly looks down at her and softly grins at her.

"Yeah, the bath is to make sure that your back doesn't get an infection, plus the medicine will have a better effect when your pores are opened," Ty says. "And I can't put you in the shower. For one, you can't stand, and second, like I said, your back."

Krysta stares at the bathwater for a second, then she slowly leans against Ty's chest, making Ty look completely down at her. Then he turns his head to the wall.

"Okay, um… I guess I'll go."

But before he could move, Krysta holds on to his shirt. Ty looks at her but she keeps her head on his chest.

"Okay," Ty softly says.

Ty then guides Krysta to the tub. He slowly takes off his shirt from Krysta's body. Krysta slowly puts her legs into the tub, then Ty slowly helps her lean down into the tub. Ty then slowly turns around, leaning back against the tub, and lets Krysta clean up. After about ten minutes, Krysta looks at Ty whose back is still toward her. She takes a low deep breath, then she looks back up at Ty.

"Um… I can't get my back. It still hurts," Krysta softly says.

Ty slowly nods his head, then he slowly turns around and looks at Krysta. She's leaning against the tub so he can't see her body, but she's still facing him. He nods his head, then he moves over to her while still on the floor. Then he leans himself up on his knees, he gently takes the facecloth from her hand. Krysta slowly puts her head on his shoulder and Ty slowly puts the facecloth in the water, then he gently puts it on Krysta's back. He slowly and very consciously rubs her back, Krysta grips tightly onto his shirt as she jumps in pain. Ty looks at her as he pauses for a minute then slowly continues rubbing her back.

After Ty finishes rubbing Krysta's back, he takes the small container and fills it with new water from the tub faucet then slowly pours the water over her back. He pours water over her a few times, then he and Krysta look at each other, Ty feeling bad and Krysta in pain. Then Ty slowly stands up and walks over to his bathroom closet, he pulls out a new towel for Krysta. He walks back over to her then he leans down and Krysta looks up at him. Krysta lifts her arms then Ty wraps the towel around her. He gently picks her up by her arms then they go into the bedroom. He stands her up so she can dry off as he gets her a new one of his shirts. Once again, Ty puts his shirt on backward so the back can be opened. Krysta lies on her stomach for Ty to put medicine on her back. They look at each other for a minute, then Ty slowly stands up.

"I'll let you get some sleep…night," Ty gently says.

Krysta softly smiles at him then she watches Ty leave the room. He softly closes the door, and Krysta stares at the door for a minute then she slowly closes her eyes. After about an hour, Ty comes into the room and sees that Krysta is asleep. He grins at her then he walks over to his closet. He takes out some clothes then he walks into the bathroom and closes the door. He puts the shower on so that it can get to the right heat level. As he waits for the heat to get right, he goes to get a towel. Ty slowly takes off his clothes then gets into the shower and closes the curtains. After about forty-five minutes, Ty comes out of the bathroom with his hair in a ponytail, dripping wet, wearing black shorts with a red muscle shirt. Ty looks at Krysta and sees that she's fast asleep still. He goes out to the living room, sits on the couch, and puts the TV on and keeps the volume low but enough for him to still hear. As Ty is watching TV, Krysta is starting to have a nightmare. She wakes up screaming, making Ty quickly drops the control, jumps over the couch and into the bedroom.

"Krysta, Krysta, it's okay, it's okay," Ty gently yells.

Tears fall from Krysta's eyes and she wraps her arms around Ty's neck. She puts her head on his shoulder. Ty puts one hand on her head then the other hand on her arm. Ty then slowly leans away from Krysta, he slowly let's go of her hand and walks over to the chair. He picks up his chair and brings it closer to the bed. He sits on his chair then he looks at Krysta as he gently takes her hand, holding it. She looks at their hands then up at Ty who is grinning at her.

"It's okay, I'm right here," Ty gently says.

Krysta smiles, then she slowly closes her eyes. Ty watches her fall asleep, then he takes a deep breath. He slowly leans his head back on the chair and also falls asleep.

Next morning, Krysta wakes up and sees that Ty's not in the chair. She looks around, then she sees that Ty's bedroom door is opened. She slowly tries to get up but her back starts to hurt, causing her to fall to the floor. As she falls to the floor, Ty is walking into his apartment. He looks around with confusion, then he walks into the bedroom and sees Krysta on the floor, trying to get up. He quickly walks over to her and kneels down in front of her. She slightly looks at him but then looks back down to the floor. Ty slowly shakes his head.

"Krysta, what are you doing?"

"You weren't here so I tried to get up. But my back started hurting and I fell," Krysta shyfully explains.

Ty looks at her, almost as if he wants to laugh, but he takes a deep breath.

"Okay, come on. Let's get you up," Ty says.

Ty gently helps Krysta off the floor, then he brings her into the living room. He sits her on the couch, he walks over to one of the bags he has. He takes out a DVD and walks over to Krysta. Ty kneels down in front of her and she looks at him, Ty shows her the DVD he has in his hand.

"Okay, this is a workout DVD for women," Ty says.

"What, you think I'm fat?" Krysta quickly replies.

Ty laughs but mostly at her pouting face and pouting voice.

"No, Krysta. It's to help you so your body doesn't get stiff. It's hard for you to walk. It's just to help you so you don't fall like you just did," Ty explains.

"Oh, thank you," Krysta says.

Ty grins at her, then he stands up and walks into the kitchen. Krysta watches him go into the kitchen, then she looks back at the DVD. As Krysta looks at the DVD, she jumps for the doorbell rings. She slowly begins to panic, but then, Ty comes into the living room to the door. He opens the door and Krysta sees that he ordered Chinese food. Ty closes the door and sees that Krysta let go of a deep breath.

"You okay?" Ty asks with a grin.

Krysta nods her head, then Ty walks over to Krysta and sits on the couch next to her. She looks at him and he looks at her.

"I pretty much ordered just about everything," Ty says.

Krysta laughs, then Ty gets up and walks over to his TV stand. He opens the cabinets and moves to the side so Krysta can see. Krysta gets a shocked look on her face.

"What movie do you want to watch?" Ty asks.

Krysta couldn't count how many movies Ty has. She stares at the movies for a minute, then she looks at Ty.

"I've… I've never seen any of these movies before," Krysta says.

Ty stares at her for a minute with complete shock.

"Okay, name a type of movie you want to watch," Ty asks.

"What…do you mean," Krysta asks.

"Like action, drama, romance, comedy," Ty replies.

"Oh." Krysta nods her head. "Um…comedy."

"Comedy," Ty says.

Krysta nods her head with a smile and Ty slowly nods his head with a grin.

"Okay, um how about this one?" Ty asks.

Ty pulls out one of the movies he has and Krysta looks at it.

"*Ride Alone*…okay."

Ty puts the movie into the DVD player then goes back and sits down next to Krysta. Ty then picks up one of the food containers and takes the chopsticks out of the wrapper. As he waits for the previews to go by, he slowly begins to eat. Then he looks at Krysta who is having a fight with her chopsticks. Ty slightly laughs.

"You have used chopsticks before, right?"

Krysta looks at him with a pouting yet guilty look on her face as she shakes her head no. Ty stares laughing even harder, making Krysta pout and look down at her food.

"Okay, sorry. I'll teach you how to use them," Ty says, laughing still.

Before the movie starts, Ty shows Krysta how to use her chopsticks, Ty still slightly laughing and Krysta also laughing. That night, Krysta laughs so hard that she has tears coming out of her eyes. After about three movies Ty starts to clean up everything, Krysta watches him, then she starts to looks around and sees some of his art around. She looks back over at Ty.

"Is this okay?" Krysta asks.

Ty turns his head and looks at her.

"What do you mean?"

"Don't you have to go to work?" Krysta asks.

"Oh, no. Not right now," Ty replies.

"That's not what I mean. For the last few days, you have been taking care of me. Won't they get mad that you're not in the studio?" Krysta asks.

Ty walks over to her, then he kneels down in front of her with a grin on his face.

"Krysta, I'm an artist. Plus I just did an art show for two weeks. So it's fine…and speaking of art show," Ty says.

Ty then gets up and walks into his bedroom for a minute. Then he comes out holding something in his hand. He walks over to Krysta and kneels back down in front of her, he hands her a packet that is in his hand.

"I promised you I'd take pictures for you." Ty grins.

Krysta looks at him with a smile, then she gently takes the packet from Ty and he finishes cleaning up. Krysta slowly opens the packet with a look on her face as if she's about to cry. She gently takes out the pictures and looks through them, she then looks over to Ty who slowly turns his head to her and they both give each other small smiles that's saying more than it looks.

Chapter 3

Krysta has been living with Ty for about two to three months, and it's now the middle of fall. Her bruises are completely gone and her back is almost healed. She can walk around but still is too afraid to leave Ty's apartment. Ty goes to work and Krysta stays and cleans like when she was with Ford. But there is a difference when Ty comes home. Ty walks into the apartment and Krysta looks at him, she's wearing one of the shirts that Ty gave her to wear.

"Hi, welcome back." Krysta smiles.

Ty closes the door and smiles at her.

"Hi…um, how long have you been cleaning?"

"Since I got up, um, around noon," Krysta says. "Are you hungry? What do you want me to cook you?" Ty stares at her for a second.

"Krysta."

"Yes," Krysta replies.

Ty walks over to her and stops her from going into the kitchen.

"You have been on your feet cleaning all day. Go sit down and put your feet up and I will cook," Ty says.

"But I—" Krysta is cut off.

"Krysta…" Ty pauses, "don't make me to glue you to the chair again."

Krysta looks at him like she wants to laugh.

"Okay."

Ty then watches Krysta walk over to the couch and sit down. Ty goes into the kitchen and starts cooking. Krysta looks at him, then she slowly gets up and walks over to the kitchen table, looking to make sure Ty doesn't see her. Ty's back is to her, Krysta still has that look. As if she wants to laugh but is holding it back. Krysta slowly starts to set the table, but then she stops after about a minute. She's about to laugh as she slowly turns around and there is Ty, staring at her with a grin on his face and one eyebrow up.

"What are you doing?" Ty asks.

Krysta slowly shakes her head.

"Nothing." Krysta smiles.

Ty looks over her shoulder and looks at the table.

"Looks like you're setting the table."

"N-no." Krysta smiles.

Ty stares at her for a second then shakes his head. Then he takes her hand and takes her into the kitchen.

"If you need something to do, cut those," Ty says.

Krysta smiles, then she starts to help Ty cook the food. As the food cooks, Ty and Krysta both set the table. After the food was done, they both put it on the table, Ty pulls out Krysta's chair then he sits on his. They both say their grace as they hold hands, then they start to eat and Krysta asks Ty how his day at work went.

"So what new project are you working on?" Krysta asks.

"Nothing…truthfully. I'm just helping around the studio, that's all," Ty replies.

Ty looks at Krysta for a minute and she looks at him.

"What?" Krysta asks with a smile.

"Do you want to come with me to the studio tomorrow?" Ty asks.

Krysta's smile slowly fades as she looks up at him and she shrugs her shoulders. Ty can see that she's a little afraid.

"You can't stay in this apartment forever. Plus I'll be with you and you'll be in the studio so you'll be okay," Ty explains.

Krysta smiles then nods her head with joy. Ty smiles at her and slowly shakes his head.

The next morning, Ty and Krysta both get up and have breakfast together. Then as Ty cleans up, he tells Krysta to go and take a shower. Krysta runs and takes a quick ten-minute shower. Krysta comes out of the shower and Ty walks into the bedroom, she wraps the towel around her body then walks into the bedroom. She sees Ty taking clothes out of the closet; she smiles at him, then Ty turns and sees Krysta in the bathroom doorway with just a towel on with her hair in a side braid on the right side of her shoulder. They stare at each other for a minute, then Ty takes a step to her. But as he steps to her, his cell phone rings, snapping the both of them out of their stare. Ty takes the phone out of his pocket and sees it's the studio.

"Hello," Ty says.

Ty looks at Krysta who's walking by him to see if she can find something to wear.

"Okay, I'll see you in forty," Ty says.

Ty hangs up the phone; he looks back at Krysta who's pouting. He looks at her, trying not to laugh.

"Okay, what's wrong?" Ty smiles.

"I don't have anything to wear. Just these same clothes from two, three months ago and walking outside in just your shirt. It's cold out." Krysta pouts.

Ty laughs, then he walks back over to his closet; he pulls out a shirt, then he walks over to her drawer and pulls out a pair of jeans.

"Okay, see if these fit," Ty says.

Ty puts the clothes on the bed, then he walks into the bedroom and takes a shower. Krysta listens for a minute to the running water, then she looks at the clothes on the bed. After about fifteen minutes, Ty comes out of the bathroom wearing a black T-shirt with dark-blue jean pants and black-white sneakers. He looks at Krysta with a shocked yet laughing look on his face, for Krysta is wearing the clothes Ty gave her to put on. She looks at Ty with a pouting look on her face.

"It's not funny…this shirt is too big. And even with these girl's jeans, they're still too big. How do you have girl jeans anyway?" Krysta pouts.

Ty starts laughing, then he walks over to Krysta.

"Okay, first the jeans used to be mine. But my friend thought he knew how to do clothes and they ended up like that. And those used to be my favorite pair. And put this belt on so they don't fall when you're walking. Second, tie the shirt or something," Ty says.

Krysta looks at him while she's putting on the belt. Then she looks on the shirt then back at Ty,

"Tie the shirt how?"

Ty stares at her for a minute.

"You're kidding, right?"

Krysta slowly shakes her head no, then Ty puts his hand to his face, looks back at Krysta. He walks closer to her, then he takes the end of the shirt. Krysta looks at him, then she looks back down at the shirt. Ty takes the last button on the shirt and unbuttons it and ties it. Krysta looks at him, a little nervous, because the way Ty ties the shirt, it slightly shows her stomach. They look at each other for a minute, then they both get ready to go to the studio. They go down to the stairs to Ty's bike; Ty helps Krysta on the bike. She wraps her arms around him, then Ty starts up his bike and they slowly take off.

They arrive at the studio and Ty parks his bike in the back of the building where all the workers park in the same spot. They walk to the front of the building, for they are working on the back windows and door of the building. As they are walking to the front, Krysta sees the cafe across the way. There she sees her friend, Sam, working, laughing, and acting up like she always does. Ty looks at Krysta and sees that she's worried about her friend.

"Go talk to her," Ty says.

Krysta turns her head and looks at him.

"I can't," Krysta softly replies.

"Why?" Ty asks.

Krysta slightly tilts her head; Ty grins then slowly nods his head. Then he looks back and forth across the street, seeing if any cars are coming. He looks at Krysta.

"Stay here."

Krysta looks at him with confusion, then Ty slowly runs across the street over to the cafe. Krysta gets a shocked look on her face. For Ty is walking over to Sam at the cafe. Krysta looks around then walks around the corner. Ty gets across the street, turns his head and sees that Krysta is going to hide around the corner. Ty shakes his head, then he walks into the cafe and right over to Sam. She looks at him with slight shock and confusion.

"Sam, right?" Ty asks.

"Yeah, you're friends with Krysta, right?" Sam asks.

Ty grins at her.

"When do you go on break?"

"In about ten minutes, why?" Sam asks with confusion.

"Okay, come across to the studio. Ask for Ty."

Then Ty walks away with Sam standing, watching him with confusion. She slightly looks around, then the manager slightly yells at Sam to get back to work. She snaps out of it then she walks to the counter. Meanwhile Ty walks back across the street and goes around the corner where Krysta is hiding who is slightly sitting on the ground. He looks at her, trying to hide the fact that he wants to laugh. Krysta looks at him like she's pouting but happy that he did that. He walks over to her then helps her stand up. They both then walk to the front of the building and head into Ty's studio.

After about ten minutes, Sam is going on her break. She goes across the street to the art building but she stands outside of it for a minute, thinking. Thinking if she should go in or just wait till she sees him again. But she takes a deep breath then goes into the building to the welcome counter. Sam asks for Ty. They nod their head then they pick up the phone and dial a number. After about a minute, Ty comes out of the elevator and slightly walks over to the welcome counter. Sam looks at him, and he just grins at her. She walks over to him.

"Okay, I have no idea why I came. B—" Sam's cut off.

"Come with me," Ty says.

Sam looks at him for a second. Ty turns around and starts walking back to the elevator with Sam slowly following him. They walk into the elevator. Sam just keeps looking at Ty as she stands in the back of the elevator. They go all the way up to the fifth floor. They both get off the elevator and Sam follows Ty to where he takes her. They come to a door and she sees that his name is on it.

"Where the hell have you taken me?" Sam asks in a nervous tone.

Ty looks at her as he opens the door.

"My studio."

Ty completely opens the door, and Sam sees a lot of people working. Sam slowly walks in and looks at everything with amazement. Ty gently taps her on the shoulder, making her look at him.

"What you're looking for is over there," Ty says.

Sam looks at what Ty is pointing at. She looks at him then slowly walks over to the person he is pointing at. Ty watches for a second, then he goes over to everyone helping him set up his studio, making sure that everything goes where he wants it. Sam walks over to the person and gently taps their shoulder. The person slowly turns around, and Sam gets a shocked look on her face. For the person is Krysta! Sam slightly screams and pulls Krysta into a tight hug and Krysta hugs her back.

Chapter 4

As Ty is working on a new painting idea, Sam and Krysta are talking.

"I can't believe he did that to you," Sam says.

"But I'm okay," Krysta says.

Sam slowly shakes her head.

"Even so, Krysta! You have to go to the cops. You have to tell them what happened to you."

Krysta looks at her.

"Sam, you know I can't do that."

"You have to do something. He's been looking for you," Sam says.

Krysta looks at her with shock and concern.

"What?" Krysta softly says.

"Yeah, days that you work or sometimes at night to see if you're going to pop up," Sam replies.

Krysta slowly looks down at the floor with a really nervous look. Sam sees the look on her face, then she looks up and sees Ty. She smiles then looks at Krysta.

"So…what's up with you and that guy over there?" Sam smiles.

Krysta looks at her with a small smile, then she looks slightly over to Ty.

"Nothing…he's just a friend," Krysta replies.

Sam stares at her for a minute with a small lift of her eyebrows.

"That's why you turn red when you look at him. What? I'm just saying. He has a body that makes you say, 'Pick me up,'" Sam says.

Krysta looks at her, then they both start laughing. Ty looks at them with eyes, then he grins as he looks back at everything. Sam stays with Krysta her whole hour break plus her lunch break. Sam and Krysta are both eating lunch together in the cafeteria, laughing, with Krysta telling Sam how her life has been living with Ty. As Krysta explains how her life is living with Ty, Sam can see how happy Krysta is talking about Ty. Sam stares at her for about a minute, then she smiles.

"I have a question for you." Sam smiles.

Krysta looks at her.

"How long have you been living with Ty again? Two, three months?" Sam asks.

"Yeah, why?" replies Krysta.

Sam stares at her for a minute, still with a smile.

"So was it before or after you started living with him that you started to fall in love with him?"

Krysta looks at Sam with shock, but then, she looks at Ty who is sitting at the table, across from them, with his friends, laughing. Krysta slowly looks back at Sam. She's about to say something but Sam cuts her off.

"It's okay. You're not with Ford, and in a way, you never were. I'm going to be straight with you, girl. You were more of a housekeeper than a girlfriend."

Krysta looks down at her food and thinks about the time she was with Ford. He never once did anything romantic with her. Then she thinks about her time with Ty, and even though they're not an item, Krysta has more fun with Ty than she ever did with Ford. Sam sees that Krysta understands what she's saying. But she also can see that she's not completely sure about her feelings for Ty. After lunch, Sam has to return to the shop.

"I'm sorry. I have to head back," Sam says.

"Okay, sorry, I would walk you down…but…" Krysta says.

"It's okay, I get it. Just find a way to contact me. And maybe you should talk to Ty about Ford. You've been with him for two months. I don't think he'll think any less of you or anything," Sam says.

Krysta looks at her and slowly nods her head with a small smile. They give each other a hug, then Sam heads back to the shop. Krysta watches Sam go back to the shop through the window. She smiles then she goes back to Ty's studio. As she walks into the studio, she sees Ty talking to some of the other workers. Ty turns his head and sees Krysta standing beside the door. He can see that she has a happy yet sad smile on her face. Ty tells everyone what else to do, then he walks over to Krysta. Krysta looks at Ty standing in front of her.

"Are you okay?" Ty asks.

Krysta stares at him for a minute, then she slightly puts her head down. Ty tilts his head, trying to see her face. Krysta slowly starts to move closer to him, she gets close, then she starts to gently wrap her arms around him. Ty looks at her, then he slowly wraps his arms around her.

"Thank you," Krysta says softly.

Ty grins then gives her a small kiss on the head, making Krysta hold him a little tighter.

The day goes on and Ty finishes up his work in the studio. As Ty is finishing his work, Krysta thinks about what Sam told her, telling Ty about Ford and what happened to her. After the workday is over, Ty and Krysta are still in the studio. Everyone has gone home. They are both cleaning up the studio. Ty looks at Krysta. He walks over to her. She looks at him, he gently takes her hand.

"Come here."

Krysta follows Ty, he has her stand beside one of his studio windows. He slowly turns her head, making her look out the window.

"Okay, don't move," Ty says.

Ty gets his camera and starts to take pictures of her. She looks at him, then she tries to hide her face. Ty runs over to her.

"Krysta stop." Ty laughs.

"I can't believe you're taking pictures of me. I look terrible," Krysta whines.

"No, you don't." Ty laughs.

Ty puts the camera down and tries to get Krysta to stop hiding her face. Then when Ty gets Krysta's hand out of her face, they look at each other, right in the eyes. Their eyes look deep into each other, making their bodies freeze. They snap out of it when the janitor walks by. They look back at each other.

"We should go," says Ty.

Krysta nods her head, then they both walk to the door and Ty shuts down the studio. They get into the elevator and go down to the first floor. They come out the backdoor where Ty's bike is. Ty gets on the bike and starts it up, then Krysta walks over and he helps her on. She wraps her arms around him, and they slowly head to Ty's apartment. They walk into the apartment and Ty sees the time.

"Damn, it's late," Ty says.

Krysta looks at him and grins at him. He slowly shakes his head.

"It's late, I'll just order us some pizza and have them deliver it, okay?"

Krysta gently smiles and nods her head. Then they walk into the kitchen and get the number for the pizza. He asks Krysta what she wants on her pizza. All she tells him is whatever he wants so Ty gets two medium pizza, one cheese and one pepperoni. They wait for the pizza, about fifteen to twenty minutes. Ty opens the door and pays for the pizza. Ty brings the pizza into the kitchen and calls Krysta. Krysta comes out of the bedroom and sees that the pizza is here.

"Okay, I got the pizza so you pick the movie," Ty says.

Krysta smiles at him, then she walks over to the TV and looks for a movie to watch. Krysta picks another movie that she has not seen. She picks *Killers* with Katherine Heigl and Ashton Kutcher. They finish their pizza and the movie is still playing. Krysta puts her head on Ty's shoulder. Ty slightly looks at her and grins. Then he puts his head down on Krysta's head. They both fall asleep not long before the movie is over.

They both wake up the next morning and see that they fell asleep on the couch. Ty doesn't have to go to work today. He tells Krysta that he's taking her to get some clothes. They both get up, take their own showers, and get dressed. Ty takes Krysta to a friend's clothing store and Krysta looks around. Then a young woman comes over to Ty and Krysta. Krysta looks at her as she gives Ty a hug. Krysta tries her best to hold a smile.

"Krysta, this is my friend I told you about," Ty says.

Krysta smiles at her.

"Hi."

"Hi," the woman says back.

"Krysta, this is Max, short for Maxseen. And, Max, this is Krysta," Ty introduces.

Max and Krysta look at each other. Ty tries not to laugh.

"Max is married to one of my high school friends."

Krysta looks at him then back at Max.

"Really?" Krysta says.

"Yeah, we got engaged our second year of college," Max explains.

Krysta nods her head with guilt yet awkward.

"So from the looks of it, you need clothes," Max says.

"Yeah." Krysta nods her head.

Krysta follows Max to show her some clothes she may like. As Krysta looks around the clothes, Ty is talking to Max at the counter.

"I think she likes you." Max smiles.

"No, she doesn't," Ty replies.

Max looks at him, trying not to laugh.

"Yes, she does. Didn't you see the way she looked at me when we came face-to-face?" Max says.

Ty looks at her, then he slightly looks over to Krysta. After about ten minutes, Krysta asks is she can try on the clothes she picked out. Max lets her into the room and stays with her while Ty stays at the counter. Ty waits for about twenty minutes for Krysta to try on all her clothes. After Krysta was all done trying on the clothes she picked, she comes to the counter.

"I can't buy all of these. I don't have enough," Krysta says.

"It's okay," says Max. "I owe Ty a lot. So don't worry about it, I'll just scratch this as one of them."

Krysta stares at Max, then she looks at Ty who is grinning at her then he winks at her. She smiles at him, then Max bags the clothes.

She walks with them to the front door. As Ty and Krysta are leaving, Krysta says her thanks then Max calls to Ty.

"Hey, Ty," Max yells.

Ty and Krysta stop and look at her.

"You know that I'm right about that."

Ty slightly tilts his head and shakes it while Krysta looks at the both of them with confusion. They both then continue walking back to Ty's apartment. As they get back to the apartment, Krysta wants to show Ty the clothes she got. Ty sits on the couch and waits for Krysta to show him her clothes. Krysta goes into the bedroom to put on one of the outfits she got. Ty shakes his head at all of them, at all ten outfits, laughing. Krysta is laughing also, then she goes to put on one of Ty's T-shirts that he gave her. They both then get ready for bed. Both of them are in the bathroom brushing their teeth. Ty then leaves the bathroom to go change his clothes while Krysta stays to braid her hair. Ty then comes to the bathroom door, and Krysta looks at him. He grins at her and she smiles back at him.

"Good night, Krysta."

"Good night, Ty."

Ty then goes into the living room to sleep on the couch. Krysta feels bad that Ty is sleeping on the couch and he lets her sleep in his room. But Ty has told her, over and over, that he doesn't mind and that he would make her sleep on the bed either way. Krysta turns off the bedroom light, then she slowly starts to fall asleep. Ty is lying back on the couch with his arms crossed, already asleep. Krysta is not sleeping peacefully; she's moving all over the bed. The she wakes up screaming, making Ty quickly wake himself up. Ty jumps over the couch and into his bedroom. Krysta looks at him and he sees that she's about to cry. Ty slowly walks over to her and gently puts his hand on her face.

"It's okay, you're safe," Ty softly says.

Krysta slowly nods her head, then Ty gets ready to walk away but Krysta grabs his hand. Ty turns and looks at her, they stare at each other for a minute in the eyes.

"Can you stay here?" Krysta softly asks.

"Sure." Ty softly nods his head.

Ty then gets ready to pull the chair over but then—"Not there."

Ty turns his head and looks at Krysta. She moves slowly over to the side of the bed. Ty sees that she wants him to lie next to her. Ty slowly moves over to the bed, then he slowly leans back. He and Krysta look at each other, then he lifts his arm. Krysta smiles softly, then she moves over to him. Krysta lies down and she puts her head on Ty's chest and Ty wraps his arms around her. They both fall asleep in each other's arms, for the first time in a long time, Krysta sleeps peacefully.

The next morning, Ty is already gone but he leaves Krysta a note.

"Left early this morning. Couldn't wake you up, for you looked so at peace. I'm not going to be gone all day. I'll be back around early to late noon. Ty."

Krysta smiles at the note, then she looks at the time. She sees that it's only going on 10:30 a.m. Krysta slowly gets up then goes into the kitchen. She looks around to see if there is anything that she can cook for Ty. But there is not a lot of food in the apartment for her to cook him anything. Krysta then remembers that there is a small store a few blocks away from the apartment. Krysta goes to put one of her clothes outfit on a gray sweat suit and get ready to head out. Even though Krysta never leaves, Ty always leaves her a spare key if she ever did. She takes the key, a little of the money Ty left for her, just in case she wants to order some food. Krysta comes to the front door and takes a deep breath before she opens the door and leaves the apartment. She slowly starts to walk out and looks around to see if anyone is around. And the part that makes her chuckle is that she wasn't afraid or nervous. Krysta then walks out the elevator and heads to the store, but as Krysta is walking to the store, she looks to make sure she has the money Ty left her. Causing her not to look where she's going, Krysta ends up bumping into another person. Krysta doesn't drop the money but she does cause the person to drop their phone. Krysta looks down at the phone and picks it up.

"I'm so sorry, here you…go."

As Krysta lifts her head, her face turns into shock and fear, for the person she bumped into is none other than Ford! Krysta slowly stands up, and Ford just stares at her with a plain look on his face. Krysta hands him his phone. He looks at the phone then at Krysta. Ford snatches the phone from her, then he walks around her. Krysta takes a breath of relief and starts walking.

"Hey, you."

Krysta stops with slight panicked look on her face. She slightly turns around and looks at Ford. He stares at Krysta and she stares back at him.

"Have me met before?" Ford asks.

Krysta stares at him for a minute, then her shocked face slowly turns to a plain look. She slowly shakes her head.

"No."

Even though she shakes her head and looking at Ford with a plain look, Krysta's body is shaking. Ford stares at her for a minute; he can't really tell its Krysta, for she's not dressed like the Krysta he knows. Since its middle of fall, she's wearing her gray sweat suit, with a white shirt and sneakers, and her hair is up in a high ponytail. Ford looks at Krysta up and down, then he walks away. Krysta takes a breath, then she continues walking away, trying to get out of sight. She turns a corner and stands against the wall, almost slamming herself, breathing heavy in a panic. Then she slowly slides down the wall and sits on the ground, holding her legs, putting herself into a ball. Hiding her head in her legs, then it starts to down pour.

Meanwhile Ty comes home and sees that Krysta is not home. He walks around as he puts his things away, then he walks into the kitchen and sees that Krysta left a note. He sees that Krysta said she was going to the store down the street. He grins but that grin quickly fades when he sees what time she left. Krysta has been gone for almost two hours. Ty quickly grabs his keys and runs out the door. He runs down the streets to the store, not caring that it's raining. He runs down the street to the corner store, the store is down the street but is on the other side of the street from Ty's apartment. Ty runs across the street and down to the store. Ty runs into the store and over to the counter. Ty is out of breath.

"Have you seen a girl come in here?"

"There are a lot of girls that come in here," replies the cashier.

"The one you saw me with last time," Ty slightly yells.

"Oh, that pretty girl. No, I haven't," replies the cashier.

Ty then runs back out the store, he runs across the street to see if she came that way. As Ty comes back to his apartment, he looks around the corner and sees Krysta sitting in a ball. He slowly walks over to her and kneels down in front of her.

"Krysta," Ty says.

Ty says her name as if he's making sure it's really her, Krysta slowly lifts her head and looks at Ty. Ty looks at her with slight shock, for Krysta has that same look in her eyes when he first found her in the alley, two and a half to three months ago. They stare at each other for a minute, then Ty gently puts his hand on her hand. He takes his other hand to her arm and slowly helps Krysta off the ground. He keeps hold of one of her hands, then he puts his hand around her waist.

They slowly walk back to Ty's apartment. Ty opens the door and Krysta slowly walks in. Ty closes the door behind them gently. Ty looks at Krysta who is just standing there. He walks over to her, then he slowly guides her into his room. She stands there again, and Ty goes into the bathroom and puts on the shower. He comes back into the bedroom and slowly takes Krysta into the bathroom. He sits Krysta on the sink and helps her take off her shoes. He looks at her, then he slowly takes his shoes off. Ty helps Krysta off the sink, then they both go into the shower with their clothes on.

After about twenty minutes, Ty helps Krysta out of the shower. He leaves her in the bathroom for a minute. He goes into the bedroom to get something for her to wear after she takes off her wet clothes. Ty comes back into the bathroom after five minutes. He put new clothes on and his wet clothes in the bathroom to dry in the shower. He walks over to Krysta and takes a deep breath. He then helps her out of her wet clothes without looking at her body. He puts her wets clothes next to his to dry, then they walk into the bedroom. Ty gently sits Krysta on the bed, then he takes a dry towel to dry her hair. Ty puts the towel over Krysta's head and gently moves the towel. But then Krysta slowly moves her hand to Ty's arm, causing Ty to stop drying Krysta's hair and look down at her. There is a pause for a minute.

"Ford," Krysta softly says.

"What?" Ty gently asks.

Krysta doesn't say anything, making Ty slowly kneel down in front of her. He gets a slight shocked look on his face, for he sees that Krysta is crying. Ty can see that she's trying to hold it all back.

"Krysta, stop holding it back. And let it go, I'm here," Ty gently says.

Krysta looks at him, then she jumps into his arms, causing him to fall on the floor. With Krysta lying on top of him, with her arms wrapped around his neck, crying. Ty looks at her, and he slowly wraps his arms around her.

After about eight minutes, Ty is able to get Krysta up. They both lie on the bed, Krysta on her side and Ty on his stomach. Both of them looking at each other. Ty has his head on one of his pillows with his arms crossed. Krysta has one of her arms on the other pillow with her head down and her other hand just on the bed. Ty takes a breath, then he looks back at Krysta.

"Who's Ford?"

Krysta looks away from Ty for a second while she takes a deep breath. She looks back at Ty.

"Ford…is my ex-boyfriend. The one that beat me up."

Ty just stares at her.

"Okay, hope you're ready. Cause you're probably wondering why I stayed with a guy like that."

Ty doesn't say anything. He's still just staring at her.

"Okay, I met Ford because he's the son of my father's boss. The reason I stayed with Ford is because he's all I had. My parents died not that long after I finished high school. My whole family is gone, both of my parents were only children. My grandparents passed when I was in grade school. So Ford was it, plus I was still just a kid. I didn't have a job because of all the after-school things I did. Then I went to college and Ford waited for me. I did two years. After that, things changed. Ford started acting different. He didn't want me to do anything, didn't even like the fact that I have friends. It wasn't that he was bad, he understood the fact that I was never ready to make that step in the relationship. But that doesn't mean he didn't find it elsewhere. Not that long after I met you, I found out that Ford was cheating on me. Times I went home, the place was a mess. And I had to clean it up and make dinner, I had to be home at a certain time. If I wasn't, I had to sleep on the couch. Sometimes with no blanket. There were times that I got slapped for being late getting home. So I get slapped and sleep on the couch," Krysta explains.

Ty just stares at her as he listens to how her life was when she was with Ford. How they never talked to each other to how she always has to be home for dinner, mostly to make it. Had to have the table set, pull out his chair when he sits, and every time he's done, she had to take his plate even if she's not done with her food. After he's done with his food, she can't finish her food, for she was to clean the dishes, table, and the rest of the apartment. And if she wasn't done by the time Ford was going to bed, she had to sleep on the couch. Then she tells Ty about the girls that he cheated on her with. How she comes home and the apartment was mess and she had to clean it. Even tells him one time, she had to make dinner for Ford, herself, and one of the girls he was cheating on her with. Krysta tells Ty that she lied to Ford so she can be his model. As Krysta tells Ty everything, she slowly comes to a pause.

"Then there was the night that you found me," Krysta says.

He walks over to her and stands next to her, but she doesn't look at him.

"I think we should take our relationship to the next level," Ford says.

Krysta stops chopping the carrots and slightly looks up but still doesn't look at Ford. Her face shows that she's tired yet aggravated. She doesn't say anything for a minute, then she slightly tilts her head to Ford.

"Why? You get in everywhere else," Krysta says.

Ford quickly looks at her, then he grabs her by the arm and turns her to him. He slaps her across the face—hard! Krysta moves back, almost losing her balance, and her face turns. But then, she looks back at Ford. She looks at him for a second, then she slaps him across the face, making his face slightly turn. Ford is in shock.

"I'm sick of this. We are done... I'm out of here," Krysta says.

Krysta then walks to the front door. Ford slowly turns his head to her. But before Krysta can open the door, Ford grabs her by the back of her hair; she slightly screams.

"So you think you can fight now. Let's see how well," Ford says.

Then he throws Krysta to the floor, hard, and looks down at her. Ford looks down at her, and Krysta slowly turns her head to him with fear in her eyes. Krysta slowly backs away from him but Ford grabs her by the ankles and pulls her back to him. He sits on top of her, so she can't get away, and punches her face a few times. Krysta bites his hand hard, enough to get him off of her. She turns to cover her face but Ford just grabs her by the back of her head. He makes her stand up just to throw her over to the wall. He slams her to the wall, then he throws her back to the floor, hard. He slowly walks over to her, then he looks at her. Then he kicks her in the thighs and stomach. Ford then quickly kneels down and turns Krysta over to her back.

"You will be mine," Ford yells.

Ford starts to rip Krysta's clothes but then Krysta knees him. Ford slowly falls off from on top of her. Krysta tries to move. She turns her body but her legs will not move. Ford looks at her, then he sees a wire that's not in use on the floor. He picks it up then slowly walks over to Krysta whose back is to him. Krysta then screams in deep pain, for Ford is whipping her with the wire. Ford whips Krysta about twelve to fourteen times before he stops. Then he quickly kneels back down and turns Krysta onto her back.

"You will be mine," Ford yells.

Krysta keeps trying to stop Ford from ripping more of her clothes off. Then when she turns her head, she sees the small lamp that she was going to throw out. She reaches for it because Ford is too angry to see what she's doing. Krysta is able to grab the lamp, she quickly hits Ford on the head, hard, knocking Ford out, making him fall off of Krysta. Krysta slowly leans up but her legs will not move. Tears will not stop falling from her eyes.

"Move, Krysta, move!"

Krysta slowly is able to get up but her body is shaking. She goes out of the apartment and over to the stairs but falls down them. She looks up at the apartment and gets a shocked look on her face. For she can see Ford's shadow. She slowly gets up and walks away as fast as she can.

"I fell in the alley and that's when you found me," Krysta says.

Ty is in complete shock from what Krysta had told him. His head is no longer down on his pillow but up and staring at Krysta. Krysta looks at him, then she puts her hand over her face and cries. Ty moves closer to her and wraps his arms around her, causing Krysta to wrap her arms around him. Krysta cries so hard and so much that she falls asleep in Ty's arms, and Ty watches her sleep. As he watches her sleep all night, thinking about what she told him, Ty also thinks about why she never wanted to go to the hospital or the cops. But he also thinks that something must have happened to make her want to talk about what happened to her all of a sudden.

The next morning, Krysta wakes up but Ty is not there. She slowly gets up and walks over to the bedroom door; she slowly opens it. She sees Ty sitting on the couch, watching TV. She walks over to the couch and Ty turns his head and looks at her.

"Morning," Ty says.

"Morning," Krysta says.

She gives him a small smile. Ty lifts one of his eyebrows.

"Why are you looking at me like that?" Ty asks.

Krysta walks a little closer to him.

"Um…about last night—" Krysta's cut off.

"Look, there are a few things I still don't get. But you finally just started talking about what happened to you with me. So I'm not going to have you tell me everything in one sitting, okay?" Ty says.

Ty can see that Krysta doesn't know what to say but is also happy. Ty then slowly gets off the couch and walks over to Krysta. They look at each other.

"Well, I don't have work today. What do you want to do?" Ty asks.

Krysta smiles at him, and he gently smiles back at her.

Chapter 5

"You okay back there?" Ty yells.

"Yeah," Krysta yells back.

Krysta wanted Ty to take her on a motorcycle ride. They don't have anywhere special to go, they are just riding around. Krysta puts her head on Ty's back and just relaxes. Ty looks at her with his eyes for a second when they come to a red light. He grins at her, then he looks back and the light changes to green. Ty takes Krysta down to the water; they don't get off the motorcycle but they do drive around it. Ty slows down so Krysta can see all the boats coming and going. She smiles, then Ty thinks of another place to take Krysta. He wants to take her to the park that she saw him taking pictures. They pull up at the park and Ty turns off his motorcycle. Krysta gets off the bike first, then Ty slowly follows. Krysta waits for Ty as she looks at the park and everyone walking around, smiling. Ty walks up next to her, they look at each other, then Ty takes Krysta's hand. Ty starts walking and Krysta follows as they hold hands.

"Okay, out of this part of the park, what do you like?" Ty asks.

Krysta looks at him, then she looks around the park, then she smiles.

"I think I like this part of the park." Krysta smiles.

Ty takes her hand and gently pulls her closer to him, then he hands her his camera.

"All right, take a picture," Ty says.

Krysta looks at him, then she looks at the camera. She slowly takes the camera and Ty slowly shows her how to work it. Krysta takes the picture, and Ty helps her find more in the area that she likes. She sees what he sees the park as and how he takes his picture, causing Krysta to smile at how Ty sees things before taking them. She looks at Ty who is petting a dog that came over to him. She slowly kneels down and takes a few pictures of him. Ty looks at her and softly smiles at her. Krysta slowly puts the camera down but still is in her hands. The dog then runs back over to its owner and Ty slowly stands up. Krysta slowly gets up as Ty walks over to her. They look at each other.

"So you hungry?" asks Ty.

"Yeah," Krysta replies with a smile.

Then they both walk back to Ty's bike. As they are walking to Ty's bike, Krysta looks at Ty's hand. She slowly reaches for it but she stops. Ty sees in their shadows that Krysta was going to grab his hand but stopped. Ty grins then he stops and turns to Krysta. She looks at him, then Ty reaches his hand out to Krysta. Ty gently takes Krysta's hand, then he turns back around and they continue walking. Krysta smiles and holds onto Ty's hand, then she slowly gets closer to him. They look at each other as they walk side by side.

They ride around, talking about what they are going to eat for lunch. They end up at a little corner café that sells sandwiches. As they sit, eating, Krysta asks Ty about a job at the building he works at.

"You want to work at the art building?" Ty asks.

"Yeah, I can't keep taking money from you. Plus I'm living with you. I want to do something. Or I can find something else," Krysta explains.

Ty looks at her with a grin, then he nods his head.

"Okay, I'll see what happens. We'll go tomorrow," Ty says.

Krysta smiles, then she gives Ty a hug. They look at each other, then Krysta goes to the bathroom. As Krysta goes to the bathroom, Ty watches her till he can't see her then he takes his cell phone out and calls his job. Ty talks on the phone till Krysta comes back. As Krysta is walking back, Ty hangs up and puts his phone back into his pocket. Krysta sits down and they finish up their food. Ty then takes their trash to throw it away. They both get onto the bike and ride off.

Ty then takes Krysta to another one of his favorite spots; he takes her to one of the beaches. He slowly pulls up to the beach and Krysta looks at it with amazement. Ty looks at her and smiles. Krysta slowly gets off the bike. She slowly walks over to the beach sand; the way the sun hits the water makes Krysta smile. Ty slowly walks behind her. She turns to Ty.

"Where are we?" Krysta asks.

"Midland Beach Veterans Memorial," Ty replies.

Krysta looks at him then back at the water.

"You've been here before, right?" Ty asks.

Krysta slowly shakes her head no and slowly start to walk away. Ty just watches her walk on the shoreline. As Krysta walks on the edge of the water, Ty can see a picture in his head that he wants to draw. Krysta walks to the shoreline, then she turns to look at Ty who is sitting on the sand, drawing in his sketchbook. Krysta slowly walks over to him but Ty doesn't look up at her. She walks around him to see what he is drawing. Krysta gets a surprised look on her face, for Ty is drawing a picture of Krysta on the shoreline. With her in a long summer dress, she can't tell much, for he hasn't put color into it yet. She stands there, watching Ty sketch her. But then, Ty stops and slowly turns his head and looks at Krysta. She looks at him and they both smile at each other. Ty then slowly closes his sketchbook and slowly stands up, but they both are still looking at each other. They stand facing each other, then they turn their heads to the sunset. Krysta then looks down at Ty's hand, wishing to hold it but stops. Ty sees in their shadows that Krysta was about to grab his hand. Ty slightly laughs under his breath, then he looks back at their shadows. Then he gently takes Krysta's hand, making her get a shocked but happy look on her face. She looks back at the sunset as she and Ty hold hands. As the sun completely leaves the sky, Ty and Krysta walk back to his motorcycle.

Ty and Krysta go out to eat after they leave the beach. As they sit there, eating and laughing, Krysta is asking Ty more about himself.

"Okay, so you came from LA? But you came out here to New York for the program they had," Krysta says.

"Yeah, my mother and father live in LA. But my grandparents live in Tennessee," Ty says.

"Wow, you do get to see them, right? I mean..." Krysta says.

"Yes, I see them. A few times on holidays, birthdays, and every year, there will be a small family get together or a family reunion," Ty says.

"Wow, sounds like it's going to be fun." Krysta smiles.

Ty looks at her and grins.

"You tell me. I want you to come with me."

Krysta stares at him with a little shock on her face.

"Yes, Krysta, I'm asking you to come with me to LA." Ty grins.

Krysta smiles at him, then she puts her head down, trying to hide how much she is blushing. Ty slightly starts laughing under his breath, putting his head down. Krysta looks at him and he looks back at her.

"I would love to go."

*****

Three weeks have gone by and Krysta has gotten a job at the art building that Ty works at. She works on the same floor as Ty, working the front desk, working the phones with another woman. Her name is Lynne; she's light-skinned, about 5'4" feet tall, very short light-brown hair, dark-brown eyes, and is married with two boys, four and five years old.

"You're getting really good at this, Krysta." Lynne smiles.

"Thank you, Lynne. And thank you for teaching me and putting up with me." Krysta smiles.

"Oh, no, thank you. Now I don't have to do everything by myself anymore." Lynne smiles.

"I just don't want everyone to think that I got this job because of Ty," Krysta says.

"He got you an interview, that's all," Lynne says.

Krysta smiles and Lynne slightly laughs. As they get back to work, a few a board members come out of the elevator. They both look over to them, then they look at each other and slightly shrug their shoulders. Then Ty comes around the corner and walks over to the desk and slightly leans on it next to Krysta. Lynne slightly laughs, for Krysta doesn't know that Ty is standing next to her. Krysta looks at her, then she turns her head and jumps but starts laughing as she puts her hand on her chest.

"Hi." Ty grins.

"Hi." Krysta laughs.

"You ready to go?" Ty slightly laughs.

"Yeah, I'm ready." Krysta laughs.

Krysta laughs, then she walks over to Ty and they both start walking to the elevator.

"I'll see you in a little bit," Krysta says.

Lynne waves to them as they walk into the elevator and she smiles.

"That's going to happen soon."

As Lynne keeps working, Ty and Krysta are slowly coming out of the elevator on the first floor, laughing.

"So where do you want to go for lunch?" Ty asks, still with a small chuckle.

Krysta looks at him and slowly shrugs her shoulders. As they walk out of the art building, they slowly start walking down the street, talking about what they want to eat. As they are walking across the street, there is Sam, looking at them with a smile on her face.

Ty and Krysta finish their lunch break, then they slowly start walking back to the art building, talking about going to LA to see Ty's family. They walk into the building, still laughing; but as they are walking, one of the women workers is looking down at them from the floor above them. She looks at them with anger in her eyes. As she watches them walk into the elevator, she slowly walks away. Ty and Krysta are talking in the elevator. Krysta looks at Ty as if she has a question but is too nervous to ask. She puts her head down, causing Ty to look at her with a little confusion with a lift of his eyebrow. As Ty stares at her, he gets a grin on his face.

"Okay, Krysta, what do you want to ask me?"

Krysta looks at him with a nervous smile.

"What makes you think I want to ask you something?"

Ty just looks at her, causing Krysta to get even more nervous.

"Okay, this is an out-of-the-blue question and I should have asked awhile go but—"

"What's the question?" asks Ty.

"Where's your girlfriend. I mean...you're an amazing guy. So you can't tell me there's not anyone in your life," Krysta asks.

Ty looks at her and slowly nods his head.

"There was someone in my life. But I broke up with her."

"Why?" Krysta asks.

"Because... I found her cheating on me. With a no-longer-best-friend of mine," Ty replies.

"I'm so sorry, I didn't know. I shouldn't have asked," Krysta says.

"Krysta, it's okay. This happened my second year of college. And she and I only dated for about four to five months," Ty explains.

"Even so," Krysta says.

Ty slowly smiles at her, causing her to smile back at him yet her smile has a little sadness in it. Ty can see it but doesn't get a chance to say anything for the elevator doors open. They look at the doors and Ty gets an angry look on his face. Krysta looks at Ty then looks back out the door. There is a young woman standing in front of the elevator door. She is light-skinned, about 5'5" feet tall, short brown hair, and brown eyes. She looks at Ty then slowly looks at Krysta who moves a little closer to Ty.

"What is it Amy?" says Ty.

"Nothing, just going down. You?" says Amy.

"Getting off," Ty says.

Ty gently takes Krysta's hand and they both walk out of the elevator as Amy walks into it. Amy watches them but Ty doesn't look at her and Krysta looks at Ty with concern. Ty walks Krysta back to the front counter, but Lynne wasn't there. Krysta sits down in her seat but looks at Ty who is walking back to his studio. She watches him with concern, then she turns her head when she hears the chair beside her move. Lynne is slowly sitting down, then she looks at Krysta who has a concerned look on her face.

"I know I just got back from lunch but—" Krysta says.

"Go, it's a slow day," Lynne continues with a smile.

Krysta smiles at her, then she gets up and quickly walks down to Ty's studio. As she comes to Ty's studio, she sees everyone slowly walking out of it. Everyone walks around her, then she slowly comes to the studio doorway and sees Ty staring out the window with one hand on his hip and the other leaning on the wall with his head leaning against it. Krysta stares at him for a minute, then she slowly starts to walk over to him. She comes up right behind him, causing her not to be seen by him. She pauses at first, then she slowly wraps her arms around Ty's waist, causing Ty to slowly yet quickly lean his head from his arm and look behind him. He sees that it's Krysta who has her head gently on his back. He grins, then he slowly moves his hand from his hip and gently puts it on Krysta's hands. They both stay that way for a while, then Ty slowly turns around and Krysta looks up at him. Ty then slowly leans back against the wall and Krysta walks closer to him. She doesn't say anything; all she does is stand in front of him with a worried look on her face.

"Amy," Ty says.

Krysta still doesn't say anything.

"The woman that we saw when we came out of the elevator is Amy. Also…she is the one that cheated on me in college," Ty continues.

Krysta looks at him with shock.

"I worked in this building longer than she has. She was transferred here a few weeks after I met you," Ty continues. "This would be the second time we have talked since she has been here."

"Wow, are you okay? I mean seeing her? It looks like it still hurts to see her," Krysta asks.

Ty looks at her with a small grin.

"No, it hurts because every time I see her, all she asks me is if we can get back together. And I don't know how many ways you can say no to someone till you snap."

Krysta slightly and slowly shrugs her shoulders. Ty slightly laughs under his breath, then he looks back at Krysta.

"Thank you," Ty says.

Krysta slightly tilts her head and looks at him with small confusion.

"For what?"

"For just listening. Sometimes that's all someone needs to just to be heard without saying anything," Ty replies.

Krysta smiles.

"Anytime."

Then everyone slowly starts to walk back into the studio, making Ty look up and Krysta turn her head to everyone. They look back at each other, then they say that they will see each other after work and Krysta walks back to the front counter. Ty watches her walk, then he looks at everyone who is staring at him with smiles on their faces.

"What?" Ty says.

Then everyone slowly starts to get back to work and Ty looks back at the studio door. He stares at it for a minute then he smiles as he goes back to work. Meanwhile as Krysta is walking back to the front counter, she sees Amy walking to her. Krysta just stares right past her and keeps walking. But then, as Krysta walks past her, Amy stops and turns around, looking at Krysta walk right by her. She doesn't say anything; she just watches her for a minute then she continues walking. As she is walking, she pauses in front of Ty's studio and she stares at Ty but he doesn't see her. Then she takes a deep breath and walks into the studio, right over to Ty. Everyone sees her coming into the studio, then they look at Ty. Ty is looking at colors, then he looks up and sees that everyone is staring at him. He looks at them with confusion, then he slowly turns his head and gets an angry shocked look on his face. He stares at her for a minute, then he turns his head and tells everyone what colors he wants for the photo shoot. Amy takes a small breath.

"Can we talk, please?"

Ty takes a deep angry breath, then he slowly turns around and looks at Amy.

"Fine, you have one minute. And I mean one minute," Ty replies.

Ty looks at everyone, then everyone slowly starts to walk out of the studio. Amy watches everyone leave the studio room. Ty stops one of the guys.

"Be back in here in one minute—one minute," Ty says.

The guy nods his head and looks at the clock on the wall and sees that it's 3:25 p.m. Then he slowly walks out of the studio. Ty then looks at Amy.

"What do you want?"

"I'm sorry," Amy says.

Ty slowly shakes his head.

"Sorry? It's been almost three and half years and you want to say sorry to me now? Why? Because you saw me with another woman," Ty says.

Amy just looks at him.

"You cheated on me with my best friend. For how long, I don't know nor do I care. I said everything I had to say to you when I broke up with you in college. There's nothing more to say, now get out of my studio. I have work to do," Ty says.

Before she can say anything, everyone starts to come into the studio. Amy looks at them all and Ty walks away from her. She takes a breath, then she storms out of the studio and heads back to her office. As she is walking to her office and stops and looks at Krysta at the front desk, answering the phones with Lynne. Amy stares at her for a minute, then she walks over to her quickly. She stands in front of Krysta and slams her hand on the desk. Krysta jumps as her looks at her. Lynne looks at Amy then at Krysta.

"What is it about you that makes him want to stay with you?" Amy asks.

Krysta looks at her with confusion, then she looks at Lynne, and she just shrugs her shoulders. Krysta looks back at Amy. Amy looks at Krysta up and down.

"Pathetic."

Krysta slightly glares at her. Amy then walks away from her, but Krysta gets up and walks around desk.

"Who do you think you are?"

Amy stops and turns around to look at Krysta. She then slowly walks over to her and they stand right in front of each other. They stare at each other without saying anything; Lynne stands up and walks over to them. Lynne gently pulls Krysta back and she tells her to go get some air. She watches Krysta walk away, then Lynne looks back at Amy. Amy just gives her a cocky grin, then she continues walking back to her office. Lynne then goes over to the desk and picks up then phone and presses three numbers.

"Can I talk to Ty?" Lynne says.

Later on the roof, Ty comes out of the door and sees Krysta leaning on the railing, looking at the sunset. Ty walks over to her and slowly leans on the railing next to her. He doesn't look at her; they just watch the sunset.

"Sorry," Ty says.

Krysta looks at him with confusion.

"For what?" Krysta asks.

"For Amy, that she came and got in your face," Ty replies.

Krysta slowly starts to smile.

"It's not that she got in my face. She called me pathetic."

Ty looks at her.

"And I am," Krysta continues.

"How is that?" Ty asks.

Krysta looks back out to the sunset and Ty can see her eyes watering.

"'Cause… I'm hiding from what happened to me."

Ty looks at her with confusion.

"Krysta, what happened to you is not something you can just stand up to. And on top of that, you got out. You didn't stay and put up with it, and since we know who he is, trying to fight that is not easy," Ty says.

Krysta looks at Ty and he grins at her, tears slowly running down her face, and Ty slowly leans off the railing. He moves over to her, and Krysta slowly leans off the railing. They look at each and Ty slowly opens his arms. Krysta slowly walks closer to him and Ty gently wraps his arms around her as Krysta wraps her arms around him.

Ty then gives her a small kiss on her head, making Krysta hold him a little tighter. Ty then looks down at her and Krysta looks up at him.

"Let's go home," Ty says.

Krysta nods her head and they both slowly start to walk back into the building, still holding each other. As they walk down the stairs, one of the guys that is working with Ty on the photo shoot comes running up the stairs. Ty looks at him and asks him what he wants. He tells Ty that everyone is looking for him. Ty looks at Krysta and she looks up at him. Ty tells him that the photo shoot will continue tomorrow. He nods his head, then he runs back down the stairs and goes to tell everyone what Ty said. Ty looks back at Krysta and they continue walking down the stairs. They both leave the building and walk over to Ty's motorcycle. As they leave the building, a guy walks right in after them. He walks up to the front desk and asks to see the art producer. The art producer comes down to meet the guy and the guy turns around.

"Ford, it's been a while. What can I do for you?"

Meanwhile Ty and Krysta pull up at home and they walk into the house. Ty looks at Krysta and sees that she still has a little on her mind. He walks over to and gently wraps his arms around her. She looks back to him. Then she slowly turns around and wraps her arms around him. Ty then takes a breath.

"I have an idea," Ty says.

Krysta looks at him with a little confusion, then Ty tells Krysta to get dressed. She smiles at him then she goes to change. After Krysta has changed, Ty goes to change and she waits for him as she gets a glass of water. Ty comes out of the room and looks at Krysta. She smiles back at him and he grins back at her.

"Okay, where are we going?" asks Krysta.

Ty slowly shakes his head as he takes her hand and they slowly leave the apartment. They head down to Ty's motorcycle. Ty takes her to a nightclub, Krysta looks at him like he lost his mind and he slightly smiles at her. They both get off the motorcycle and Ty walks right up to the front door.

"Don't we have to wait in line?" Krysta asks.

Ty looks at her and gently takes her hand, and she follows him to the front door. The bouncer at the door looks at Ty and smiles. He moves the rope and tells Ty that they both can go right inside. Krysta looks at Ty and smiles as they walk into the club. Ty looks at her and gives her a wink. They walk into the club and Krysta gets a smiling shocked look on her face with the music, the lights, and the energy that everyone is giving off. Ty looks at her.

"You have been to a nightclub before, right?"

Krysta looks at him and shakes her head, no making Ty smile.

"This is going to be fun."

Ty takes Krysta over to the bar and they take a seat. The bartender walks over to them and asks them what they want to drink. Krysta looks at Ty and he says he wants a beer, then she looks back at the bartender. Ty looks at her, trying not to laugh, then he looks back at the bartender and tells him she's having a Sex on the Beach. Krysta quickly looks at Ty and he just starts laughing, then he looks at her. Then the bartender comes back over to them with their drinks and gently puts them down in front of them. Krysta looks at them, then she looks at Ty who looks at her then at her drink.

"Please tell me you at least had a drink before," Ty asks.

Krysta slowly shakes her head, then Ty takes a laughing deep breath.

"Okay, well, try it and see if you like it," Ty says.

Krysta looks at her drink, then she slowly puts it up and takes a small sip. She slowly nods her head, noting that she likes it. Ty grins at her and they look at each other for a minute. They both lift their glasses and gently put them together. Then they both take a drink, then they look out to the dance floor. Krysta finishes her drink and asks the bartender for another. Ty looks at her then back out to the dance floor. Krysta looks at him then out to the dance floor.

"You can go out there if you want to."

Ty looks at Krysta and she looks at him with a smile on her face.

"Why?" Ty says.

"Because you look like you want to go and dance," Krysta replies.

"Okay, I'll go. But only if you come and dance with me," Ty says.

Krysta looks at him with a little shock.

"I don't think so."

"Why not?" Ty asks.

"I can't dance, I never did it before," Krysta replies.

"Well, you're never going to know if you don't try," Ty says.

Ty then takes her drink and puts it down on the bar and gently pulls Krysta off her seat over to him. He slowly guides her to the dance floor. He turns to her and sees that she has a nervous look on her face. Krysta is looking at everyone on the dance floor and sees them all dancing, making her think of how she dances. Ty takes his hand and gently turns Krysta's face to look back at him. He smiles at her and nervously smiles back at him.

"Just follow me. I got you."

Krysta slowly nods her head and Ty takes her hands, pulls her close to him, and they slowly start to move side to side. They start to move faster as the music gets louder and Krysta starts to smile normally. Krysta and Ty start to salsa, laughing as they dance together. Ty looks at one of the other dancers on the dance floor and starts to talk Spanish to him. Ty then spins Krysta around and the other guy gently takes Krysta by the waist. Ty gently grabs one of the girls dancing alone and starts dancing with her. Then a circle of dancers form together and they all start dancing together. At the end of the song, Ty and Krysta end up back together with smiles on their faces. They look at everyone and they all start laughing and smiling at each other. Then Ty and Krysta walk back over to the bar. They ask for new drinks, laughing and talking, Krysta saying how much fun she is having.

The night goes on and Ty, with the bartender, can't stop laughing at Krysta. The club is starting to close with everyone slowly leaving.

"You know, I have never been on a dance floor in years. The last time I was on the dance floor was…at my school prom high," Krysta says.

"You mean your high school prom," Ty repeats.

"That's what I said," Krysta replies.

"Okay, Krysta I think you've had enough," Ty says.

Krysta looks at Ty with a drunken glare, causing Ty to cover his mouth, trying not to laugh, then he looks at the bartender who is still laughing.

"You, mouth shut, mind it," Krysta says.

Ty laughs as he shakes his head then slowly gets out of his seat and gives the bartender the money for the drinks. Then he moves over to Krysta and helps her out of her seat, and they get ready to walk away. But then the bartender calls Ty over for his change. Ty walks back over to him and Krysta looks up, tilting her head, looking at one of the fans. Then she starts walking and falls; Ty comes running over to her and kneels down next to her. He shakes his head, for Krysta is laughing. Ty then helps her stand up, then they slowly start to leave the club with Ty trying to keep Krysta from falling as they walk to Ty's motorcycle. Ty looks at his motorcycle, then Krysta, and takes a deep breath. Ty gets onto his bike first, then he gently helps Krysta onto his bike but she doesn't get on the back. Ty has her sit on his lap, then he slowly starts to drive off with Krysta leaning back against his chest.

They both get home with no problems. Ty gets off the bike and helps Krysta. They slowly walk up the stairs and into the apartment. Ty brings Krysta into the bedroom and over to the bathroom. Ty leans Krysta back against the sink and Krysta looks at him as he is getting something from the cabinet. Ty stands in front of her, looking down, opening a small bottle, and Krysta slowly and gently puts her hand on his face. Causing him to look up at her.

"You're a really handsome guy. Why couldn't I have met you sooner, then I wouldn't be this damaged girl. I don't deserve to be happy. I was in a relationship but I started caring for someone else who makes me feel dizzy. I'm no good," Krysta says.

Ty looks at her with confusion, then Krysta's eyes are starting to get heavy and Ty then quickly opens the bottle. He takes out two pain pills and gets a glass of cold water. He gently helps Krysta take the pills and the water. Then he gently picks her up and slowly carries her back into his bedroom. He sits her on the bed and takes off her shoes, then he slowly lays her back onto the bed. He stares at her for a minute, watching her sleep. Ty kneels down next to the bed, watching Krysta with a guilty look on his face yet a little happy. Ty then moves a piece of hair from Krysta's face and grins.

"Same here," Ty whispers.

For about two hours, Ty watches Krysta sleep, then he slowly falls asleep on his chair.

The next morning, Krysta wakes up with a pounding headache. She quickly puts her hands to her head as she looks around, wondering how she got home or into Ty's bed. Then Ty walks into the room with a grin on his face, then he slowly walks over to her and Krysta has no idea he is in the room. He leans down and takes a quiet deep breath, then he yells in Krysta's ear.

"*Morning*," Ty yells.

Krysta jumps, causing her to fall out of the bed on the other side of Ty and making him laugh hard enough that he moves back to the wall to help him stand. Then he looks at Krysta who slowly leans up onto the bed, giving him a tired glare. Ty then walks over to the bed and kneels down as he puts his arms on the bed, still with a grin on his face.

"How you feeling?" asks Ty.

"My head hurts. Why did you yell in my ear?" Krysta whines.

Ty smiles at her.

"Because your face was priceless."

Ty then slowly gets up and walks into the bathroom and Krysta watches him, still with a pouting look on her face. Then Ty comes out of the bathroom with a glass of water. He puts it down on the nightstand. He then walks over to Krysta on the other side of the bed and helps her back onto the bed. He gives her the glass of water; she slowly drinks it, then she looks back at Ty who is walking into the bathroom. Ty comes out of the bathroom. He and Krysta look at each other for a minute.

"Okay, I'm going to let you get some sleep," Ty says.

"Ty," Krysta softly says.

Ty stops and turns to her.

"Yeah."

"Will you say with me? Watch some TV with me," Krysta asks.

"Sure." Ty grins.

Ty walks over to the bed and slowly sits down on the bed next to her. Krysta leans back, and Ty puts the bedroom TV on. They watch TV for about three hours before Ty sees that Krysta fell back asleep. He grins at her, then he slowly gets up and gently puts the blanket over her. He turns the TV off. He leaves the room and goes into the kitchen. He gets himself a beer, then his cell phone rings.

"Hello," Ty says. "Hi, Ma, yes. I will be coming down in a couple of weeks for the holidays. Um…about that…there might be someone with me. No, Ma, she's not my girlfriend, not like that. It's a long story," Ty says.

Ty slowly shakes his head as he hangs up his phone, then he takes a breath. Then the doorbell rings. He looks at the door with a little confusion, then he looks at the bedroom door. He slowly walks over to the door. He looks out the peephole and sees that its Amy, causing him to shake his head, then walks away from the door. He sits on the couch as he puts the TV on and listens to the doorbell ring. As the doorbell is ringing, Krysta comes out of the bedroom with a tired look on her face. Ty turns his head and looks at her, then Krysta looks at the front door. Ty then looks at door. Krysta slowly walks over to the door and Ty quickly gets up, jumping right in front of Krysta, stopping her from getting to the door.

"That damn doorbell is killing my head," Krysta says.

Ty grins at her, then he nods his head. He takes a deep breath, then he walks over to the door and slowly cracks it open.

"Hi," Ty says.

"Hi," Amy replies.

"What the hell are you doing here?" Ty quickly asks.

Amy smiles at him.

"Well, can I come in and talk to you?"

"No," Ty quickly replies.

Ty shakes his head, then he quickly slams the door. He turns and sees Krysta is looking at him with a plain look on her face. Ty looks at her, trying not to laugh.

"If she rings that doorbell one more time—"

"Krysta, I got it. But first, why don't I help you back to bed?" Ty says.

Krysta gives him a tired smile, then she slowly nods her head. Ty guides her back into the bedroom and onto the bed. She lies on the bed and Ty sits next to her, then he gently moves the piece of hair from her face. Krysta smiles at him, then she slowly starts to fall back asleep. Ty grins at her. But then the doorbell rings again, and Ty takes a deep breath as he rolls his eyes. Then he gets up and goes to the front door. Ty quickly opens the door and walks out but gently closes it behind him. He turns to Amy as he crosses his arms, staring at her with a plain glare, slightly shaking his head.

"What do you want, Amy?" Ty says.

"Look…um. What I did to you was wrong and I'm sorry. I miss you… I've been missing you, Ty. I want us to go back to the way things used to be or try," Amy says.

Ty stares at her for a long minute without a word, looking at Amy with unbelief and slight shock.

"Amy, the closest you and I are ever going to get now," Ty pauses, "is when we see each other at work. Now get away from my apartment," Ty says.

Ty then walks back and goes back into his apartment, closing the door behind him, leaving Amy outside, stunned. Ty takes a breath, then he looks at the bedroom door and grins. He slowly walks over to it and gently cracks it. There is Krysta, sleeping peacefully, causing him to slowly and gently close the door. He goes back over to the couch and continues to watch TV as he drinks his beer.

Later that night, Krysta wakes up. She comes out of the bedroom and sees Ty on the couch, watching a basketball game. She slowly walks over to the couch and Ty slowly turns his head and looks at her. Krysta smiles at him and he grins back at her.

"Feeling better?" asks Ty.

Krysta nods her head, then she walks around the couch, over to the other side of the couch, and sits down next to Ty. He lifts his arms and Krysta puts her head on Ty's shoulder. Ty gently puts his around her neck. They both watch the game, not saying anything with small smiles on their faces. As they watch the game, Ty tells Krysta that he told his mother that he's bringing her with him to LA. Krysta quickly but slowly leans up and looks at him with a nervous look. Ty looks at her with a grin as if he is going to laugh.

"What am I supposed to do? What if she doesn't like me?" Krysta asks in a panic.

Ty smiles at her then slowly leans up and they come eye to eye.

"She is going to love you. Trust me when I tell you, we don't leave for a couple of weeks. So we are good."

Krysta smiles at him, then she slowly leans back down and Ty puts his arm back around her neck.

Chapter 6

Time goes by and it's just about a week before Ty and Krysta get ready to go to LA for the holidays. Krysta gets more and more nervous every day, making Ty have this urge to mess with her every chance he gets.

"You know, we are taking the late fight so our plane leaves in about ten minutes, right?" Ty says.

"*What,*" Krysta yells in a panic.

Then she runs into the bedroom and looks for things to pack, but then she stops when she hears Ty laughing. She slowly walks out of the bedroom and looks at Ty. He looks at her, causing him to want to laugh even harder. For Krysta is looking at him with a pouting look on her face, then he slowly walks over to her.

"I'm sorry." Ty smiles.

"Why do you keep doing that to me?" Krysta whines.

"Because you make it easy, and you're cute when you pout," Ty replies.

Krysta turns her head, then she looks back at Ty who is still smiling at her, making her slowly smile back at him. Then they both walk into the kitchen to clean up the dishes from their dinner that they made. As they finish cleaning up, Krysta goes to the bathroom to freshen up and Ty cleans up the other dishes. Meanwhile in the bathroom, as Krysta is drying her hands, she looks in the mirror and gets a fearful panicked look on her face. For she sees Ford in the mirror, causing her to scream. Ty is drying off his hand when he hears Krysta scream, making him run right to the bathroom. He comes into the bathroom and sees Krysta in the corner on the floor in a ball, covering her face, slowly rocking back and forth. Ty slowly walks over to her.

"Krysta," Ty softly says.

But she doesn't reply nor does she look up at him. Ty slowly kneels down in front of her and slowly reaches his hand out to her. He gently touches her shoulder and Krysta jumps, looking at him. Ty looks at her with deep concern. Krysta looks at him, shaking, and she looks as if she's going to cry.

"Okay, what happened?" Ty gently asks.

Krysta slowly starts to shake her head.

"I don't know. I came in here to clean up, and when I looked in the mirror, I saw Ford."

Ty looks at her with a little shock but still deep concern, not sure what to say to her.

"Okay…um. Well, let's get you off the floor," Ty says.

Krysta nods her head, then Ty helps her off the floor and they walk into the bedroom. Ty gently helps her sit on the bed. He tells her to change out of her clothes and he will be right back. Krysta nods her head, then Ty leaves the room for a minute and goes outside of the apartment. But he stays in front of the door. He stares at it for a minute, then he pulls out his cell phone. He takes a deep breath then he dials a number.

"Hi, I had a couple of questions to ask you. Um, if someone… went through something tragic and they were fine for a while, can that come back to them randomly?" Ty asks. "Okay, so seeing images of what happened to them can come back anytime…even if they seem fine," Ty continues. "How do you help them out of it?" Ty asks. "Okay, thank you," Ty says.

Ty hangs up the phone and looks back at his apartment door as he breathes heavy, then he slowly walks back over to it. Ty walks back into the apartment and goes over to his bedroom to see how Krysta is doing. But he sees that she hasn't changed out of her clothes and that she is looking down at the floor. He walks over to her and she looks up at him and he grins down at her.

"Let's get you out of these clothes," Ty says.

Krysta nods her head, then Ty helps her stand up and gently helps her out of her clothes. After Ty helps Krysta get out of her clothes and into a long nightshirt, she lies down on the bed. Then Ty changes out of his clothes and was about to walk out of the room but Krysta gently calls his name, and he looks back at her. Krysta then softly asks him to stay with her, for she doesn't wish to be alone, and Ty nods his head. He walks over to the other side of the bed and gently moves over to her. Ty slowly wraps his arms around Krysta and she holds on to his hands tight, slowly helping her to stop shaking. Ty smiles at her as he watches her sleep, then he slowly falls asleep himself.

The next morning, Krysta wakes up and Ty is sitting next to her, still on the bed, watching TV and flicking. Krysta slowly leans up, and Ty slowly turns his head, looking at her. He grins at her and she smiles back at him. Ty stares at her for a minute, then he puts the TV on mute then looks back at Krysta.

"Truthfully… I have no idea what happened. What made me see him or anything that happened," Krysta says.

Ty doesn't say anything. All he does is move closer to her and gently puts his arms around her. Krysta puts her head on his chest. Later on that day, Ty and Krysta go out to eat then they go out for ice cream in a medium cup.

"It's cold," Krysta says.

"You're the one that wanted ice cream in the beginning of winter," Ty replies.

Krysta looks at him with a grin on her face as if she is going to start laughing. They are walking around as Krysta eats her ice cream. As they are walking, Krysta ask Ty more about going to LA. Ty looks at her, then he takes her ice cream. Krysta starts laughing and Ty starts to tell her more about LA and some of the places he wants her to see. She smiles, then they come close to the area of the apartment. As they are walking, they see some people outside, playing music from their cars. Krysta looks at them with a laughing smile in her face, then she looks up at Ty who looks at her.

"It is freezing out here. Why are they out here playing music?" Krysta asks.

Ty looks at her and he grins, then he gently takes her hand. She looks at him and he guides her over to the guys playing music. He spins her around and gently pulls her close to him, slowly moves his arms around her waist. They look right into each other's eyes and softly smile at each other.

"Dance with me," Ty says.

Krysta smiles even more and they slowly begin to dance to the music the guys are playing, making other people walking by look at them and some even join them. Everyone starts laughing and start having fun with one another. Krysta and Ty take a break from dancing. Ty goes over to the guys playing music and Krysta looks at everyone. The guy comes over to Krysta and she slightly jumps and her smile turns to a nervous smile. He starts talking to her and she gets a little more nervous. Ty turns his head and sees her talking to another guy but also sees that she's a little nervous. He grins, then he slowly walks over to her. He walks up right behind her and gently wraps his right arm around her waist. Krysta turns her head and sees that it's Ty, making her quickly wrap both of her arms around his arm tight. She breathes, a little more relaxed, and Ty reaches his hand out to greet the guy. The guy shakes Ty's hand, then he slowly walks away and goes over to talk to another girl. Ty looks down at Krysta then at his arm. He sees and feels that she is holding on to him as if she is going to fall. Ty then whispers in her ear, asking her if she wants to go. She slowly nods her head, then they both say night to the guys playing music and slowly start to walk home. They come to the apartment. Ty opens the door, Krysta slowly walks in, and Ty closes the door. He looks at her and how she's breathing.

"You okay?" Ty asks.

Krysta slowly turns her head to him and slowly shakes her head no. Ty slowly walks over to her as she puts her head down. Ty slowly lifts her head and she looks at him and Ty slowly wraps his arms around her. Causing Krysta to wrap her arms around him and gently put her head on his chest. Krysta's eyes become watery.

"He's taken everything from me. I can't even talk to a guy alone. He took my life, didn't he?" Krysta says.

Ty gently kisses her on the head, then he looks at her and she looks up at him.

"Why don't we get away early then?"

Krysta smiles at him and slowly nods her head, then they slowly hug each other again.

The following day, Ty and Krysta get ready to go to LA. Both of them are in the cab driving to the airport. Ty looks at Krysta and gets a huge grin come on his face as if he is trying not to laugh.

"Krysta, we are not even at the airport yet and you're nervous," Ty says.

Krysta looks at him and nods her head quickly and nervously, and Ty starts laughing, making Krysta pout. They arrive at the airport and the driver helps them take their bags out of the trunk, and Krysta looks around. Ty gives the driver the money, then he and Krysta head to their gate for their plane. Krysta looks around, and Ty just keeps walking. Then they get to the seats to wait for their plane. Ty is on his phone, and Krysta is looking through the photo book that Ty brought along for his family to see. Krysta looks up, then she sees a guy walking over to them dressed up in a suit. She looks at Ty who is still on his phone, then he looks up and sees the guy walking over to them. Ty stands up and shakes the guy's hand, then he looks at Krysta an tells her to come over and say hello. She slowly stands up and walks over to the guy and gently shakes his hand. Then he helps Ty and Krysta with their bags. They hold hands as they walk to their gates. Krysta looks at everyone that is waiting for their plane but they are just walking to one of the gates with no one waiting. Then as they are going through the gate outside to the plane, Krysta gets a shocked look on her face. For they are walking to a jet. Krysta quickly looks at Ty and he slowly looks down at her.

"You have a jet?" Krysta asks.

"No, my parents have a jet. They say since they can't buy much for me anymore since I moved out and lived on my own, the least they can do is use their jet for me to go and see them. Can't fight them unless I want to see my mother fake cry," Ty says.

Krysta starts softy laughing, and they both continue walking to the jet. They slowly get into the jet and sit on their seats. After they are all set and ready, the pilot slowly starts up the jet. He tells everyone to sit on their seats and get strapped in. Then they get the sign that they are good to go. The jet starts to ride down the runway, then it slowly takes off. Krysta looks out the window and smiles while Ty is just looking through a magazine.

As they are flying, Krysta looks out to the sky and Ty still just looks through his magazine. But after a couple of hours, Krysta falls asleep on the long seat in the jet. Ty looks over to her with a grin, then he sees a picture that he can draw for how the sun is coming through the window. He slowly pulls out his sketchbook from his bag and slowly starts to draw Krysta sleeping, but he draws her as if she is sleeping on the clouds with the sun shining on her. After about an hour, Krysta wakes up and Ty is still sketching. She slowly gets up and walks over to him but Ty slowly closes his sketchbook. He looks up at Krysta with a laughing grin as he slowly shakes his head. Krysta gives him a smiling pout, then Ty takes out some of the pictures he had taken and shows them to Krysta. She smiles with joy as she gently takes the picture book from Ty and Ty puts his sketchbook away. Krysta starts to ask him where he took the pictures. Ty slowly tells her about some of the pictures he took and she smiles at all of them. As Krysta looks at the pictures, she looks at Ty and he looks at her. She quickly looks back at the pictures. Ty slightly laughs under his breath, then he looks back at the pictures with Krysta and she slowly looks back at him.

"If you want to ask me something, just ask me." Ty grins.

Krysta slightly smiles.

"Can you tell me more about your family?" Krysta asks.

"Like?" Ty asks.

"I don't know, mostly are they—" Krysta is cut off.

"My family is going to love you. This is the first time I'm bringing a girl home with me. But heads up, my mom, um…she can drive you crazy. But in a good way that you want to run away nicely from all her questions," Ty explains.

Krysta smiles as Ty tells her more about his family. Time goes by and the pilot tells them that they have to put their seat belts on. Krysta looks out the window as she puts her seat belt on and she smiles. As the plane is landing, Ty just looks through another magazine and Krysta just keeps looking out the window. Ty and Krysta then wait for the seat belt sign to turn off, letting them know that they are able to get out of their seats. They both get their things and slowly start to depart from the plane. As they walk down the steps, Krysta stops with a slight shocked yet confused look on her face. For there is a limo waiting for them right as they get off the plane. Ty walks right over to the driver who is standing right next to the limo. The drive takes Ty's bags as he and Ty greet each other, then he takes them to the trunk and gently puts them away. Ty opens the limo door, then he stops and slightly turns around to Krysta who is still on the plane steps.

"Are you coming?" Ty asks.

"Ty…that's a limo," Krysta says.

"Yes, and?" Ty replies.

Krysta then slowly walks down the steps, looking at the limo with disbelief as she walks over to Ty. Then the driver walks over to them. Ty grins and Krysta looks at him.

"Joe, this is Krysta. And, Krysta, this is Joe. Known him my whole life. He's been with the family since I was a kid," Ty says.

"May I take your things, ma'am?" asks Joe.

Krysta slowly nods her head as Joe gently takes her bags. She looks over to Ty and he just grins at her as if he is going to laugh. Then they both slowly get into the limo with Joe slowly closing the door behind them. Then he walks to the front of the limo to get into the driver seat and slowly takes off. Krysta looks around the limo with amazement. Ty looks at her, slightly laughing under his breath, slowly shaking his head. Then they come up to a tall metal gate and Krysta looks out the window with complete shock. For the metal gate stops in front of a driveway that goes up to a very large house! Krysta slowly turns her head to Ty who just looks up at her, then he looks around her out the window and up to the house. Then he slowly looks back at her with that same grin.

"What?" Ty asks.

"Okay, Ty. First there is a jet, next there's a limo and driver, now we have that! Start talking…who the heck are you?," Krysta says.

Ty stares at her for a minute, slightly laughing, as the limo starts to drive up the driveway.

"Okay, my father is an owner of a business and my mother is the vice president of that business. And that is how they met…next here I am," Ty explains.

"And what business is that?" asks Krysta.

"I don't know much about it but it is a stock business," Ty replies

"But if your dad runs it. Isn't he going to get mad that you're not taking over it?" Krysta asks.

"No, because my older brother is taking over it," Ty replies.

Krysta stares at him for a minute with a blank stare.

"Older brother…"

"Yes, his name is Lucas," Ty replies.

"I have no words right now," Krysta says.

"Good 'cause now we're here," Ty replies.

Krysta looks over to the door, for Joe slowly opens it and Ty slowly gets out with Krysta very nervously following him. Ty gently takes Krysta's hand and they both walk into the house. And Krysta looks around with complete amazement. Ty looks at her.

"Okay, few things. You don't have to answer things you don't want to. Yes, there are a few housekeepers and beware of my mother. My father, not so much, and my brother…he likes to talk, just go with it," Ty says.

Krysta smiles at him, then they hear a woman shout out Ty's name from around the corner. Ty's mother comes running around the corner right over to Ty with her arms wide opened. She pulls Ty right into a hug and Ty gently hugs her back. Then Ty steps back and gently pulls Krysta closer to him to meet his mother.

"Krysta, this is my mother, Kate. Mother, this is Krysta," Ty introduces.

Krysta smiles at Ty's mother as Kate stares at Krysta with amazement. She smiles at her and gives her a loving hug.

"Nice to meet you," says Kate.

"Nice to meet you too," Krysta replies with a joyful smile.

Kate is light-brown skinned, is about 5'5" feet tall, short brown hair, brown eyes, and has a thick yet slim body. Kate smiles at Krysta, then she looks over at Ty who looks over to her, slowly shaking his head as he slightly laughs under his breath. As they all stand there, they hear laughter coming from the hall. Coming from the hall, laughing, is Ty's father and older brother, Lucas, who stops when they see Ty standing next to Krysta. They look at each other, then they slowly walk over to Ty and Krysta.

"Krysta, this is my father, Nick, and my older brother, Lucas. Dad, brother, this is Krysta," Ty introduces.

"Nice to meet you," says Nick.

"Pleasure is all," says Lucas.

Krysta smiles at the both of them with a slight laugh.

"Nice to meet both of you."

Nick is six feet tall, brown eyes, dark-brown hair, skin is a little lighter than Kate, and slightly thick, not very buff. Lucas is about 6'1" tall, brown skin, brown eyes, light-brown hair, and a little buffer than Ty.

Ty slowly shakes his head, then Kate calls for the butlers and maids. They come over to them and Kate tells them to take Ty and Krysta's clothes to their rooms. Looks at them and slightly sees herself.

"No, it's okay. I got it," Krysta says.

They all look at her. Ty grins, then he looks over to his family and agrees with Krysta.

"Yeah, it's okay, we got it. If you guys can just show us the way?" Ty asks.

The butlers nod their heads and they slowly show Ty and Krysta to their rooms as they help them with some of their bags. The maids show Krysta to her guest room, and the butlers help Ty to his old bedroom. Ty says his thanks, then he looks around his room and sees that his parents didn't change a thing since he was last here. Then he looks to the door and slowly walks out. He walks down the hall to

Krysta's room. Ty gently knocks on the door and slowly opens it and sees Krysta staring out the window. Ty slowly walks over to her.

"You okay?" Ty asks.

Krysta turns her head to him and slightly smiles.

"I'm sorry, just seeing them come and take my things made me think."

"It's okay. I get it. But there is a difference between you and them. One they're not in a relationship like that, and second, it may sound wrong but it's their job. And we don't yell at them if they don't do it right away. They do get time off. Sometimes we have to make them. And some of them, I've known since I was little," Ty says.

Krysta smiles at him and he grins back at her. Then the door slowly opens and Kate walks in, smiling. Ty and Krysta look at her, then each other, trying not laugh as Kate walks over to them as if she is going to start dancing. She tells them to come downstairs for some late breakfast and to talk about how they came to meet one another. Ty and Krysta look at each other, then they slowly follow Kate downstairs and outside to the balcony where everyone else is waiting for them to have breakfast. Krysta smiles at them. Kate tells her and Ty to sit next to another with a happy joyful smile on her face. Ty slowly shakes his head as he slightly grins, Krysta looks at her then at Ty. Everyone is sitting in silence. Krysta looks at all of them, then she takes a breath.

"This is a beautiful home you have," Krysta says.

"Oh, thank you," Kate replies.

Causing Kate and Krysta to talk a little more makes everyone slowly jump into the conversation. Soon everyone is talking and laughing about things that have happened in their home. As they all sit on the balcony, Lucas has everyone laughing, telling one of his stories.

"Okay, Lucas, let's give everyone a break. For I have a question for Ty and Krysta," says Nick.

Ty and Krysta look at him then at each other with slight nervous looks. They turn their heads back to Nick.

"I'm just wondering how the two of you came to know one another," asks Nick.

Ty slightly looks over to Krysta who is looking at Nick with a small smile and a slight chuckle under her breath.

"Um… Well, we met at the same café that I used to work at," Krysta replies.

"Oh, really?" says Nick.

"Yeah," Ty replies.

"Is that all? Are you going to tell us more?" asks Kate.

Ty and Krysta look at each other, trying not to laugh, even though their faces show that they are a little nervous about answering.

"Um, I asked Krysta if I can sketch her…face," Ty replies.

"That's how you pick up girls now?" asks Lucas.

"No, I just asked. She didn't have to if she didn't want to. It was just a question," Ty replies.

Ty and Krysta told them how they both came to know each other but the one thing they didn't talk about was what happened to Krysta. Everyone listens with enjoyment, then Kate asks Ty to see some of his sketches of her. Ty nods his head and Krysta looks at him, then she turns her head from being shy. Ty gets up and goes to get his sketchbook for everyone to see. Krysta looks at them with a small smile. Ty comes down, back out to everyone, and gives Kate his sketchbook. She looks at Ty's sketchbook with amazement, then she leans over to Nick and Lucas to show them. They look at Ty's sketches with amazed shock, they look up to the two of them. But Ty and Krysta are looking at each other with grins and smiles, Ty leaning back against his chair and Krysta slightly biting her index finger. The three of them look at one another with big smiles on their faces.

*****

Ty and Krysta have been in LA for almost a week, Ty and his brother have been hanging out with each other, getting to know what's been going on with each other. Ty keeps changing the subject every time Lucas asks about him and Krysta's relationship. Krysta has been spending time with Kate with some girl time. Kate doesn't ask her anything about her and Ty's relationship, for she already has an idea. Kate and Krysta have been going shopping with each other just about every day since they have been in LA. Ty sometimes go to the office with his father and brother. No one has any idea about Krysta's past, not just about her relationship, also about her family. But then one day, as Kate and Krysta are heading back home from shopping.

"So, Krysta, where are your parents? Are you going to go see them for New Year's?" asks Kate.

Krysta looks at her with a smile that she's trying to keep, but then she takes a deep breath

"I'm not going to see them," Krysta replies.

Kate looks at her with confusion.

"Um…my parents passed away in a car accident. Not that long after I graduated high school," Krysta continues.

Kate looks at her with shock.

"Oh, honey."

"No, it's okay… I didn't…" Krysta says.

"How…would you…that's not something you just bring up in conversation," Kate says.

Krysta smiles at her, then they pull up to the house and they both slowly get out of the car. They walk into the house and bring their bags to their rooms. Kate walks downstairs and sees the guys in the kitchen, talking and laughing. She walks over to Ty. He looks at her and he can see that something is bothering her.

"Can I talk to you?" asks Kate.

Ty nods his head, then they both leave the kitchen, leaving Nick and Lucas in wonder, but then they go back to talking. Ty and Kate go into the other room. Kate turns to Ty and he looks at her with confusion.

"Um, Krysta just told me that her parents passed away in a car accident," Kate says.

Ty takes a deep breath as he nods his head, then he looks over to her.

"Is that all she told you?"

"What do you mean?" Kate asks with confusion.

Ty shakes his head.

"Nothing, never mind."

Ty then walks back into the kitchen. Kate looks at him, then she walks into the kitchen with the guys.

Krysta is in her guest room, looking at her new clothes that she got with a smile, but her smile is a little sad. Then she looks out her window as she slowly walks over to it and takes a deep breath. She stands there, looking out the window with a look on her face, almost as if she's going to cry, but she breathes. She sits down on the window seat, she stays there and watches the sun go down. As the sun comes close to an end, Krysta is still sitting down and Ty is watching her from the doorway.

"You okay?" Ty asks.

Krysta turns around and sees Ty in the doorway, leaning against it. She gives him a very small smile, then she looks down at the floor. Ty leans off the doorway wall and walks over to Krysta and sits down next to her. He looks at her, then he takes his hand and gently lifts her head, causing her to look at him.

"Mother told me that you told her about your parents," Ty says.

Krysta nods her head, and they stare at each other for a minute.

"Is that all you're thinking about right now?" Ty asks.

Krysta stares at him, then she slowly shakes her head.

"But I'm okay."

"You sure?" Ty asks.

Krysta nods her head.

"Okay, well, um, dinner in going to be ready," Ty says.

Krysta smiles with a small laugh, then Ty gets up and takes her hand, causing her to get up and they both walk out of Krysta's room and downstairs to everyone. Kate looks at Krysta and sees that Ty has her laughing. They come over to the dinner table and sit down next to each other, start listening to Lucas tell one of his stories. Kate stares at Krysta for a second, but then she starts laughing with everyone.

Later on at night, when everyone is sleeping, Krysta can't sleep. She wakes up and slowly leans up, looks around, slightly breathing heavy. She slowly gets out of her bed and walks over to her bedroom door. She opens the door and looks to see if anyone is around. She slowly walks out of her room and gently closes the door behind her. Then she quietly walks down the hall to a door and quietly opens it and closes it behind her. There she sees Ty sleeping soundly. She walks over to the end of his bed. Then she crawls on the bed, up to the side of Ty, causing Ty to feel his bed moving. He slowly opens his eyes and sees Krysta lying beside him, looking at him. He slowly leans up and looks at her with confusion.

"Krysta, what's wrong?" Ty asks.

"Nothing," Krysta says.

Ty lifts on of his eyebrows and stares at Krysta. She then slowly nods her head. She slowly leans up.

"I had a dream about Ford."

Ty nods his head.

"So when I asked you if you were okay, you lied."

"Yes, and no. I thought I was okay," Krysta replies.

Ty then takes his arm and puts it around Krysta's waist. She puts her head down on his shoulder, then he kisses her on her head.

"Why don't you just stay here?" Ty says.

"No, it's okay—" Krysta is cut off.

"Krysta, just stay," Ty says.

Krysta smiles and breathes with relief, then she slowly nods her head as she looks up at Ty. They look into each other's eyes, then they both lean back and lie down. Ty lifts his arm, telling Krysta that she can lie close to him. She moves closer to him, putting her head on his chest and wrapping her arm around him as he wraps his arm around her. They then both slowly start to fall asleep.

The next morning, Ty wakes up and smiles, sees that Krysta is still there, sleeping with her head still on his chest and arm around him. He gently gives her a kiss on the head. He sees that Krysta slowly starts to wake up. She looks up at Ty and smiles at him, then she turns her head, hiding that she wants to laugh. Then she leans up and Ty slowly leans up. He puts his chin on her right shoulder. She slightly turns her head to him and smiles.

"How did you sleep?" Ty asks.

"Better than ever," Krysta replies.

Ty lifts his head up.

"Really?"

Krysta laughs as she covers her face with the sheets, and Ty laughs. Krysta looks up at him, slightly covering her face. They look at each other, laughing, then they hear someone knock on the door. They both look over to the door, then Krysta quickly hides herself under the sheets and Ty looks down at her, gently laughing. Then the door slowly opens; it's one of the butlers. He bows to Ty and Ty smiles at him, trying not to laugh.

"Sorry, sir," says the butler.

"For the hundredth time, it's just Ty."

The butler bows his head again.

"Your mother just asked me to see if you are up and if you are coming down for breakfast."

Ty slightly laughs.

"Yes, I'll be right down. And don't worry about Krysta. I'll make sure she gets up."

The butler nods his head, then he gently closes the door. Ty looks down at Krysta, then he quickly takes his hands and starts to tickle her. She starts laughing and gently kicking, causing the sheets to slightly moves off of her to show her face. She tries to move away from Ty but he grabs her by the waist and pulls her back to him. She turns her head to him and their faces come very close, just about two inches apart. That causes both of them to stop laughing and look right into each other eyes with heat!

"We should um…head downstairs," Ty softly says.

Krysta nods her head, then they both get out of bed and walk over to the door. They slowly head downstairs. They come out to the balcony, and everyone is sitting and talking to each other, then they turn and look at Ty and Krysta. They look at each other, then they look back at everyone and slowly go to sit down. They sit down, then they look at each other from across the table, trying not to laugh. Everyone looks at them with confusion yet curiosity.

"So what's up with you two?" asks Lucas.

Ty looks at him while Krysta puts her head down.

"What's up with you?" Ty replies.

Kate and Nick start laughing. Krysta covers her mouth, trying not to show that she's laughing, and Lucas looks at Ty with a shocking laugh. Then he and Ty start laughing with everyone. They all eat and laugh.

"So tonight is an early Christmas party. Are you two going to be ready to go?" asks Kate.

Krysta quickly looks at Kate.

"A…party? I didn't know there was a party?" Krysta says.

"Yes, don't worry we're going to look for a dress later. For you to wear at the party," Kate says.

Krysta looks at Ty who has his head leaning on his right hand as he shakes his head, softly laughing under his breath.

Later after everyone finishes breakfast, Kate takes Krysta to go and find a dress while the guys go to the gym. The guys go to a boxing gym; they all talk about anything that comes to mind and Lucas starts to ask Ty more about Krysta. Ty is punching the bag while Lucas holds it.

"Lucas, let it go," Ty says.

"No way. What happened last night?" asks Lucas.

"Nothing, okay? She just couldn't sleep so she came to me," Ty replies.

Lucas stares at him for a second, smiling.

"Yeah, I don't know how long you are going to keep hiding it from everyone. Or I should say from yourself because everyone can see. But you two are falling for each other," Lucas says.

Ty stops punching the bag and looks at Lucas. He takes a deep breath, and Lucas shrugs his shoulders.

"All right, Lucas. What do you want me to tell you?" asks Ty. "That you're right?"

"Well, yes, and as your brother, I want you to be happy. And she's it," Lucas replies.

Ty shakes his head and the both of them laugh, then they both go back to working out. Nick is over talking to one of his friends that go to the gym. Meanwhile Kate and Krysta are shopping in all different dress shops, trying to find something for Krysta to wear. They have gone to about five to six different dress shops. They come to the last shop. They both walk inside and look around; Kate goes to the women at the counter while Krysta slowly walks upstairs. As she walks upstairs, she sees a dress right away. She walks over to the dress and stares at it. It is an elegant red V-neck, off the shoulder left-slit long cocktail dress. Kate comes upstairs, looking for Krysta, and sees her looking at a dress. She walks over to Krysta and she looks at her.

"You like this dress?" asks Kate.

"Yes," Krysta replies.

"Okay, let's take it," Kate says.

Kate then gently asks the woman to come over, then she takes Krysta into the back to see if they need to do anything to the dress to make it fit. A few others follow to help, and Kate waits for them. After about a half an hour, Krysta comes out from the back and she is holding her dress. Kate stands up and walks over to Krysta and gives the woman her credit card. Krysta quickly looks at Kate.

"I can't take this. It's too much and I can't have you pay for it," Krysta says.

"Oh, stop. I want you to go to the party and have a nice dress," Kate replies.

Krysta smiles.

"Thank you. I wish there were more words."

Kate looks at her smiles, then one of the women takes Krysta's dress and covers it. After Kate gets her card back, they both say their thanks then they leave the store. As they pull up to the house, they see that the guys are also just getting home themselves. Kate opens the limo door and looks at them with small shock.

"What are you guys doing? You are now just getting home?"

Krysta slowly gets out of the limo and tries not to laugh, then the driver comes over to Krysta and hands her the dress. Krysta smiles at them, then she gently takes her dress and thanks them. Kate makes everyone go into the house to hurry and get ready.

Chapter 7

$\mathcal{E}$veryone is ready for the party and waiting for Kate and Krysta to come downstairs. Kate walks into Krysta's room and sees her standing in front of the tall mirror, looking at herself nervously. Kate smiles and walks over to her.

"You okay?" Kate asks.

Krysta turns her head to her, then she looks back into the mirror.

"I've never been to one of these. I don't know what to do."

Kate walks over to Krysta and helps her with her hair. She puts a comb, silver hairpiece, in her hair, helping her hair stay to the side. As she helps Krysta, she looks at her face through the mirror and sees that Krysta looks like she's going to cry.

"You know, I think someone might just have a hard time taking their eyes off you tonight," Kate says.

Krysta smiles with a small laugh.

"You know, they are also watching you too," Kate says.

Krysta looks at Kate through the mirror.

"Thank you…for everything."

Kate smiles.

"Well, let's not keep the guys waiting more than we are."

They both laugh, then they both slowly walk out of the room and head downstairs to the guys. As they walk downstairs, they all look at Kate with joy. She is wearing a long black cocktail dress that ties in the back behind her neck and her waist. She walks over to

Nick and they give each other a kiss. Krysta takes a deep breath, then she slowly walks downstairs and Ty gets a shocked look on of his face. He looks at Krysta with amazement, not just her dress but her hair and makeup. Kate helped Krysta put her hair to the side, hanging over her right shoulder with curls and two pieces on both sides of her face, braided. Her makeup has a red outline above her eyes and white-silver eyeshadow with clear lip gloss. She replies to Ty's face with passion in her eyes and a gentle smile. She walks over to Ty and he can't find the words to speak.

"I wish I had words to tell you how beautiful you look right know," Ty says.

Krysta just smiles at him, then she shyly puts her head down. Ty gently lifts her head, and they look into each other's eyes as they softly touch foreheads. Everyone smiles at them, then Kate sees the time.

"Oh, we have to go. Let's go, let's go. You too, love birds."

Then everyone runs out of the house and to the limos: Kate and Nick in the first one, Lucas and his date in the middle one, with Ty and Krysta in the last one. Everyone gets into their limos and they slowly drive off to the destination. They arrive at the building that they are holding the party. Ty helps Krysta out of the limo, and she looks at the building with amazement. Ty looks at her and gently smiles, then he holds out his arm. Krysta looks at him and smiles as she takes his arms. They both walk into the building, and it's filled with hundreds of people and Krysta gets a little nervous. Ty looks at her and puts his other hand onto her hand then around her arm. Krysta looks at him and she softly smiles. Then one of the people working comes to them holding a tray that has glasses of champagne. Ty takes two, then he gives one to Krysta but she looks at him.

"Um, I don't think that I should drink," Krysta says.

Ty slightly laughs.

"It's okay, you wouldn't get too bad. I promise," Ty says.

She smiles at him with a small laugh, then she slowly takes the glass from him. They smile at each other, then they gently touch glasses and take a sip. Then they walk around the party. They come across a few people that remember Ty when he was a kid and some that work for his father. Some of the people walk over to Nick and Kate and ask them about Krysta, who she is to Ty. Kate and Nick smile and tell them that they are waiting for Ty and Krysta to admit to themselves their feelings for each other. They all laugh as they look back at Ty and Krysta who are walking onto the dance floor and slowly dance with each other.

The night goes on and slowly starts to come to an end with everyone slowly leaving. Ty and Krysta slowly walk to their limo with Nick and Kate not too far behind. Kate looks around for Lucas.

"Ty, have you seen Lucas?" Kate asks.

Ty looks at looks at her.

"Yeah, he's not coming home tonight. He'll be home in the morning," Ty replies.

Kate rolls her eyes with a very small laugh, then she looks back at Nick who is talking to a friend. Ty and Krysta continue walking to their limo and get inside. Kate and Nick watch them slowly drive off and smile. Meanwhile as Ty and Krysta are driving home, Krysta is laying her head on Ty's shoulder and he lays his head on her head.

"You know Christmas is about four days away and I never asked you what you want," Krysta says.

They both look at each other and Ty gently smiles.

"What makes you think I want anything?" Ty asks.

"I don't know. I just… Everything you have done for me… I want to at least get you something," Krysta softly replies.

"Okay, I'll let you know as soon as I think of something," Ty replies.

She smiles with a slight bite of her bottom lip as she slightly looks down, causing Ty to take a deep breath. They pull up to the house and the driver comes to open the door. Ty gets out of the car, then he helps Krysta. They both thank the driver, then they walk into the house; the lights turn on when they walk into the house. Krysta looks around then at Ty; he looks at her.

"The lights are on a timer till everyone goes to bed. That's when they get turned off," Ty says.

Krysta laughs as she shakes her head. She walks into the other room and takes her shoes off, then she looks over to the balcony.

Meanwhile Ty is listening and looking at his phone massages. She walks over to the doors and gently opens them; she walks out onto the balcony. She walks over to the railing and gently puts her hands on them as she looks over to the lights of LA. Ty walks into the room as he takes off his tie and unbuttons two buttons on his shirt, then he looks over to the balcony. He sees Krysta standing there; he slowly walks over to the balcony doorway. Ty stares at her for a little with a grin. He slowly walks over to her, then when he comes up behind her, he gently wraps her arms around her waist. As he wraps his arms around Krysta, she puts her arms to his and leans his face down to her face and they touch. They both look out to the lights and stay that way. Then they look at each other with passion in their eyes and slowly move their faces closer to each other. Their lips are about inches apart but then they hear Kate and Nick come into the house, causing them to part from each other. They look at each other, then Krysta walks into the house and Ty slowly follows as he takes a deep breath.

The next morning, Krysta is still sleeping, Ty is at the gym, and Kate and Nick are sitting down, eating. Then they hear the door open and see Lucas walking into the room and his clothes are a mess.

"Late night?" asks Kate.

Lucas sits down and gives her a goofy smile, and Kate slowly shakes her head with Nick laughing as he reads the newspaper.

"Where's Ty?" asks Lucas.

"He's at the gym," Nick replies.

"This early? "Lucas asks. "And Krysta?"

"She's still sleeping," Kate replies.

"Oh, okay," Lucas says.

"No, nothing happened between those two last night," Kate says.

"You think that's going to happen here?" Lucas asks.

"Why not?" Kate asks.

"Mother, this is your house. He's not going to do anything in this house. Why do you think he's at the gym?" Lucas says, softly laughing.

Kate looks at him with confusing shock, then she looks at Nick who is still reading his newspaper, softly laughing, shaking his head. Kate looks back at Lucas.

"You know I want grandbabies. This a big house. I want to hear little feet running around again," Kate says.

"Wow, Mom, really?" Lucas replies.

"Yes, they can't resist each other much longer," Kate replies.

"What, you think I can't give you grandchildren?" Lucas asks.

"Legally," Kate quickly replies.

They all start laughing. Nick puts his newspaper down, Lucas leans back in his chair while covering his face, and Kate holds her drink. Meanwhile Ty walks back into the house and hears everyone laughing. He walks over to the dinner room and looks at everyone like they are crazy. He slowly moves back and goes to his room. He puts his bag down, then he walks into the bathroom and takes a shower. After Ty gets out of the shower, he comes out of the bathroom with a towel around his waist and he slightly jumps. For Lucas is sitting on a chair in his room.

"Lucas, what are you doing in here?" Ty asks.

"Nothing, just wanted to see my little brother," Lucas replies.

Ty looks at him with confusion then slightly looks around.

"No, I know you want something," Ty says. "The only time you say little brother is when you want something."

"Okay, since you asked. I need your help in getting gifts for the parents," Lucas replies.

"You could just say that," Ty asks.

"No," Lucas quickly replies.

Ty and Lucas stare at each other, Lucas with a goofy grin and Ty with no emotions.

"Lucas, I have to get dressed," Ty says.

"Oh yeah, go ahead," Lucas replies.

"Lucas, get out," Ty slightly yells with a soft laugh.

"Right," Lucas says.

Lucas leaves Ty's room and Ty softly laughs as he shakes his head and goes to get dressed. Ty comes downstairs and into the living room, and there he sees Krysta talking to Kate. They both look at each other and softly smile. Then Lucas comes around the corner and tells them that he's taking Ty for a while. They both take their leave then Kate asks Krysta if she wants to have girl time. Krysta gently laughs and nods her head, then they both get ready to go. Nick has left for an emergency at his office.

As Kate and Krysta are shopping, Krysta is trying to find Ty a present for Christmas. She asks Kate if she can help her find something for Ty. They look around, then they come to a store. Kate walks around and Krysta sees something that she thinks Ty might like. She smiles, then she looks around but doesn't see Kate. She then gently picks up her gift then walks over to the counter-cashier. Krysta gets her gift for Ty, then she looks for Kate who is outside on the phone. Krysta goes outside and they both smile at each other then get back into the car. Kate asks if there was anything else she wanted to look for but Krysta says that she doesn't need anything. Then they head home. As they come up to the house, they see Lucas and Ty walking into the house. Krysta and Kate come into the house and see Ty and Lucas coming downstairs. They see Krysta and Kate; Kate sees that Krysta is hiding her gift for Ty behind her, causing Kate to tell them that she needs their help. They look at each other with confusion, then they go to help their mother. As they walk in to help, Krysta runs upstairs to her room and hides her gift for Ty.

*****

Days go by and Christmas is the next day. Everyone is putting decorations on the tree and laughing. They all sit around the tree, having drinks and talking about anything that they can think of. Later on in the night, everyone is in their rooms wrapping their gifts. Krysta finishes her gift, then she goes to bed.

The next morning, Kate and Nick are awake, waiting for everyone to get up while making breakfast. Lucas comes downstairs and smells the food cooking; he walks into the kitchen and sees that his parents are finishing up breakfast. He walks over to the dining room and sees that the table is all set. He walks back into the kitchen and looks at his parents.

"What time did you two get up?" Lucas asks.

They both look at him, then they slowly start to bring things into the dining room. Lucas helps brings more things into the room. Meanwhile upstairs, Ty wakes up and slowly gets out of bed. He goes to see if Krysta is also awake. He walks into her room quietly; he sees she is sleeping soundly. He grins, then he slowly walks into the room. As he gently closes the door, he walks over to Krysta. He kneels down next to the bed, then he slowly leans over to her and whispers in her ear. Krysta slightly moves that causes Ty too move back and look at her. Her eyes slowly start to open. She sees Ty softly smiling at her; she softly smiles back, then she slowly leans up on the bed. Ty slowly stands up, then sits on the bed. They look at each other and Ty slowly moves Krysta's hair from covering some of her face. He gently puts his hand on the side of her face, causing Krysta to put her hand on his hand. They stare into each other's eyes, then they slowly lean closer to each other. But then they hear everyone downstairs; they look at the door then back at each other. They both get up and head downstairs. They see that everyone is at the table, laughing. They see Ty and Krysta. Nick tells them to come and sit with them to eat before they all go to open gifts. They sit down, start to make a plate and laughing at what they are listening to what Lucas is talking about.

After everyone is done eating, they all slowly go into the living room and see that the tree has a lot of gifts under it. They all go to sit down. Ty and Krysta sit down next to each other on the floor, Nick and Kate sit down on the couch while Lucas sits on the recliner. Kate tells Lucas to pass around the gifts since he's sitting right next to the tree. Lucas looks at the gifts and stares at them for a second, then he looks back over to Kate. They all start laughing, then Lucas slowly starts to grab a gift. He looks at the name and sees that it's for Kate from Nick. He gently passes the gift to Nick to give to Kate. Lucas keeps giving gift to everyone and Krysta watches with a smile on her face. Then she gets a shocked look on her face for Lucas gives her a gift. She gently takes the gift and looks at the names. The gift is from Kate and Nick. She turns and looks at them and they both smile at her. She smiles back at them then looks back at her gift. Everyone opens their gifts and smile with joy. Krysta looks at her gift with joy and tearful eyes, for Kate and Nick have gotten Krysta a real diamond bracelet. She gets up and gives them both hugs, Lucas and Ty look at her then each other, smiling. Then Lucas calls to Krysta and she turns to look at him.

"Look, you have another one." Lucas smiles.

Krysta looks at him with shock, then she walks over to Lucas and gently takes the gifts and sits back down next to Ty. Everyone opens another gift. Krysta gently laughs for the next gift that she has gotten was from Lucas. He got Krysta one of the newest cell phones. She looks at him, trying to hold her laugh in. She gets up and walks over to Lucas and gives him a hug. She walks back over to Ty and sits down next to him. Everyone finishes opening their gifts but Kate and Nick tell Ty that they have another gift for him but it's not ready. He looks at them with a grin yet a little confused. Then Krysta gets up and walks over to the tree. They all look at her.

"Okay, it's not much. I don't know much of what you guys like but…" Krysta says.

They see Krysta pick up a bag that was behind the tree and walks back over to Ty. She sits down and they all look at her. Then she pulls out gifts; she gives one to Kate and Nick then hands one to Lucas. Krysta has given Kate a locket with her family picture in it. She smiles at Krysta. Nick was given a gift of a wristwatch with his name engraved on it, and Lucas's gift is a Personalized Engraved Ballpoint pen set for his office. He looks at Krysta and smiles. Krysta then slowly pulls out her last gift for Ty. He looks at Krysta as she hands him his gift; he gently takes the gift and slowly opens it. Then he gets a shocked look on his face for the gift Krysta has gotten him is a whole new art set. He looks at her and she smiles.

"I saw that the ones you have are getting a little rundown," Krysta says.

"Thank you," Ty says.

Everyone gets excited, then they all slowly get up but then Kate turns and looks at them.

"Oh, don't forget that we are going to Mike's house for a late lunch, early dinner. So get ready."

They all nod their heads and get ready to head to their rooms but Krysta stops Kate and Nick to thank them again.

"Thank you so much for this. You really didn't have to do this," Krysta says.

"Oh, Krysta, you have given us something much more," Kate says.

"You make our son happy," Nick continues.

Krysta smiles at them, but then her smile slowly moves to tears, causing them to look at her with confusion yet smiles. Krysta looks at them, then she takes a deep breath. Kate takes a step toward her.

"Krysta, is there something on your mind?" Kate asks.

"I can't say. Not on this beautiful day," Krysta says.

That causes Kate and Nick to look at each other with confusion then back at Krysta, who is about to walk away, but Nick stops her. He and Kate ask Krysta to tell them what she has to tell them. Krysta looks at them. She asks if they can sit down to tell them. They go into the other room and they all sit down. Krysta sits down across from them.

"Um…it's hard, for it's a beautiful day and holiday."

"Krysta, there's more to a holiday than gifts, and the day will seem better if you talk about it," Kate says.

Krysta takes a deep breath, then she slowly starts to tell them.

"Um… I use to have a boyfriend. I lived with him for years because I had nowhere to go. No money, no family, nothing. The job that I had didn't pay enough for me to have a place of my own because of the hours that I worked. I should say, what he allowed me to work," Krysta says.

Nick and Kate look at her with confusion yet with deep concern and Krysta continues to explain what happened to her and how she and Ty became so close. Krysta tells them how she and Ty first came face-to-face, who her ex-boyfriend was, about the women he had been with that she had seen. Then she tries to hold in her tears as she slowly starts to tell them both about what happened to her the night she broke up with Ford! As she is telling them about that night, Kate looks at her with complete shock as she covers her mouth and Nick is staring at her with shock with his left hand to his head. After

Krysta tells them everything that happened to her, Kate gets up and walks over to her; she hugs her. Nick gets up and walks over to them and kneels down in front of Krysta and holds her hand. Krysta then starts crying as she hides her face in Kate's shoulder and holds tight to Nick's hand. They hold onto Krysta for a while till they hear Lucas in the hallway getting ready to come downstairs. They look at each other, and she smiles at them.

"Why don't we go and get ready?" Kate says.

Krysta smiles at her as she nods her head, then she looks at Nick and he nods his head. Then she gets up and goes to her room to get ready. Kate and Nick look at each other as they watch Krysta leave the room. Kate then walks away and Nick follows her. Kate knocks on Ty's door then opens it and Ty looks at her as he puts on his shirt.

"Sure, Ma, come right in," Ty says. "And you're not ready."

Kate doesn't say anything, she just walks over to him and hugs him, causing him to be confused, then he looks over to Nick who slowly walks in. Kate looks at him and he sees as she has been crying.

"Ma, what's wrong?" Ty asks.

Kate takes a deep breath, then she looks at Nick who walks over to them.

"Krysta just told us everything," Nick says.

Ty looks at them with confusion, then he knows what they are talking about, causing him to nod his head.

"We're proud of you," Nick says.

Ty doesn't say anything; he just slightly grins, then Kate and Nick goes to get ready. Ty then goes to Krysta's room. Krysta is coming out of her bathroom wearing a bathrobe. She sees Ty walking to her and she gets a little nervous. But Ty just walks up to her and gives her a hug; she quickly hugs him right back. Ty can feel that she's shaking a little. He gives her a kiss on her head as she hides her face on his chest. They stay like that for a minute, then Ty and Krysta look at each other. He asks her if she is okay, and she nods her head with a small smile. Ty then slowly starts to walk away so Krysta can get ready. Ty and Lucas are downstairs, waiting for everyone to come downstairs. Krysta comes down, wearing a black and white dress that goes down to her knees. She walks over to Ty, and they all wait for

Nick and Kate. After about twenty minutes, Nick and Kate come downstairs. Lucas walks over to the stairs.

"What the hell were you two doing? Ma, you told us to hurry."

Kate softly laughs and Nick just shakes his head, then they walk past Lucas and continue walking to the front door. Lucas quickly turns his head to them as he puts his arms in the air.

"No, I wasn't talking!"

He looks over to Ty and Krysta as he puts his arms down and sees that they are trying not to laugh at him. They then start walking to the front door. Lucas watches them walk by him, slightly pouting. He stays there for about a minute, then he slowly starts to follow everyone outside. Outside is one limo where Kate and Nick are waiting for them with Joe holding the door open for them. Joe closes the door and goes to the front of the limo, to the driver seat; he drives to Mike's house.

Joe gets out of the car then he goes to open the door for everyone. They all thank Joe and walk up to Mike's front door. Nick knocks on the door and Mike opens the door. He smiles and tells everyone to come in, and they all slowly follow Mike into the house. There they see that some more people came over.

After about three hours, everyone has had a little to drink. Krysta is standing next to Ty as they talk to Mike's son and soon-to-be wife. They are all laughing, trying not to spill their drinks with each laugh. The sun is gone from the sky, and some of the people slowly start to leave to other houses. Kate and Nick tell Lucas, Ty, and Krysta that they are getting ready to leave. They all nod their heads and get ready to leave. After they say their goodbyes, they all slowly start to leave and there is Joe, waiting for them with the limo door opened. They all get into the limo and Joe takes them home. They arrive home and they all look tired. Everyone is yawning, and they all head upstairs to bed.

Next morning, everyone gets up late at noon. They all go downstairs as if they are dead. Ty goes to sit outside near the pool. Kate and Lucas look for something to eat and Nick gets some water. Krysta asks for some water for her and Ty; Nick gives her two glasses of water. Krysta smiles, then she walks outside to the pool and sits down next to Ty. He looks at her and gently takes the glass of water. They relax outside, talking about last night. Everyone then slowly come outside and sits down; they all enjoy the noon sun.

*****

Time goes by and it's now New Year's Eve! Everyone is getting ready for the New Year's Eve party at Nick's building. They get all dressed up, Kate and Krysta go to get their hair done. Kate has her hair in banana curls and up in a clip with a long green cocktail dress. And Krysta has her hair in waves with most of her hair to the right side and completely out; she has a long silver cocktail dress on. It's silk with hints of glitter, one shoulder on her left that slits on the right side, up to her thigh. Kate helps Krysta with her makeup and they are both laughing and talking while Ty and Nick are downstairs waiting for them, drinking water and laughing, since Lucas has already left to get his date. But then they completely stop when they see the girls coming downstairs. Nick walks over to Kate and softly takes her hand; they walk to the door. Ty walks up to Krysta and she gets a shy nervous smile as she looks down to the floor. Ty gently lifts her head and their eyes meet. He gently moves the hair from her face.

"You look beautiful."

She smiles even more slightly, and gently biting her bottom lip, they move closer to each other where their lips are close to touching. But then Nick and Kate call them, causing them to look over to them. They slightly laugh, then they take each other's hands and follow Nick and Kate outside to the limos. They arrive at the party and Krysta holds onto Ty's hand a little tighter, causing Ty to look at her and see that she's nervous. He gives her a kiss on the head then and she looks at him, smiling. She relaxes and starts to enjoy the party with everyone, talking and laughing. The night goes on and everyone sees that it's getting close to midnight! Ty and Krysta stand side by side and everyone starts to count down.

"Happy New Year!"

Everyone gets excited; Ty and Krysta look at each other with excitement, then unexpectedly, Ty and Krysta give each other a small kiss! They slowly move their faces away from each other and look deep into each other's eyes. Then Nick comes over to pull Ty away to talk to one of his friends. Krysta stands there and waits for Kate who is walking over to her.

Chapter 8

The party is slowly coming to an end, and everyone is slowly heading home. Ty and Krysta say good night to Nick and Kate who are staying behind to wait for everyone to leave. Ty and Krysta don't say anything to each other the whole ride home. They come into the house and slightly look at each other, then Krysta quickly says good night. She then quickly runs up to her room. Ty watches her go upstairs, then he slowly walks up to his room and gently closes the door.

"That did happen," Ty says to himself.

The night goes on and Ty is lying on his bed, looking up at the ceiling with one hand behind his head and the other just on his stomach. But then he hears his door open, causing him to lean up to look at why his door opened. He gets a small shocked look on his face, for he sees that Krysta is the one to open his door. She gently closes the door behind her and Ty slowly gets off his bed. They walk over to each other and slightly stare at each other.

"I'm sorry about what happened," Krysta says.

Ty stares at her for a minute.

"And if I don't?"

Krysta looks up at him and he stares at her.

"Ty, I'm no good for you… I don't ever want to hurt you. Look at my life," Krysta says.

"I don't care," Ty whispers.

"But—" Krysta is cut off.

Krysta is cut off by Ty who pulls her into a kiss, and she quickly kisses him right back. Their kisses turn into deep heated passion, both breathing heavy. Ty slowly moves his hands down to Krysta's thighs and picks her up. She wraps her legs and arms around him as he walks over to his bed. Ty slowly leans down to the bed and softly lies on top of Krysta, both still kissing each other. Ty then stops and looks at her.

"We should stop," Ty whispers.

Krysta slowly shakes her head as she pulls Ty back into another kiss, and he kisses her right back. Then he leans up and slowly takes off his shirt; he leans back down, they both kiss. Ty then leans back up but gently pulls Krysta up with him, both still kissing. He slowly then starts to take off the nightshirt she is wearing. They look deep into each other's eyes and kiss each other with deep passion. Ty kisses Krysta on her neck as he gently moves her hair from her neck. Krysta tightly yet gently holds onto Ty's hair with one hand and her other hand on his chest. Then Ty and Krysta look at each other with heat in their eyes as they move closer to kiss. Their kisses get deeper and more fire in it as they hold each other tightly. Then they lean back down to the bed, and that night, Ty and Krysta made love! The joy of being touched makes their whole bodies burn. Both of them melting in each other's arms with heat and desire. As if they are being tossed by waves, just feeling something unmatched by any other feeling.

Early the next morning, the sun has not fully come up in the sky. Krysta wakes up and she sees that she's not in her room. Then she feels her hand on skin. She slightly moves her head and sees that her head is on a chest. Causing her to pick up her head slowly and see that it's Ty, sleeping right next to her peacefully. One of his arms behind his head under the pillow and the other arm around Krysta. She stares at him for a minute, then she remembers what happened last night, causing her to put her hand to her lips for a minute. She leans closer to Ty and gently gives him a kiss on the cheek. In that moment, Ty's eyes twitch, causing Ty's eyes to slowly start to open. As he opens his eyes, he sees Krysta gently smiling at him; he replies also with a gentle smile. He slightly leans up to her and they give each other a kiss that starts to become more passionate. Ty leans back down and Krysta follows; he gently wraps his arms around her. Krysta puts one hand gently on the side of his face and keeps her other hand on his chest. They slowly roll on the bed, then Ty is gently on top of Krysta and she wraps her arms softly around his neck. A few hours later, Krysta is walking around Ty's room, wearing one of his button-up T-shirts. While Ty is on his bed, leaning back against the backboard, watching her walk around. She sees pictures of Ty and she turns her head to him, smiling.

"I didn't know you boxed," Krysta says.

Ty grins at her.

"Wasn't anything big? I did for a while until my junior year in high school."

"Do you still do it?" Krysta asks.

"Here and there, for a work out. Remember, I paint, need my hands," Ty replies.

Krysta smiles as she slightly bites her bottom lip, walking over to Ty, and he still grinning, slightly laughing under his breath. Krysta then crawls on the bed up to Ty.

"Why, you want to learn how to box?" Ty asks.

Krysta kisses him and he kisses her back, then they look at each other.

"Why, would you teach me?" Krysta asks, smiling.

"Maybe, if you're a good girl," Ty replies, smiling.

Krysta starts laughing, causing Ty to laugh with her; he looks at her and they stare into each other's eyes.

"You know what, as long as we have been here, I have not shown you my view of LA," Ty says.

Krysta smiles, and she shakes her head.

"No, you didn't."

He gently puts his hand on the side of her face, caressing her face.

"I'd love to see it," Krysta says.

"Then I guess we need to get out of this bed," Ty says.

They give each other two kisses, then Krysta gets up and softly runs to her room as Ty gets out of bed. They both take a shower, get dressed, but Ty gets to Krysta's room before she is done getting ready. He knocks on the door then walks in, closes the door behind him, and there is Krysta, putting on her shirt. She slightly starts laughing.

"You're supposed to wait for me to tell you to come in," Krysta says.

Ty walks over to Krysta, softly smiling as if he's going to laugh.

"And you're shy because? Did the shower give a blur of last night?"

Krysta's jaw drops, as if she's going to laugh, but she looks at Ty with a pouting smile. Ty puts his arm around her waist and she puts her hands on his arms.

"You're not cute." Krysta slightly laughs.

"Sure about that?" Ty replies, smiling.

"You can't not always be a smart-ass." Krysta smiles.

Ty slightly nods his head. He and Krysta kiss. They look at each other.

"You ready to go?" Ty asks.

Krysta smiles as she nods her head, then she finishes buttoning her shirt, then they both head downstairs. Everyone is in the dining room, dealing with a hangover. They hear Ty and Krysta coming downstairs. They see them heading to the front door.

"You two are not going to eat?" Kate slightly yells.

Ty and Krysta stop and look at each other, trying not to laugh. Ty shakes his head. Then they both walk over to the dining room doorway and look at everyone. Ty starts laughing at how everyone looks, and Krysta looks at them with concern yet about to laugh.

"Not funny, man, not funny," Lucas says.

"No, it's hilarious," Ty replies, laughing. "You guys drank that much?"

"Are you two going to eat?" Lucas asks.

Ty shakes his head.

"No, we're going to get something later."

They both say their byes, then they walk away and head outside to Ty's car. Lucas looks at them with confusion while Kate and Nick look at each other with a smile. Then Lucas looks at them both with even more confusion for the way they are smiling.

"What are you two smiling at?" Lucas asks.

They both look at him and slightly start laughing.

"If you can't see it, Lucas, don't worry about it," Nick replies.

Meanwhile Ty is taking Krysta to all of his favorite spots and takes her to his favorite places to eat. He takes her to the gym he goes to, also where he used to train for boxing. He walks in and his old trainer sees him walk in.

"Well, if it isn't my favorite student, Ty," yells the trainer.

Ty turns his head and sees his old trainer walking to him. Ty's old trainer is light-skinned, brown eyes, blond buzz-cut hair, is about 5'7" tall. He comes up to Ty and Krysta; he and Ty shake hands with a little hug. Then he turns his head to Krysta

"And who is this beauty?"

"This is Krysta, and, Krysta, this is my old trainer, Tommy," Ty says.

Krysta smiles and says her hello, and Tommy grins at her. Then he looks back at Ty.

"Krysta, she your girlfriend?"

Ty looks at him, smiles as if is he's going to laugh.

"That's right so don't touch."

Tommy starts laughing, then he tells them that he has to get back to work and tells Ty and Krysta that they can do whatever they want. Ty thanks him, then he takes Krysta in the back to show her around. As they are walking, she sees pictures of Ty. She smiles and continues to follow Ty to the back.

Ty and Krysta travel all over LA till it starts to get dark. Ty is driving with the top down.

"Are we going to head home now?" Krysta asks.

Ty shakes his head.

"No, not yet. I want to show you something first."

"Okay," Krysta replies, smiling.

Ty takes Krysta to a hilltop that looks over the water where the water and sky look as if they are touching. He parks the car, and Krysta walks almost to the edge with amazement, and Ty slowly comes out of the car. He then sits on the hood of the car and leans back gently against the glass, Krysta watching the sunset as it reflects in the water. She turns her head to Ty who is softly smiling at her, then she walks over to him. She crawls up on the hood of the car, up to Ty, and they kiss. They look at each other, then Krysta leans back on the hood with Ty as she puts her head on his chest. He gently rubs her head, and they stare at the sunset.

"This is where it all happened for me," Ty says.

Krysta looks up and him with her eyes.

"I found this place one day when I was little. I got mad that my parents were busy with work and Lucas was out with his friends. Plus I couldn't stand the babysitter, so I ran out of the house. No one could find me. The babysitter called my parents, and they came right home. They called Lucas to see if I was with him, then he came home. I walked around and saw this hill and just walked up it, and then I saw the sunset. Don't ask me why because I don't know but I had a notebook and a pencil with me. The sunset made me so calm I started sketching, I stood there for hours until the sun was gone. Then I realized the time…so I got up and started to walk home. I went home and there were cops, my parents and Lucas were freaking out. I was too calm to freak out or anything. I just walked over to them. They were happy I was okay, got mad, and after that, it was all good," Ty explains.

"I can't see you mad at your parents or Lucas," Krysta says.

"Yeah, it's different now. I told them why I was mad at them. They got it. That's when it all changed with my parents. Lucas, you get mad at him every day. It's just Lucas," Ty replies.

Krysta laughs and that causes Ty to laugh, then Krysta leans up and they both look at each other.

"It's beautiful." Krysta smiles.

Ty leans up and kisses Krysta and she kisses him back; their kisses slowly starts to turn to passion. They look at each other, then they look at each other deep in the eyes with fire that is growing.

Ty and Krysta return home. Ty gently slams Krysta to his bedroom door while kissing each other. He puts his hand to Krysta's thighs to pick her up, she wraps her legs around him, and as he opens his bedroom door, he quickly closes the door behind him, both still kissing deeply and passionately. Then they both gently but quickly fall to the bed, Ty slightly on top of Krysta, still kissing; then they slowly start to remove each other's clothes. Krysta then leans back and Ty follows, looking at each other, panting, as they hold each other's hands tight. Krysta moves her face to Ty's, kissing him, and he kisses her right back. He kisses her neck as he wraps her arms around his neck, then they kiss each other.

The next morning, everyone wakes up and meets each other downstairs; and there, they see breakfast already on the table, then they hear noise outside. Kate, Nick, and Lucas walk to the backdoor screen, and there, they see Ty and Krysta in the pool. They look at each other, then they slowly slide the screen and walk outside. Ty picks up Krysta and throws her back into the water. She comes up from the water and starts laughing but Ty is nowhere to be seen, she then feels something under her. Ty comes up from under her and flips her over him into the water. He moves his hair and the water from his face as he turns to Krysta, laughing, and Krysta comes up from the water with her hair covering her face. Ty slowly walks over to her and gently moves the hair from her face. They both start laughing.

"Well, well, what's going on out here?" asks Lucas.

Ty and Krysta turn their heads and see everyone staring at them; they look at each other with their eyes, then they start laughing again.

Chapter 9

$\mathcal{E}$veryone is outside, sitting on lounge chairs, but Lucas and Krysta are in the pool. Nick is on the phone with work, while Ty and Kate are talking.

"So when is she and I going to look for wedding dresses?" Kate asks.

"Mother," Ty says with a small laugh.

"What? Lucas may not figure it out yet. But I know what happened, a mother knows. And I'm happy for you, you smile a lot more now. And she's a beautiful young woman, inside and out," Kate says.

"Yes, Mother, I'm very happy. And I'm sorry to tell you but we have to leave," Ty replies.

"What, already?" Kate whines.

"What do you mean already? We were supposed to leave two weeks ago, Mom," Ty replies.

Kate smiles as she slightly rolls her eyes, then she looks back at Krysta and Lucas in the pool, laughing.

"I know, I don't want you to leave. What mother wants her child to leave?" Kate says. "But before anything? Um, I think you should go and help your brother because your girlfriend is beating him in the pool."

Ty looks at Krysta and Lucas who is being flipped my Krysta and both are laughing very hard. Causing everyone else to start laughing with them; Ty stares at Krysta as she smiles and laughs with joy.

He watches her beat Lucas, then he looks at Kate who tells him that he should go help his brother. Ty nods his head as he slowly stands up and walks over to the pool; Lucas swims over to him as Ty kneels down to him.

"Your girlfriend is crazy," Lucas says, out of breath.

Ty nods his head as he looks up at Krysta who is on the other side of the pool, laughing to the point that she has to hold onto the side of the pool. Ty puts his hand out to Lucas and he slaps his hand, then Ty jumps over Lucas into the pool. Krysta turns her head and Ty comes up from the water over to Krysta. Krysta smiles at him and he returns with a smile as he slowly swims over to her.

"What are you doing to my brother?" Ty asks.

Krysta slowly wraps her arms around Ty and gives him a quick kiss. They look at each other as they touch foreheads. Ty then moves his face closer to hers and they kiss. Lucas gets a shocked look on his face. With Kate and Nick both looking at each other, smiling.

"Some brother, you were supposed to avenge me," Lucas slightly yells.

Ty and Krysta stop kissing as they slowly start to laugh, then they turn to Lucas and everyone, then they look back at each other.

Later that night, everyone is in the house, Ty and Kate in the kitchen while Krysta, Lucas, and Nick are in the living room, playing chess. Lucas is playing Krysta with Nick watching them, laughing at them.

"It's on, Krysta, you got me in the pool. But I'm going to get you in chess," Lucas says.

"Okay." Krysta laughs.

Meanwhile in the kitchen, Kate and Ty are talking and getting drinks for everyone.

"Mother, we have to go back tomorrow," Ty says.

"Why? Can't you stay a little longer?" Kate whines.

"Really, Mother, I told you today. We stayed two weeks longer. Now we have to go back early tomorrow," Ty replies.

"Can't you go later? I mean after lunch or dinner," Kate whines.

"No," Ty says, trying not to laugh.

"Tyler Smith," Kate says.

"Okay, after lunch, but that's it," Ty replies.

"Fine, I'll make sure that the jet is ready." Kate smiles.

Ty shakes his head as he slightly laughs, then they both start walking to the living room. They see that Lucas and Krysta are playing chess. Ty sees that Krysta is having a little hard time; he smiles, then he walks over to her. He puts their drinks down on the coffee table, then he sits behind her and puts his chin on her right shoulder. Kate gives Nick and Lucas their drinks and sits down next to Nick and watches the game. Krysta is thinking about what to do; Ty looks at her with his eyes and he grins. Then he gently whispers in her ear, she gently smiles then she makes a move and looks at Lucas. Lucas looks at the chessboard, stunned, then he looks at Krysta and sees that Ty has his chin on her shoulder. He slowly starts to shake his head.

"Oh no, you can't be giving her any help."

Everyone starts laughing. Ty and Krysta look at each other and gently touch foreheads with everyone looking at them with happiness.

Next morning, everyone is up and exploring LA before Ty and Krysta have to leave. Krysta bought Lynne and Sam gifts while everyone watches her. As it gets close to lunchtime, everyone goes to find a place to eat. They are all laughing, talking, and joking with each other, Lucas almost choking from laughing and everyone coming to tears from laughing at him. But slowly, the laughing comes to an end as the hour comes close for Ty and Krysta to leave. They go to the airport, Ty says his bye to Lucas and Nick. They look at back to Krysta and Kate; they see that Kate is whining. The three of them walk over to them.

"Mom, you have to let her go," Ty says.

Kate looks at him.

"I don't want to until you guys say that you're going to come visit," Kate whines.

"Yes, Mom, we will come visit. Promise," Ty replies with a small smile.

Kate looks at Krysta who is smiling at her with joy all on her face. Kate then gives Krysta a hug, then she gives Ty a hug while Krysta gives hugs to Nick and Lucas. Ty and Krysta then get into the jet and head back to New York. They both fall asleep on the way back to the New York.

*****

Three days have passed since Ty and Krysta returned to New York and got right back to work. Ty is helping with the new art opening and Krysta was given a new position at work as an assistant. She is now the assistant to the director of the art shows as well as the daughter of the owner of the art building. Ty is in his art studio with other workers, coming up with ideas for the art show coming up. Thinking about how they can set up the gallery. As they are talking, Krysta walks in. They all turn their heads to her and she smiles at them; Ty gets up and walks over to her. They all stare at them for a minute with confusion yet curiosity; Ty and Krysta stand really close to each other, smiling and talking. Though no one can hear them, for they are too far, it didn't stop them from trying. Ty turns his head to them and they all move back to their places. Krysta slightly laughs, then she and Ty look back at each other.

"Okay, I just came to give you the update. They're just waiting to see how you guys are going to theme it," Krysta says.

"All right, we have a couple ideas. Just trying to see which one seems better," Ty says.

"Okay, am I getting a ride with you or going home with Lynne?" Krysta asks.

Ty smiles, slightly shaking his head.

"No, you're going home with me."

"Yeah, you like that truck your parents got you." Krysta laughs.

Ty just laughs, then he and Krysta give each other a small kiss. Then Krysta leaves and Ty walks back over to everyone. Everyone looks at him with big grins on their faces, and he looks at them as if they are crazy.

"What are you so happy about?" asks one of the workers.

"You mean the newest model of the navy-blue Ford-350 pickup truck I got for Christmas from my parents?" Ty replies.

"*No*, you and Krysta. What's going on?" asks another worker.

111

Ty looks at all of them who are looking at him like they are waiting for him to answer, but Ty grins at them, then he goes back to talk about what the theme is going to be for the art show. The workday comes to an end and Krysta is walking to Ty's studio; she walks in and sees that he's shutting everything down. He turns his head and sees that Krysta is waiting for him in the doorway. He walks over to her as he turns off the last light, and they wrap their arms around each other's waist. They get into Ty's truck and head home; they walk into the apartment. Krysta walks into the kitchen and Ty puts his coat on the rack. He looks over at Krysta who is getting some water to drink. He stares at her with a grin; Krysta slowly turns her head to him and smiles as if she's going to laugh.

"Why are you looking at me like that?" Krysta softly asks.

Ty slowly shakes his head as he shrugs his shoulders, then he slowly starts to walk over to her. He comes up to her and she lifts her head to look him in the eyes as she smiles slightly, biting her bottom lip. Ty puts his hand to her face softly.

"Stop that."

Krysta giggles. Ty takes his other hand to her waist and pulls Krysta closer, and they kiss. Krysta slowly wraps her arms around his neck, and Ty wraps his arms around her waist. They look each other in the eyes, they kiss again, and it starts to get deep. Ty then gently picks up Krysta and she wraps her legs around him; Ty then slowly start to walk to his bedroom. He opens the door, walks in, and closes it by gently pinning Krysta to the door. And Krysta, not paying any mind, Ty locks it. Krysta looks at him as he gently puts her down. She slowly starts to look at him with a seductive smile. They kiss again and slowly start walking, Krysta walking forward and Ty walking backward. They look at each other, then Krysta looks at him with that seductive smile again. Then she gently pushes him onto the bed, he softly laughs, and Krysta is still looking at him the same. She slowly crawls on to him and they slowly kiss. As their kiss start to get more passionate, they start to removes each other's clothes. They make love!

Later that night, as Ty and Krysta are sleeping, someone walks into the apartment and closes the door behind them. They look over to Ty's bedroom door and slowly walks over to it; they feel the door is locked but that doesn't stop them. They slowly pull a key out of the pocket and unlocks the door, slowly opening it. They see that Ty is sleeping but not alone, they look at Krysta as they walk over to the bed. They see that Ty has his arm around Krysta, they kneel down, looking at Krysta's face. Both sleeping peacefully till Krysta's eyes slowly start to open and she sees someone staring at her. She screams as she quickly leans up, causing Ty to also quickly wake up and lean up.

"What…what happened," Ty says.

He looks over to the person and breathes with relief but a little angry then turns to put on the light on his nightstand. He turns back.

"Bobby," Ty slightly yells.

Krysta moves closer to Ty, holding the sheets over her body, looking back at forth between Ty and Bobby. Bobby has light skin, short black hair, brown eyes, about 6'1" tall.

"Who's this?" Bobby asks.

Ty looks at him as if he's crazy, slowly shaking his head.

"What are you doing here? How did you get in here?" asks Ty.

"I live here," Bobby replies.

"My room, Bobby," Ty says.

Bobby looks around then back at Ty.

"You made another key, didn't you?" Ty says.

Then Ty looks at Krysta who is looking at him, confused.

"Um, Krysta, this is Bobby. The roommate that is never here. Bobby, this is Krysta. My girlfriend," Ty says.

Bobby looks at Krysta who is gently smiling at him, but Bobby just stares at her, causing Krysta to look at him with a little confusion.

"Well, it's about damn time," Bobby quickly says.

Bobby looks at Ty who rolls his eyes as he slightly shakes his head. Then Bobby looks back at Krysta and smiles.

"Well, nice to meet you," Bobby says.

"Bobby," Ty slightly yells," what are you doing in here?"

Bobby looks at Ty.

"Oh, me and my girl got into another fight. So she told me to get out," Bobby replies.

"And you come into my room at almost three o'clock in the morning because?" Ty asks.

"That hurts, man, you're support to be my boy, my friend. So I come to you, me and my girl are having problems," Bobby replies.

Ty stares at him with a plain look for about a minute. Krysta looks at him as if she's going to laugh.

"Bobby, go to bed. I worked, I'm tired, and it's three o'clock in the morning. Bed, now," Ty says.

Bobby nods his head.

"Good point, and if I remember your work schedule, you don't work tomorrow, so I'll talk to you about it then," Bobby says.

Then he gets up and walks over to the door, slowly opens it, then turns back to Krysta and Ty as he stands in the doorway.

"About time," Bobby says.

Bobby walks out of Ty's room and gently closes the door, heading to his room. Ty slowly shakes his head, Krysta smiles at him, then gently kisses his cheek. Ty looks at her.

"You will get annoyed soon."

Krysta slightly laughs, then she moves closer to Ty and they give each other a small kiss.

"You look really tired," Krysta says with a small smile.

Ty slowly nods his head, then they both lie back down and fall back asleep.

The next morning, Ty wakes up and Krysta is still asleep. He gives her a gentle kiss on the side of her head, then he slowly gets out of bed. He walks over to his door and walks out of his room, closing the door quietly behind him. As he comes out of his room, there he sees Bobby, sitting on the couch, watching TV. Ty walks over to the couch and sits down next to Bobby, both watching TV.

"So what happened this time?" Ty asks.

"I don't know. I come home from work and she starts yelling at me. I tried to get her to tell me what's going on but she wouldn't. She just yelled," Bobby replies.

"Something was bothering her, she just took it out on you," Ty replies. "So just give her some space. That means that till she comes to you, don't go running back to her again."

Bobby looks at Ty who is looking at the TV, then he looks back at the TV himself. As he looks at the TV, he gets this look as if he has something on his mind as he slightly looks at Ty.

"So how long have you—" Bobby is cut off.

"Don't go there," Ty says.

"She's cute," Bobby says.

Ty slightly laughs under his breath as he shakes his head.

"I take it that you want a few beers tonight?" Ty says.

"Do you even have to ask?" Bobby says.

"It wasn't a question," Ty replies.

Bobby gently laughs, then he gets up and goes into the kitchen; he gets a bottle of water. As he gets ready to walk back over to the couch, he sees Ty's bedroom open. Krysta comes out of Ty's room wearing one of his zip-up sweaters. Ty leans his head back as she walks over to him and they give each other a kiss. Bobby stares at them for a minute with a grin on his face as he watches them kiss each other. Then he walks over, he makes a sound as if he's clearing his throat. That makes Ty and Krysta look at him, they both slightly laugh then Krysta asks them if they are hungry. Then she goes into the kitchen to make some food; she's making them breakfast. Ty then gets up and walks into the kitchen to get something to drink, but then he looks over at Krysta. He walks up behind her and wraps his arms around her waist; he gives her a kiss on the shoulder. She smiles with a small laugh.

"It's almost done," Krysta says.

Ty shrugs his shoulders.

"I think Bobby is dying more than me. I don't think his girl cooks."

Krysta turns his head, she and Ty are looking face-to-face.

"Then why didn't you cook?" Krysta asks with a smile.

"I was not cooking for him, hell no," Ty replies.

Krysta starts laughing, then she asks Ty to put the food she cooked on the table. Ty slowly removed his arms from around Krysta, then he takes the food and puts in on the table. Ty tells Bobby to come and eat; he quickly gets up, walks into the kitchen. The three of them sit down and start eating and laughing. Bobby almost had Krysta choke on her food a few times from laughing too hard while Ty's eyes start to water and Bobby just keeps going.

Later that night, Ty gets Krysta to come out with him and Bobby to have a few drinks but only if she gets one of her friends to come, Sam. Sam meets them up at the club; she and Krysta are on the dance floor, having a good time while Ty and Bobby are talking at the bar. Ty looks out to Krysta and sees that she's having fun with Sam, then he sees that Bobby is checking out Sam.

"Bobby, no," Ty says.

Bobby looks over at Ty who is looking over at Krysta, dancing with Sam still. Then she turns her head and sees Ty looking at her, grinning. She smiles at him, then Sam takes her hand, gently pulls her over to Ty and Bobby.

"I'm going to take a break but Ty, this is Krysta's favorite song," says Sam.

Ty slightly laughs, then he looks at Krysta; he slowly gets out of his seat and takes her hand. They both go to the dance floor while Bobby and Sam watch them. They start to dance to salsa; Sam and Bobby take out their phones and start to record them. Sam then looks at Bobby and asks him if he would like to dance. He nods his head and they both go and join in with Ty and Krysta. They all drink and dance, but Bobby has had a little too much to drink, Ty and Krysta take Sam home. Then they look at each other, trying not to laugh at how Bobby is acting in the back seat.

"Bobby, you puke in my truck, you will clean it with a hang-over," Ty says.

Bobby looks out the window.

"Something is on the window."

Krysta covers her face and starts laughing. Ty is shaking his head.

"That's your reflection, Bobby."

They drive into the parking garage. Ty and Krysta get out of the truck and walk over to the back. Ty opens the door, and Bobby slowly comes out of the truck as if he's crawling out of the truck. Ty stares at him while Krysta walks behind Ty with her head on his back, shoulder laughing. Ty is looking at Bobby with a laughing shocked face, then he walks over to Bobby and helps him walk. He then picks Bobby up over his shoulder and Krysta slowly follows them into the building. Krysta opens the apartment door and Ty walks Bobby to his room; he plops Bobby onto his bed, then he leaves Bobby's room. He walks into the kitchen and sees Krysta getting some water. She smiles after she feels Ty wrap his arms around her waist and gently kiss her neck.

"How's Bobby?" Krysta softly asks.

"Fast asleep, thank you," Ty gently replies. "How about you, you feel okay?"

Krysta turns her head to Ty and she gives him a kiss, then she smiles at him. She tells him that she's tired, Ty gently laughs. Then he slowly takes the glass of water out of Krysta's hand then picks her up, causing her to slightly laugh as he carries her to the bedroom. They both change out of their clothes, then they slowly head to bed.

The next morning, Bobby wakes up with his head pounding; he looks around and sees that he's in his room. He slowly gets out of bed, then he walks to the bedroom door, almost hitting it. He slowly opens the door then walks into the kitchen and gets a bottle of water; he sees Ty's bedroom door. He looks around then slowly walks over to it, he puts his ear to the door then slowly opens it. He sees Ty and Krysta fast asleep, Ty with one hand behind his head and the other arm around Krysta who has one hand on Ty's chest, slightly below her face that is also resting on Ty's chest. Bobby slowly walks into the room and over to Ty's side of the bed, then he starts to poke Ty. Ty slowly starts to wake up, he turns his head and sees Bobby, almost giving him a shock. Ty looks over at Krysta and sees that she's still fast asleep, then he looks back at Bobby, slightly glaring. Bobby slowly waves his hand at Ty who is taking a deep breath. Then he slowly moves, trying not to wake Krysta, gets out of bed, then quickly grabs Bobby by the back of the neck and walks him out of the room. Ty gently closes the door and looks at Bobby.

"Why, why, just why?" Ty asks.

Bobby slightly scratches his head.

"I woke up and I was all alone. So I came to see you."

Ty stares at him for a second.

"My girlfriend is asleep. I was enjoying sleeping next to my girlfriend. So I'm going to go back sleeping next to my girlfriend. Get your bottle of water and relax," Ty says.

Ty then takes a couple steps back, opens his bedroom door, and walks back into his room with Bobby watching him. Ty slowly closes the door behind him, then he walks over to his bed and slowly lies back down. He wraps his arm around Krysta with her back to his chest; he slowly falls back asleep.

Later in the day, late that afternoon, Ty and Krysta wake up; they look at each other and smile. Then Ty hears yelling outside of the room. He and Krysta look at the door then back at each other. They both slowly get out of bed and walk over to the door, slowly opening it. There they see Bobby and a girl yelling back and forth at each other; Krysta looks at Ty and he looks at her.

"That's Bobby's girlfriend," Ty says.

Bobby's girlfriend is a light-skinned, brown hair, brown eyes, and she's 5'3" tall, and her name is Anna. Ty and Krysta stare at them.

"Should we do something?" asks Krysta.

Ty shakes his head no, then he walks away from the door and goes into the bathroom. Krysta gently closes the door and watches Ty walk into the bathroom. She looks back at the door then follows Ty into bathroom. Ty is in the shower, Krysta stares at the shower for a minute, then she hears Bobby and Anna. She walks over to the shower and slowly gets into the shower; she wraps her arms around him. Ty looks down and sees her arms around him, causing him to slowly turn to her. She looks up at him and smiles. Ty lifts one eyebrow and shakes his head with a small grin.

"No," Ty says.

Krysta gives him a pouting smile, Ty slowly shakes his head again with a laughing smile.

"The answer in still n—" Ty is cut off.

Krysta cut Ty off with a kiss, and he kisses her back as he wraps his arms around her. They look at each other and gently touch foreheads. Ty then grabs the loofah mesh sponge and slowly starts to wash her back. Krysta looks at his hand then back at him and he looks at her; they give each other another kiss. That slowly starts to become passionate, Ty drops the loofah mesh sponge and pulls her closer to him. But then, they hear a crash, Ty takes a deep breath, then he turns the water off. He reaches out to grab two towels; he gives one to Krysta and wraps the other one around his waist. Ty gets out of the shower and goes to put some clothes on; Krysta slowly gets out of the shower. She goes into the bedroom and sees Ty put a white T-shirt on and black basketball shorts. Krysta puts on one of Ty's button-up shirts and watches Ty walk to the bedroom door. Still hearing Bobby and Anna yelling at each other! He quickly opens the door, causing Bobby and Anna to stop yelling. Ty sees that Bobby and Anna broke a lamp, he takes a deep breath. He looks up at Bobby and Anna who is looking at him nervously. Ty just stares at them.

"What the hell is going on?" Ty slightly yells.

Anna takes a step to Ty.

"Ty, can you believe that he has been cheating on me. All this time, and here I was, feeling sorry for him," Anna slightly yells.

Ty just stares at her, then he looks at Bobby. Anna walks closer to Ty and puts her hands on his chest. She gives him a seductive smile, but Ty just stares at Bobby. Anna looks at Bobby and smiles at him.

"Maybe I should be with Ty," Anna says.

"Like hell."

Anna looks around, Ty moves away and leans back against the bedroom door wall and Krysta walks out from behind Ty. She and Anna stare at each other, Anna wondering who she is and Krysta stares as if she's challenging with death.

"You keep your hands off my man," Krysta says.

Chapter 10

*A*nna looks at Ty who crosses his arms, looking at Krysta then at Anna. Anna then slightly turns her head to Bobby then back at Ty.

"Who the hell is she?" Anna asks.

Krysta takes a step toward Anna, but then Ty walks up behind her and gently wraps his arms around her.

"Krysta, this is Anna. Anna, this is Krysta. My girlfriend," Ty says.

Anna looks at her with shock then at Ty who is grinning at her.

"You have a girlfriend? Since when?" asks Anna.

"That's not your business," Ty replies.

She looks at Krysta with a slight glare, but Krysta just stares at her. For Ty is keeping her next to him, trying to keep her calm. Ty then unwraps his arms around Krysta, takes her hand, and gently pulls her into the kitchen to look for something to eat. Anna turns completely to Bobby who is looking at her with a glare. Bobby walks over to her and she stares at him.

"Please tell me that you haven't been doing all this just to get close to Ty?"

Anna doesn't say anything. She looks over at Ty and Krysta in the kitchen, then she walks out of the apartment. Bobby watches her for a minute, then he follows her out of the apartment. Ty and Krysta watch Bobby leave as she slams the door. They both look at each other.

"And you wanted me to stop them from fighting. I had to stop you," Ty says.

Krysta smiles.

"No touching."

Ty grins as if he's going to laugh, Krysta then starts laughing, causing Ty to start laughing with her.

Meanwhile outside of the building, Bobby and Anna are fighting with each other again.

"*I can't believe you! You wanted Ty this whole time,*" Bobby yells.

"*No, but I can't believe you didn't tell me that he has a girlfriend,*" Anna yells back.

"*That's none of your business,*" Bobby yells. "*And that's why you're angry. Because you want Ty!*"

Anna stares at Bobby for a minute, then he slowly starts to shake his head.

"What is it about him that you like?" Bobby asks.

Anna doesn't reply. Bobby nods his head, then he slowly walks away. Anna watches him walk away, then she slowly starts to leave herself. Bobby goes back into the apartment; he stops before he closes the door behind him. He stares, for there he sees a little what makes Anna look at Ty more than she does him. Ty and Krysta are still in the kitchen; Krysta is sitting on the counter with Ty standing next to her, making a sandwich. On the other side of Krysta is a small bowl of grapes. Krysta takes one then slowly feeds it to Ty who looks at her with a smile and gently takes the grape. Then they both lean close to each other and give each other a kiss. They smile at each other then give another kiss. Bobby closes the door; Ty and Krysta look at him and see that something is bothering him. Ty then asks Krysta to give them a minute to talk; she nods her head. She jumps down from the counter then takes the grapes and sandwich into the bedroom.

"Bobby, what happened?" Ty asks.

Bobby looks at him and takes a deep breath, then he walks over to him. Bobby tells Ty everything that happened between him and Anna. Ty looks at him with shock.

"You can't believe that she was only with you because of me," Ty says.

Bobby shakes his head and shrugs his shoulders.

"Think about it. You and Anna were dating three months before I met her," Ty says.

Bobby looks at Ty, more relaxed

"Yeah, I know. I just don't know what is going on," Bobby says.

Ty grins as he shakes his head, then he puts his hand on Bobby's shoulder.

"Bobby, you feel like your heart is breaking. 'Cause you love her, but you're starting to feel like she doesn't love you."

Bobby nods his head, then he tells Ty that he's going to go out with some friends from work. Ty nods his head and asks if he wants him to go out with him. Bobby shakes his head and tells Ty to stay with his Krysta. Ty gently laughs as he nods his head, then he leaves and walks into his bedroom. Bobby watches him go into the room, then he goes to his room and relaxes before he goes out.

Meanwhile Ty walks into his room and sees Krysta lying on the bed, watching TV. He gently leans back against the door, with his hands in his pockets, and watched Krysta, slowly looking at the girl's body without her knowing he's in the room. After about a few minutes of staring, Krysta slowly turns her head and sees that Ty is staring at her. She softly smiles at him and he replies with a small grin. He slowly starts walking over to her and she looks up at him. They stare at each other, then Krysta slowly gets up, still on the bed, and wraps her arms around Ty's neck.

"Is he okay?" Krysta asks softly.

"No, but hopefully, with time, he will be," Ty gently replies.

Krysta softly smiles; she gives Ty a kiss and he gently returns it. They look at each other, then Ty kisses Krysta again; she quickly replies. Their kiss slowly becomes more passionate and deep as Ty wraps his arms around Krysta and pulls her closer to him. Krysta then slowly leans back as Ty leans forward. Ty keeps one arm around Krysta while he uses the other to stop them from falling on the bed but gently lie on the bed. Ty gently lying on top of Krysta, one hand now on her face and the other slowly moving from her leg to her thigh. Krysta has one arm still around Ty's neck and the other hand on Ty's chest. They kiss and kiss, but then, Krysta stops.

"Wait, wait, wait," Krysta pauses.

They both look at each other.

"Is this fair. I mean, Bobby is having a hard time with his girl. And we are in here enjoying ourselves while he's in the other room, pouting," Krysta asks.

Ty stares at her for a minute then looks as if he's trying not to laugh, causing Krysta to look at him with confusion.

"Do you know how long this has been going on between them? Like I told you before, it is a never-ending circle with them. They will fight, go out, have drinks, whine, pout, then out of nowhere, they are back together," Ty explains. "He'll be fine."

Krysta nods her head, then she stares at Ty.

"I want to watch the movie," Krysta quickly says.

Ty softly laughs, then he softly rolls off of Krysta to the other side of the bed and Krysta smiles as she holds her lips together. Then she slowly leans up and looks at the TV. Ty puts his head on his pillow and watches TV with Krysta.

Later in the night, Bobby is getting ready to go out while Ty and Krysta are still in the room, watching TV. Then Bobby comes running into the room; Ty and Krysta look over at him calmly. Ty still is lying down, one hand behind his head and the other one over his stomach and Krysta is just sitting on the bed.

"What's wrong, Bobby?" Ty asks.

"I don't know what to wear," Bobby replies in a small panic.

"Clothes," Ty replies.

"Funny," Bobby quickly replies.

"Do you need help, Bobby?" Ty calmly asks.

Bobby nods his head as if he's shaking.

"Yeah, a little."

Ty nods his head, then he slowly gets up and follows Bobby to his room but doesn't go in. Bobby stops and looks at him. Ty doesn't go in for all the clothes all over the floor. He leans back against the wall, with his arms crossed, with Bobby staring at him.

"Pick something, Bobby," Ty says.

Bobby shows Ty about fifteen shirts but Ty shakes his head to all of them.

"You have the boots and the jeans, but what is with your shirts?" Ty asks.

Bobby doesn't say anything; he just keeps looking for something to wear but Ty keeps telling him that it doesn't go with what he has on already.

"Bobby, I have been standing here for over twenty minutes. You already know what you want to wear," Ty says.

"Well, you know that shirt you have?" Bobby says.

"I have a lot of shirts, which one?" Ty says.

Ty then starts walking away, Bobby follows him. They walk into Ty's room, Krysta still sitting on the bed, watching TV. Ty walks over to his closet and pulls out one of his silk shirts.

"I take it, it's the red one."

Bobby looks at Ty with a goofy smile. Ty shakes his head, then he hands Bobby his shirt and Bobby runs to his room to change. Ty looks at Krysta; she smiles at him, then she gently starts to laugh. Ty then lies back down on the bed and sees what Krysta is watching. After about a two minutes Bobby comes running back into the room. Ty turns his head to him.

"You really need to knock," Ty says softly.

Bobby just looks around, then he looks back at Ty.

"The guys are here."

"Bye, Bobby," Ty says.

Bobby nods his head then leaves Ty's room quickly but gently closes the door behind him. They hear Bobby leave; Ty slowly shakes his head as he looks back at the TV. Krysta looks at Ty who is staring at the TV. She turns around and slowly crawls over to Ty, causing him to look at her. She gently puts her hand on his face.

"You look tired."

"A little but I'll be fine," Ty says. "Just looking forward for when he comes back."

Krysta softly laughs.

"Maybe I can get you to think about something else."

Ty slightly tilts his head. Krysta moves closer to him and slowly gives him a kiss. Ty slowly starts to kiss her back, then he leans up and pulls Krysta closer. Causing her to sit on his lap and wrap her arms around his neck as he wraps his arms around her waist. They look at each other, they both move closer and kiss again. Their kiss becomes deep and heavy; Ty slowly starts to unbutton the shirt Krysta is wearing. But before finishing, Krysta slowly starts to lift his T-shirt, causing them to stop kissing for a second. Ty's shirt is removed, he pulls Krysta back to him and kisses her as quickly as she kisses him back. He unbuttons her shirt and slowly slides it off her body. She wraps her arms back around him as he slowly starts to lean back, causing her to move forward. Krysta is lying on top of Ty and Ty is holding her close to him. Ty and Krysta give each other passionate kisses while making love to each other.

Late in the middle of the night, Bobby comes home and is completely drunk. He walks into the apartment, almost falling as he opens the door, closes the door behind him but still holding onto the door handle. He looks at the door and the handle, sees that he's still holding it. He smiles, then he looks over to Ty's room and sees that the door is closed. Bobby looks around then slowly walks over to the door, he goes to open it but the door is locked. He looks at the door then sticks his tongue out to it, then he wobbles to his room. Meanwhile Ty and Krysta are fast asleep in each other's arms.

The next morning, Ty wakes up; he looks over to Krysta who is still sleeping. But then her eyes slowly start to open, she looks at Ty and smiles. Ty gently kisses her on the forehead, they touch forehead.

After about an hour, Bobby very slowly comes out of his room. He sees Ty sitting at the table who looks up at him with a look as if he's going to laugh.

"Hungry?" Ty asks.

But Bobby looks at him as if he's going to pass out. Ty shakes his head. Bobby slowly sits down next to him.

"Why are you all dressed? Where's Krysta?" Bobby asks.

"She's getting dressed because we both have to get ready to leave for work," Ty replies.

"You have work today?" Bobby asks.

"Yes," Ty replies.

"But you're an artist and a photographer. You can work whenever," Bobby says.

Ty looks at him, softly laughing.

"But I also help with the shows."

They both look at each other, then Krysta comes out of the room and looks at the both of them. She sees Bobby and gently starts laughing as she walks over to them.

"Are you okay?" Krysta asks.

Bobby shakes his head. Ty stands up and puts his plate in the sink then goes back into the room. He brushes his teeth while Krysta helps Bobby with his hangover. Ty comes out of the room, Krysta walks over to him and they look at Bobby who has his head down on the table. They look at each other, then they slowly leave the apartment.

Ty and Krysta arrive at the art building. As they are going up to their floor, Krysta is looking through her paperwork. Ty is standing behind her, arms gently wrapped around her with his chin lying on her shoulder.

"Do you like your new job?" Ty asks.

"Yeah, I get to see more of the art. I don't have to find ways to sneak into your studio," Krysta replies.

Krysta slightly turns her head to Ty; they give each other a kiss. They look at each other, then they give each other another kiss and another; but then, their kisses start to get a little deeper. Meanwhile in the building, without anyone knowing, Ford is walking and talking with one of artist! The elevator comes to a stop, Ty and Krysta quickly stop kissing and move slightly away from each other with looks as if they are about to laugh, Ty slightly covering his mouth and Krysta slightly biting her bottom lip. They both walk out of the elevator and head to their areas. Krysta goes to her desk while Ty walks to his studio.

Lunchtime comes around and Krysta starts walking to Ty's studio without her knowing across the way is Ford! Krysta comes into Ty's studio and sees him talking to one of the head members who sets up for the shows. He leaves Ty's studio and Krysta walks over to him. Ty is in shock till Krysta gently touches his arm. Ty looks at her and smiles, he picks her up and starts to spin with joy. He puts her down and tells her that his artwork is going to be part of the main show hall in two weeks. Krysta screams for joy as she wraps her arms around Ty; they hug each other close, then they go to lunch. Only a few minutes after they leave, Ford walks into Ty's studio, looking for him. One of the workers tell him, "You just missed him."

"When will he be back?" asks Ford.

"Who knows? He might get an idea while he's on break," the worker replies.

Ford nods his head as the worker walks away. He looks in Ty's studio and is about to go in. But then an assistant comes up to him and tells him that they are waiting for him to start the meeting. She guides him to the meeting room. Ty and Krysta return from lunch, and before Krysta can head back to her desk, Ty gently pulls her into his studio. She looks at him and starts laughing.

"I have to get back to my desk." Krysta laughs.

"Yeah, you can in one minute. But first, I need to ask you something," Ty says.

"Like?" Krysta asks with a small happy smile yet curious.

"Well, I have enough paintings but I still need a few more pictures," Ty replies.

Krysta stares at him for a minute till she looks at him with shock. "No, no."

"Why not?" Ty slightly laughs.

"Is that what everyone is going to see in the show? Me?" Krysta asks.

"Yeah," Ty replies.

Krysta then tries to run out of Ty's studio, but he gently grabs her by the waist and pulls her back to him. Krysta starts pouting.

"Ty, no, that's not fair."

"What's so bad about it?" Ty asks as he lets her go.

Krysta walks over to the door, turns and leans back against it, still pouting.

"Everyone is going to see me." Krysta pouts.

Ty grins at her as he walks over to her.

"Yes, everyone is going to see a young beautiful women. What's wrong with that?"

"What happens if no one likes them? Then everything you did goes to waste," Krysta replies.

Ty comes up to her, leans one hand on the door, and holds Krysta's hand with the other.

"The key word in your sentence is *if*, but the way I see it is everyone is looking at you. The beauty that I see, and if they don't, sucks for them. More for me," Ty says.

Krysta looks at him, still pouting.

"So can I take the pictures," Ty asks.

"Ty—" Krysta is cut off.

Ty cuts Krysta off with a kiss that slowly becomes a little passionate. Krysta then agrees to have Ty take her picture. Ty whispers a thank you to her as he kisses her again and again. Meanwhile Ford's meeting just comes to an end. Before Ford can leave the room, the director of the show comes up to Ford.

"I heard that you are trying to meet one of my artists," says the director.

"Yes, I believe his name is Tyler," Ford replies.

"Oh, yes, Tyler," says the director.

"Yes, I've seen some of his work. And I was hoping that he could take a few pictures for me. I also understand that he's a painter, sketch artist," Ford says.

"Yes, he's a young man of many talents. But you'll have a hard time finding him. He's never really in his studio, only for touch-ups on his work or for supplies. But he will be here for the art show in two weeks. He's work is going to be part of the main show hall," says the director.

Ford nods his head, then they shake hands that they will see each other then.

Later that night, Ty and Krysta stay in the art building to work on Ty's pictures. While Krysta is changing, Ty is setting everything up for the background. Ty takes out cameras, cleans them while waiting for Krysta to come out from changing.

"Krysta, it does not take almost two hours to change," Ty slightly yells.

"I'm not coming out," Krysta yells back.

"Why?" Ty laughs.

"I can't wear this," Krysta yells back.

"Krysta, you say that about every outfit you put on," Ty yells, laughing still.

"Ty," Krysta whines.

"Do not make me come in there to get you," Ty yells.

"Fine," Krysta says.

Ty is sitting on a chair, back to Krysta, still cleaning his cameras. Ty set the studio with dim lights, the background is like that of night with the sky full of stars. With a Victorian couch, Krysta slowly comes out of the changing room. She is wearing a long silk white nightgown, her hair is wavy and completely out, no makeup, just a little clear lip gloss. Ty hears her coming out of the changing room; he slowly turns and looks at her. He stares at her, stunned, her head slightly tilted down, slightly looking at Ty. Ty slowly stands up and walks over to her, gently takes her hand, and walks with her over to the Victorian couch. She sits down and Ty kneels down in front of her, then he tells her how he wants her to lie on the couch. He wants her mostly lying on her back, slightly leaning back against the couch. Her right hand to slightly touch her forehead, her left hand lying across her stomach. Her legs crossing each other, slightly bent.

He slowly stands up and walks over to his cameras. He turns to her and tells her to keep her eyes on him; she takes a calm deep breath. Ty takes a couple steps to her and kneels down, starts to takes her pictures. After a couple of pictures, he changes his camera and tells Krysta to close her eyes with a small smile. Krysta closes her eyes, and with a small smile, Ty takes a couple of pictures. Then he tells her to open her eyes but keep that smile and tilt her head a little more. As Krysta stares at Ty taking pictures, without realizing it, her smile and face slowly turns seductive. Ty, still taking pictures, stops after seeing how Krysta is looking at him. He slowly moves the camera from his face and stares at Krysta; they stare deep into each other's eyes. He puts the camera down and walks over to her, she moves her hand from her forehead as she looks up at Ty who kneels on the couch and gently leans Krysta up to him, kissing her! She kisses him back as she wraps her arms around his neck and he wraps one arm around her and the other leaning on the couch!

Chapter 11

Two weeks pass and it's only a few hours till the opening at the art show. Ty and Krysta are home, getting ready for the show. Ty is in a black and white tuxedo but no tie, but his white shirt is completely buttoned. His hair pulls back into a ponytail; he's sitting on the bed, tying his shoes. Krysta comes out of the bedroom. Ty looks up at her and grins with amazement. For she is wearing a long black off-the-shoulder cocktail dress in a Lycra stretch fabric, zippered back, and has a slit in the middle up to her knees. Her hair over her left shoulder, silver hoop earrings, silver bracelet on her right wrist, and clear lip gloss. He stands up and walks over to her.

"Is it too much?" Krysta asks.

"You look beautiful," Ty softly replies.

"Not so bad yourself. But no tie," Krysta softly laughs.

"You know I don't like ties," Ty replies.

Krysta slowly shakes her head, then she gives Ty a kiss on the cheek. She looks at his cheek and gently wipes away her lip gloss. They both then leave and head to the art show; they are both picked up in a limo. As they are heading to the show, Krysta keeps looking at Ty who is looking out the window. Ty sees that she's looking at him through the window.

"Yes, Krysta."

"Nothing," Krysta replies.

Ty looks at her as if he's going to laugh.

"I can see that you keep looking at me. What's wrong?"

"Nothing, just are you nervous?" Krysta asks.

"No," Ty replies.

Krysta looks at him with a small smile, as if she can tell he's lying.

"I'm not nervous—terrified." Ty laughs.

Krysta laughs with Ty. She moves closer to him.

"It will be fine," Krysta says.

Ty gently lifts Krysta's chin and moves closer to her. He gives her kisses, she slowly kisses him back. They look at each other and about to kiss each other again, but then, they arrive at the art building. They look at each other, then the limo driver opens the door. Ty comes out of the limo, then he puts his hand out for Krysta. Krysta wraps her arm around Ty's arm as they walk into the building, gently waving at all the reporters taking their pictures. Ty gives Krysta a kiss on the head; the reporters tell him to do it again, and some ask who she is.

They come into the building and one of the head show members walks over to them. He shakes Ty's hand and kisses Krysta's hand as he tells her how lovely she looks. Krysta looks at Ty, smiling; Ty softly laughs. Then they both walk away to look at the others' art. Krysta looks at all the art with amazement; as they stand next to one of the paintings, a waitress comes by with a tray holding glasses of champagne. They both take a glass and say their thanks. Ty looks back at Krysta who is looking at the painting. Ty takes her hand, causing her to look at him. He tilts his head, signing that he wants her to come with him. He brings her to another painting that she looks at with amazement. Meanwhile as Ty and Krysta are looking at everyone's pictures and paintings, Ford is coming out of his limo. He walks into the building and takes a glass of champagne. As he walks around, the director comes up to him and they start talking about the show.

Ty and Krysta look at the art, but then Krysta looks at Ty. He looks at her and gently smiles.

"What?"

"Okay, I was stalling on this. But where is your work?" Krysta asks.

Ty slightly laughs, then he takes her hand and they start walking to another room. They come to the doorway, Krysta sees that the lighting is different from the lights on the floor. She looks at Ty and he gently pulls her into the room. Ty shows her the others' art but Krysta starts looking at him as if he's stalling. Ty looks at her.

"They're over here. Are you sure you want to see them? You're not going to run?" Ty says.

Krysta slowly shakes her head, then Ty guides her to his paintings and pictures. They walk over and Krysta gets a complete look of amazement. She holds onto Ty's arm; as she moves closer to him, he looks at her. Everyone looks at the pictures and paintings, talking about how beautiful they are and the girl in them.

"Told you, you're beautiful," Ty softly says.

Krysta looks at him.

"That's all you."

They give each other a kiss, then the show director comes over to Ty and tells him that someone is looking to talk to him. Krysta tells Ty to go and meet who wants to talk to him. She will stay there, waiting for him. As she's looking at some more of the art, someone is looking at her, smiling. They walk over to her, come up behind her, and she slightly looks at them with just her eyes. Krysta then slowly turns around to see who is standing so close behind her. She looks at the person with shock and fear. For the person standing behind Krysta is none other than Ford!

He looks at Krysta with amazement but also as if he's looking at her with no clothes. Krysta looks around, even though there are lots of people to see if anything happens, she is still scared.

"I never thought I would see such a beauty," Ford says.

"It's an art show. There is a lot of it," Krysta replies.

"Oh, yes, the art is beautiful. But I wasn't talking about the art," Ford says.

"Excuse me," Krysta says.

Krysta is about to walk away but Ford follows her, causing her to get more nervous. She looks at more of the art with Ford following her every step.

"For a lovely young lady to be here alone is such a shame. Maybe—" Ford says.

She slowly starts to shake but then—"There you are. What happened?"

Krysta turns and sees Ty standing slightly behind her. She quickly moves closer to him and wraps her arm around him. Ty feels that she's slightly shaking, then he slowly looks at Ford and slowly looks him up and down as he wraps his arm around her.

"And you are?" Ty asks.

Ford looks at Krysta, then back at Ty.

"Sorry, I'm James Ford."

Ford reaches his hand out to Ty who is looking at him with a slight glare then slowly down at his hand. Ty slowly grips Ford's hand and slowly shakes it.

"Ty."

They both stare at each other for a minute.

"I take it you know this lovely lady?" Ford says.

"Yes, I do. She's my date as well as my girlfriend," Ty replies.

"And you leave her alone?" Ford asks.

Ty stares at him with a small cocky grin. He very slightly tilts his head, then he looks at Krysta who looks up at him.

"I'll make it up to her later," Ty says.

Krysta slowly smiles with a little seduction in it. Ty then gives her a kiss and she returns it. They look at each other.

"Oh, by the way, Lynne is looking for you," Ty says.

They both then look at Ford, who is slightly glaring at Ty, but Ty still has that same small cocky grin. Krysta looks back at Ty then gives him a kiss on the neck then walks away to go find Lynne. Ty watches her walk away then looks back at Ford, then the director comes over to them.

"Oh, it looks like you two have met," says the director.

He looks at Ty and walks over to him, Ty looks at him.

"Ford has been looking to talk to you," says the director.

Ty looks at Ford.

"Really?"

Ford looks at the director with confusion then back at Ty.

"I'm sorry. I'm looking to speak to Tyler."

"That's me," Ty replies.

Ford looks at him with a little shock, then he looks at the director, Ty looking at him as if he's about to laugh.

"My name is Tyler but everyone calls me Ty. Well, my friends do."

Ford looks at Ty.

"Excuse me. I left my girl alone too long," Ty says.

"Oh, Ty, before you go and do that. I have someone who wants to ask you about one of your paintings," says the director.

Ty and the director walk over to Ty's paintings and start talking to one of the people who are interested in one of Ty's paintings of Krysta. Ford looks and talks around, then he sees Krysta again. He sees that she's walking to the ladies' room. He looks to see if anyone is following then follows her. He waits for her to come out of the ladies' room. She comes out of the ladies' room and stops. For Ford walked in front of her, she looks at him with shock, and he looks at her with lust in his eyes. Then a waitress walks over and gives them glasses of champagne; they both take a glass and the waitress walks away. Krysta gets a little nervous, Ford sees that and smiles.

"You seem a little nervous," Ford says.

Krysta looks at him.

"You happy that we're alone?" Ford continues.

Krysta slightly glares at him.

"Don't flatter yourself."

Krysta gets ready to walk away but Ford walks into front of her again. She looks at him then looks away as she takes a deep breath.

"You know I can make you feel a lot more than your boyfriend. And he doesn't have to know," Ford says.

Krysta quickly looks at him, then she splashes her champagne on his face.

"Go to hell," Krysta says, angry.

Then she walks away as she slams the glass to the floor in front of Ford's feet. Ford slowly wipes the champagne from his face, then he looks around to see if anyone saw them. He walks into the men's room to clean himself off.

Meanwhile Ty comes up to Lynne and asks her if she has seen Krysta. She shakes her head no. Ty then goes to look for her but can't find her. Then he goes out into the opening of the art show and looks for Krysta. He then looks up and sees that Krysta is up on the next floor. He gets into the elevator; he gets off and slowly walks over to her. She turns her head to him and sees that her eyes are watering, as if she's about to cry. He walks closer to her, then he slowly opens his arms. She walks right into his arms and hides her face in his chest.

"What happened?" Ty softly asks. "That's a stupid question. What did Ford do?"

Krysta looks up at him, then she gently puts her head against his chest and tells him what happened between her and Ford. She looks up at Ty.

"Why does he still get to me?" Krysta asks.

"Krysta, you can't expect one year to fix years of pain. Mostly when they come out of nowhere," Ty says.

She nods her head, then she softly smiles at him.

"But I still have you, right?"

"Is that a question? Because I'm not going anywhere," Ty replies.

Then the director comes up and finds them.

"There you are. I have some more people who wish to talk to you."

Ty and Krysta look at each other, then they follow the director back downstairs. They come into the main showroom, also at the same time Ford is coming out of the bathroom. He sees Krysta and Ty together with the director, he glares. Ty and Krysta are talking with the people who like Ty's artwork. Some have already bought two of his paintings and three of his pictures. The only one that no one has seen yet is the last one he took where it has Krysta in the night-gown with a night-sky theme. The director comes over to see Ty and tells him that all of paintings and pictures have been sold. He only has one left that is going to be part of the head art show that will be taking place in about ten minutes. Ty nods his head then he looks at Krysta who smiles at him and hugs him. Ford is watching them from behind; he takes another glass of champagne.

After about ten minutes, the main show is about to start. The director tells everyone to come and see the last three works of art of the night. Everyone comes together to see the last three; the director shows everyone the first two artworks. They were sold in ten minutes; the last one is Ty's picture of Krysta. The director shows it to everyone; as they look at it, they all become stunned. Everyone stares at the picture, then they all try to buy it. Ford is the only one who doesn't try to buy it. For he is too much in a daze, looking at the picture, but a woman ends up buying the picture. At that moment, Ford sees that he's too late to put in a number for the picture. Everyone walks away and Ford walks up to the picture. He looks closely at it and sees that he knows who it is. He looks over to Krysta and sees that it's her in the picture, but lucky for Krysta, he still doesn't truly know who she is!

Ford is watching Ty and Krysta talk to the woman that bought Ty's picture, how Ty and Krysta have their arms around each other. After they say bye to the woman, they start to walk to the entrance to leave, for the art show is over and everyone is slowly leaving. Ford slowly yet quickly follows them, but there are too many people leaving at once. Once he comes out of the building, he sees Krysta and Ty getting into their limo. He watches as the limo drives away; he takes a deep angry breath. Then he walks over to his limo as it slowly pulls up, he gets in then takes out his cell phone.

"Meet me at my place in ten minutes. I need to release some energy," Ford says.

He hangs up his phone then tells the driver to drive faster as he looks out the window, thinking to himself.

"Why do I feel like I know her?" Ford says to himself.

Meanwhile Ty and Krysta arrive at home. They thank the driver then slowly head up to the apartment. As they are in the elevator, Ty is talking about how excited he is about how all his paintings and pictures were sold. Krysta listens with a happy smile for Ty; he looks at her with a smile. Krysta moves closer to him and gives him a kiss, he kisses her back, then they arrive at their floor. They come into the house and sees that Bobby is not home, for all the lights are still out. Ty locks the house since they get home around two thirty in the morning.

"Do you want something to drink?" Krysta asks.

"No, I had enough champagne," Ty replies, smiling.

Krysta laughs as she gets a small glass of water. Ty walks into his room. Krysta puts her glass down then walks into the room and stares at Ty from the doorway. Ty is taking off his shoes, sitting on the bed. Krysta walks into the room as she gently closes the door. She walks over to him, standing right in front of him. He looks up at her, she is slightly biting her bottom lip. She leans down to him and kisses him. They both slowly kiss each other. They look at each other, then Krysta moves closer to Ty, slowly sitting on his lap. Ty gently puts his hands on her waist as Krysta pulls him closer to kiss her. She puts her hands on his face then slowly starts to wrap her arms around his neck. She moves her hands down to the front of his shirt, slowly unbuttons them then slowly removes it. Ty slowly moves his hands from her waist, then he gently puts his hands back on her waist. Then he slowly moves his hands up to her back then starts to unzip her dress. They look at each other. Krysta slowly stands up as Ty slowly removes her dress. Ty stands up in front of her, Krysta slowly takes the hair clip out of her hair. Krysta then moves closer to Ty then gently kisses the right side of his neck, slowly moving to his shoulder as she walks around him, kissing his back shoulder. Ty then doesn't feel her, causing him to slowly turn around. There he sees Krysta, slowly lying on the bed; they stare at each other with desire in their eyes. Ty slightly smiles, then he slowly crawls on the bed to Krysta, leaning over her. He moves down to her, they kiss slowly; but then as they wrap their arms around each other, their kiss gets more hot and passionate. They make love to each other, holding each other tightly, looking into each other's eyes with fire. Deep passionate kisses to the lips, kisses to the body that make them feel like their bodies burning with heat.

Chapter 12

A week has passed since the art show. Ty and Krysta have not been back to the art building since it has been closed due to the art show. Krysta is happy for it because she fears running into Ford. She and Ty have been spending time with their friends. Krysta has been going to self-defense classes with Sam and Lynne. While Ty is helping Bobby with his breakup-non-breakup with Anna.

"Bobby, stop," Ty says, trying not to laugh.

"What am I supposed to do? She makes it seem like she wants to get back with me and the next, she wants nothing to do with me," Bobby says.

Ty and Bobby are home, talking in the living room. Ty is sitting down and Bobby is walking back and forth. Ty is listening to Bobby, shaking his head as he covers his mouth, trying to hide the fact that he's laughing. Bobby looks at him and stares at him with a plain look on his face. Ty looks up at him and Bobby doesn't blink, causing Ty to start laughing, and Bobby looks at him with complete shock.

"I don't like you anymore. Where's Krysta? She listens to me better and with feelings." Bobby pouts.

"Bobby, you sound like a fifteen-year-old girl," Ty replies, laughing.

Bobby stares at Ty and Ty is still laughing, then the apartment door opens. They look to the door and sees Krysta walking in. She has her workout clothes on and gym bag over her shoulder. She looks at them and smiles.

"Hi, guys," Krysta says.

"Hey, Krysta," Bobby says.

Krysta walks over to Ty on the other side of the couch. Ty leans his head back as Krysta leans behind him, and they give each other a kiss.

"Hi, babe," Krysta says.

"Hi, beautiful," Ty replies.

Then Krysta looks at Bobby, trying not to laugh.

"Are you okay, Bobby?" Krysta asks.

Bobby stares at her for a second.

"No."

Ty and Krysta laugh.

"What happened, Bobby?" Krysta asks.

Bobby starts to tell Krysta everything that he already told Ty. Krysta listens as she gently massages Ty's shoulders. Krysta gently smiles at Bobby as Ty laughs under his breath.

"Bobby, I care about you. So I'm just going to tell you, you need to drop her," Krysta says.

"What? Why?" Bobby asks.

"Bobby, she's using you and you're letting her. Cut her off, even if it's just for a little while. See how much she starts begging for you, then you'll know," Krysta continues.

She then looks at Ty as he leans his head back to her.

"I'm going to take a bath," Krysta says.

She gives Ty a kiss, then she goes into the bedroom and gently closes the door behind her. Ty looks at Bobby and Bobby looks back at him.

"She listened…with feelings," Bobby says.

Then Bobby's cell phone rings and he sees that it's work. Ty watches him go to his room. Ty looks back at the TV. He turns it off, then he gets up and goes to the bedroom. He hears the water running in the bathroom, he puts the TV on as he goes and sits on the edge on the bed. After ten minutes, he hears the water turn off; he slightly turns his head to the bathroom door, then he looks back at the TV. He gets up and walks over to the bathroom door, he gently opens the door and looks at Krysta who is sitting in a bubble bath with her head leaned back and her eyes closed. He leans to the side of the door, his hands in his pockets, grinning at her. He then slowly walks into the bathroom, over to Krysta. He kneels down and lays his arms on the side of the tub. He looks to the mesh sponge then slightly back at Krysta. He gently grabs the mesh sponge. He puts a little bodywash on it then gently starts to rub Krysta's neck; her face slowly relaxes. Then she opens her eyes and sees that it's Ty who gently smiles at her. She leans her head up and smiles back at him, then she gently puts her hand to his face. Ty then pulls her closer and gives her a kiss, she kisses him back. They look at each other.

"How was class?" Ty asks.

"She pushed us today," Krysta replies with a smile.

Ty nods his head, then he tells her to turn around; she slowly turns around, then Ty slowly starts to massage her shoulders. She leans her head back, gently hitting his chest.

"I'm going to fall asleep in this tub," Krysta softly says.

Ty slightly laughs under his breath as he looks down at Krysta's face, then Krysta slowly opens her eyes. She and Ty look at each other.

"You should come in here with me. I'm sure you can use a little relaxation after dealing with Bobby," Krysta softly says.

Ty stares at her with a grin, then he slowly removes his hands and stands up. He slightly tilts his head. He slowly starts to remove his shirt, then he slowly starts to remove his pants.

"Move."

Krysta smiles then slightly moves out of the way for Ty to get into the tub. He slowly sits down as Krysta leans back, putting her back against his chest and leaning her head back on his shoulder. Ty wraps his arms around her as he gives her a kiss to the side of her head.

"Krysta, is there something else that's making you all stiff?" Ty asks.

Krysta takes a slight deep breath, then she leans her head up and looks at Ty

"We go back to work in two days. I guess I'm a little nervous about going back."

"A little?" Ty says.

"Okay, I'm freaking out," Krysta quickly replies.

"Krysta, I got you," Ty says.

Krysta smiles at him, then they give each other a kiss. They look at each other. Ty then has Krysta lean her head back onto his shoulder.

"We should do this more often," Krysta softly says.

They both gently laugh. Krysta then leans her head back up and kisses Ty, he slowly kisses her back. Krysta slowly leans up and turns around, slightly sitting on Ty's lap as she wraps her arms around Ty's neck. Ty gently puts his hands on her waist, pulls her closer to him, wrapping his arms around her. Kissing each other deeply, Ty then slightly moves his lips away from Krysta. They look at each other with heat in their eyes. Ty slightly grins as he drains the tub. Causing Krysta to look at him with slight confusion. Ty then stands up and closes the tub and puts the shower on; he looks at Krysta and helps her stand up. He pulls her right back into a deep heated kiss, Krysta kisses him right back as they wrap their arms around each other. Ty then slightly pins her to the wall as their kisses get deeper and deeper. Ty slowly moves his hands down to Krysta's thighs and picks her up. They hold each other close and tight as they give in to their passion!

*****

The two days have passed. Ty and Krysta are back at work. Ty is working with another photographer, helping him with his models. Krysta comes by to give Ty some paperwork; the other photographer sees Krysta and recognizes her from Ty's painting and photos. He walks over to her and asks her if she's a model. She looks at him with shock and shakes her head, trying not to laugh. She looks at Ty who is still looking at the paperwork, grinning, as if he's going to laugh. Then he walks over to one of his helps to see if he has the right setting. Then the photographer asks Krysta to take photos for help because he's missing a model do to the fuel. Then the boss walks into the studio to see how everything is going and he comes over to Krysta and the photographer. And the photographer asks if he can use Krysta for his last model. The boss looks at Krysta and nods his head. Krysta quickly looks at him as if he's crazy then back at the photographer. He smiles at her; she looks for Ty but he is nowhere to be found. They get Krysta to the dressing room to change, hair, and makeup. They put Krysta in a beautiful long green silk dress with small diamond flower design going all the way down on one side of the dress. Her hair braided to the side to hang over her shoulder with silver flower earrings. They walk her over to where they want her to stand; they have her set up as if she is Mother Earth. The photographer tells her to just relax and do what she did for her other photos. But as he's trying to take her photos, he's not getting the same as he saw with the other photos. He looks at her with confusion.

"What's going on? I'm not seeing what I saw in the other photos...is something wrong?" the photographer asks.

Krysta shakes her head.

"No, I'm just not a model."

Ty comes back into the studio and sees that Krysta is all dressed up but also sees that she's not taking the right photos. He walks over to the photographer and looks at Krysta, and she looks back at him. Ty looks at her, up and down, then he walks over to her; everyone is watching with confusion. Krysta slightly looks down, Ty gently takes his hand and lifts her head, causing her to look back at him.

"Come here," Ty gently says.

He takes Krysta's hand and walks over to a different area for the photo. He tells Krysta to sit down, he puts one of her hands on her lap and the other as if she's about to pick a flower. Then he calls one of his helps to bring him his camera. Then he starts to take photos, then softly, he lifts Krysta's head and gently turns it to look at him. Slightly tilting it, she looks at him gently as he steps away and takes more photos. The other photographer looks at him, then at Krysta, watching how Ty has Krysta doing all these beautiful photos. With her sitting, standing, and even lying, with eyes as if she's no longer taking photos. Just staring into Ty's eyes, calmly and peacefully. But that piece is about to come to an end, for at that same moment, Ford is walking the halls.

Ty has Krysta relaxed for she is now taking photos with the other models, smiling and laughing. Ty is no longer taking the photos, he's telling the girls what to do and keeping Krysta's eyes on him. After the photos are done, everyone slowly starts to take the studio down and the girls go to change. Krysta walks up to Ty, trying not to laugh, and Ty smiles at her. She shakes her head, then she goes to change. Ty walks over to the photographer and looks at the photos with him.

"I don't know how you did it. But these photos of her are beautiful. You and I are going to have to talk. I might need you and her again. I'll be in touch," says the photographer.

Ty nods his head. They both shake hands, then he leaves. Ty is still in the studio, waiting for Krysta to come out of the changing room. But as she comes out of the changing room, the boss walks in with Ford right behind him. Krysta sees Ford and her eyes turn to complete shock, causing her to walk fast over to Ty. Ty slowly stands up as he sees Ford walking over to him and Krysta. Ford smiles when he sees her, Krysta slightly hiding behind Ty, holding slightly yet tightly onto Ty's shirt. Ty just stares at Ford with a calm face yet his eyes say completely different. The boss comes over to them, smiling.

"And what brings you here?" Ty asks.

"Oh, Ty, Ford will be part of the company now," says the boss.

Krysta gets a shocked look on her face with fear in it. Ty slowly looks at Ford and Ford smiles at him. Ty nods his head.

"Great, but I still have work to do. So if you two don't mind?" Ty says.

"Yes, I also heard good things about you. If we can get him to be part of our company, we could be golden," the boss says.

Ty nods his head as the boss is walking away. Ford is staring at Krysta but she isn't look at him. Ty looks at him, just his eyes, causing Ford to look over to Ty. Ty tells him to leave with just his eyes, looking at the door then back at Ford. Ford slightly smiles, then he slowly starts to follow the boss out of the studio. The moment they leave, Krysta starts to breathe heavy, almost in a panic. Ty turns to her and helps her stand.

"It's okay, relax," Ty says.

Krysta looks at him and quickly wraps her arms around him, and Ty wraps his arms around her. She hides her face in his chest and Ty looks out to the door. Ty slightly leans back and gently lifts Krysta's head.

"Let's go home," Ty gently says.

Krysta nods her head. They both wrap their arms around each other as they start walking to the studio door.

*****

Time goes by, Ford keeps trying to get Krysta to talk more than work with him. Ty is getting ready for another art show for his paintings and Krysta is helping with the theme for the show. Everyone is sitting in a meeting, coming up with ideas for the show. After the meeting, Krysta is walking down to Ty's studio but Ford runs up to her. She stops, for he comes in front of her pathway.

"Yes, Ford, what is it now?"

"I thought maybe since the meeting is over, we can have lunch," Ford asks.

Krysta stares at him with a plain yet annoyed look on her face.

"No, Ford, I'm having lunch with my boyfriend."

"Did someone call me?"

Ford slightly turns around and sees that Ty is walking over to them. Krysta walks around Ford and walks over to Ty. They hug and give each other a kiss; they look at Ford.

"Need something, Ford?" Ty asks.

Holding onto Krysta as she keeps her arms wrapped around Ty's waist as he has his arm wrapped around her shoulder. Ford shakes his head, then Ty and Krysta look at each other.

"You hungry?" Ty asks with a grin.

"You have no idea," Krysta replies with a slight laugh.

Ford watches them walk away, then he walks back to his office. Meanwhile Ty and Krysta are out walking around, trying to see what they want for lunch.

"It is hot today," Krysta says.

"Well, it is summer. It's almost July," Ty replies.

"So what are we doing for the Fourth?" Krysta asks.

Ty looks at her and gently smiles.

"Whatever you want."

Krysta smiles at him, then she sees a place for them to eat and gently pulls him over.

After they finish lunch, they return to the art building. Ty and Krysta are in the elevator. But as they are in the elevator, Ty has Krysta gently pinned to the wall, both kissing each other. He's holding one of her thighs up and with his other arm around her waist while Krysta has her arms wrapped around his neck, both kissing each other passionately. They arrive at their floor and the doors open; Ty and Krysta are standing side by side, trying not to laugh. For there are people walking into the elevator. They both walk off the elevator and look at each other as the door closes. They walk down to Ty's studio and see that everyone is still on lunch, they look at each other, softly smiling. They turn to each other and hold each other.

"Everyone is still on lunch," Krysta softly says.

"Yeah, but not for long," Ty replies.

Krysta gently laughs.

"How about we go to dinner tonight? Then when we get home, we can continue what happened in the elevator," Ty says.

Krysta gives him a seductive smile.

"Okay. But maybe more of a sneak preview."

Ty gives her a return grin as he pulls her closer to him, then he kisses her and she quickly kisses him back. But after about five minutes, Ty and Krysta hear people talking and walking to the studio. They both look at each other and both slowly get off the couch; they fix themselves up then look at each other. Everyone walks in and sees Ty and Krysta standing next to each other, but they look as if they are talking about the art show coming up. Everyone walks in and gets back to work.

"See you after work." Krysta smiles.

"Yes, ma'am," Ty replies.

Krysta leaves Ty's studio, then one of the worker, a friend of Ty's, walks over to him and Ty looks at him. But he's watching Krysta leave the studio, then he looks at Ty.

"I guess I should put some Lysol on the couch."

Ty shakes his head then starts laughing softly. He tells him nothing happened but his friend just stares at him and shakes his head at him. Meanwhile Krysta is walking back to her office, but as she's walking back, Ford comes up to her. She rolls her eyes, then she stops and looks at Ford with a slight glare.

"Krysta—" Ford is cut off.

"No," Krysta quickly says.

Ford looks at her with shock.

"I'm going to tell you this one time, I have a boyfriend, Ford. And I love him., and unfortunately, you and I work together. So I have to put up with you, but if you keep following me around, either you'll get a fist in the face or a knee in the crotch so think twice," Krysta says.

Krysta walks around Ford and continues walking to her office. Ford slowly turns and watches Krysta walk away.

Later on, when office hours are over, Ford is in his office, finishing up some work. He looks up and sees that Krysta is still in her office, also working. But then he sees that Ty is walking into her office. Krysta stands up and gives him a kiss. She starts to shut down her office, then she and Ty leave. Ford watches them leave but also thinks to himself, *How do I know you?*

Meanwhile Ty and Krysta go out to dinner, having a glass wine, talking and laughing.

"So how was dinner?" Ty asks.

Krysta looks at him as she takes a sip of her wine; she gently puts her glass down.

"It was good but I think I would like dessert better," Krysta replies.

Ty slightly grins as he lifts one of his eyebrows. He then raises his hand for the waiter and asks him for the check. Ty then looks back at Krysta.

"What did you have in mind for dessert?" Ty asks.

"I have a few, just don't know which one," Krysta replies with a small smile.

"I think I can help with that," Ty replies.

Ty and Krysta gets home, Ty gently slams Krysta to the door, kissing her as he tries to open it. Ty opens the door, holding Krysta to him with his other arm, both of them slam against the wall as they both push the door close, still kissing. But then, Ty's cell phone starts to ring, they both stop kissing. Krysta gently slaps his shoulder, telling him not to answer.

"It's the bossman. It might be about the show," Ty says, breathing heavy.

"Are you kidding me?" Krysta replies, also breathing heavy.

"Two minutes," Ty says.

He gives her a kiss, then he walks away to answer the phone. Krysta puts her head back against the wall, then she looks over to Ty. She then walks into the bedroom and looks around. She sees the shirt that Ty sleeps in. She slightly bites her bottom lip. After about five minutes, Ty gets off the phone. He sees that Krysta is nowhere to be found, but then, he sees that the bedroom door is cracked open. He walks into the bedroom and sees that Krysta's clothes are on the floor. Then he hears the door close behind him; he turns around and sees that it's Krysta who is wearing his nightshirt. He lifts one of his eyebrows as he looks Krysta up and down.

"That's my shirt," Ty says.

Krysta slightly tilts her head.

"Well, you're going have to take it back, if you want it."

Ty walks over to her.

"Is that right?"

Krysta slightly smiles, then she takes Ty's hand and they walk over to the bed; but then, Krysta stops and turns to Ty. She gives him a kiss and he slowly kisses her back. As they kiss, Krysta is slowly unbuttoning Ty's shirt. Then she pushes him on the bed; Ty looks up at her and she smiles down at him, slightly biting her bottom lip. She slowly crawls on the bed, over Ty; she leans down and kisses him. Ty gently puts his hands on her hips as he kisses her back. Their kisses start to get hotter and deeper. Ty then quickly leans up and he wraps his arms around Krysta and she wraps her arms around him. Krysta removes Ty's shirt, then he slowly starts to remove his shirt that she's wearing. Then spins them around and gently lays her on the bed;

they look at each other. Deep into the eyes, they smile at each other. Krysta gently pulls Ty to her and kisses him. As the night goes on, Ty and Krysta make love to each other.

The next few days, everyone is working to get ready for the art show. Ty is working on how to set up his paintings and Krysta is helping with how to get the show ready in the meeting room. Krysta is also helping with naming some of the artwork that everyone is putting out for the show. As everyone is sitting in the meeting room, Krysta goes back to her office to get some papers for the meeting. Then Ford walks by; he sees her alone getting some papers. He looks at her, up and down, he grins then slowly walks over to her. Krysta turns around, getting ready to head back to the meeting room but slightly bumping into Ford, causing her to drop all her papers. She looks at Ford with a slight glare.

"Really?" Krysta slightly says in anger.

She kneels down and starts to pick up the papers.

"I'm sorry, I was looking for the boss." Ford grins.

Then he kneels down and starts to help Krysta pick up the papers. He hands her the papers, she looks at him and takes a low deep breath. Then she gently snatched the papers and stands up; Ford follows. But as they stand up, Ford snatched a kiss from her! Krysta gets a shocked look on her face and quickly pulls away from him. She stares at him with hate, then she quickly slaps him across the face—hard that the snap echoes and that it almost causes him to fall! Krysta doesn't say anything; she just walks around him and continues to walk back to the meeting room. Ford slowly wipes the side of his face. He looks at his hand and sees that his lips are slightly bleeding. Krysta is storming down the hall with an angry look on her face, stops right outside the meeting room, and takes a deep breath, then she walks in. She sits down and everyone continues talking about the show. Then later that night, while everyone is closing for the night, Krysta is walking to Ty's studio and sees that he's putting things away. Ty looks up and sees her standing in the doorway.

"Hey," Ty says with a small smile.

She quickly walks over to him, causing him to look at her with slight confusion. Krysta wraps her arms around him as she kisses him. Ty gets a slightly shocked look but then kisses her back as he wraps her arms around her. Krysta kisses Ty deeply and Ty returns the kisses, but he can also feel that something is wrong.

"Okay, okay, hold on," Ty says.

Ty gently pulls away from Krysta's kisses but still has his arms around her; he looks at her and sees that her eyes are sad yet scared.

"Hey, hey, what happened?" Ty gently asks.

Krysta hides her face on his chest as she wraps her arms around his shoulders. Ty can feel that she's slightly shaking.

"Krysta, what happened?" Ty asks.

Krysta slowly looks up at him.

"Ford kissed me!"

Ty's face goes to shock, and Krysta still has that look of sad yet scared. Krysta then let's go of Ty and slightly backs up. Tears run down her cheeks as she looks down to the floor. Ty takes a step toward her. She sees that he's moving to her, then she feels his hand on her chin; he gently lifts it, causing her to look at him.

"Are you okay?" Ty softly asks.

Krysta stares at him for a second, then she shakes her head no. Ty pulls her to him and hugs her. Then he says that they should go home. She nods her head, and they both head home. They both walk into the house and Krysta stands next to the bedroom door while Ty goes and gets a bottle of water. Ty looks at her.

"Tell me what happened," Ty asks.

Krysta looks at him and slowly starts to tell him. After she finishes telling him what happened, Ty stares at her, then he starts laughing, Causing Krysta to look at him with confusion.

"What's funny?" Krysta softly asks.

"Krysta, you…you clocked him," Ty replies, laughing. "Is your hand okay?"

Krysta looks at her hand then back at Ty and nods her head, but then, she slowly starts to shake it.

"*Why aren't you mad! Why aren't you yelling at me, telling me that I'm unfaithful?*" Krysta starts yelling.

As Krysta is yelling, Ty is looking at her with a slightly shocked face, but then, he slowly starts to walk over to her.

"*That I let it happen! That I should have seen it coming,*" Krysta, still yelling.

She looks up at Ty as he comes up to her.

"*I know you want to—*" Krysta is cut off.

Ty pulled Krysta into a kiss, holding her close to him, causing her not to be able to back away. Though at first, she tries; but after Ty gently pushes and pins her to the wall, she slowly starts to wrap her arms around him. Ty then looks at her and she looks at him as if she's starting to fall in desire.

"One, I don't want to yell at you. Two, I know that you're not unfaithful. Three, we both saw that coming, we just didn't know when. And to top everything off, I'm not mad at you," Ty softly says. "So stop it."

Krysta looks at him, still with a look at guilt on her face. She nods her head, then she tells him that she's going to take a shower. Ty watches her go into the bathroom and hears her put the shower on. Ty takes a deep breath, then he looks back at the bedroom door. Meanwhile Krysta is in the shower, though it's hard to see, she's crying. She keeps wiping the water from her face, and, at the same time, she's also thinking about the time Ford beat her. She washes her body as if she's trying to forget everything. But then she feels gentle arms wrap around her; she slightly turns her head and sees that it's Ty. She turns to him and wraps her arms around him. Ty then gently starts to wipe her back and Krysta starts to feel more relaxed. That night, Ty eases Krysta's worry and bad memories. Then later, he watches her sleep peacefully with a little anger on his face.

The next morning, Krysta wakes up and sees that Ty is not there, but there is a letter. Telling her that he will be back later; he just has to go into work to confirm a few things for the show. She smiles gently then slowly lays her head back down. Meanwhile Ty is at work in his studio, finishing up with some of his workers. After two hours, Ty gets ready to go home. As he's walking down the hall, he comes across Ford. Ford walks up to Ty and Ty looks at him with a plain glare but Ford looks at him with a grin. Ty walks around but stops on the side of him.

"I'm going to tell you one time, touch her again and you'll regret it."

Ty continues walking and Ford turns to look at him, but Ty just keeps walking without saying another word. Ford walks over to the railing, looking over, and sees Ty getting into the elevator and saying bye to Lynne. Ford glares at him, then he hears the boss calling him, causing Ford to walk over to him.

Meanwhile Ty returns home; he walks into the bedroom and sees that Krysta is still sleeping. He smiles as he closes the door and walks over to her. He slowly crawls on the bed and over to her. He gives her a kiss on the cheek and lies down next to her; after a few minutes, Ty falls asleep. Then late afternoon, Krysta slowly wakes up and sees that Ty is lying next to her. She gently smiles then slightly leans over to him and softly gives him a kiss on the cheek. Then she sees that Ty's eyes are slowly starting to open. Ty looks at Krysta and gently grins. He leans up and gives her a kiss and she returns it; they look at each other then gently touch foreheads.

*****

Then for the next few weeks, Krysta has been keeping away from Ford, going over to Ty every time she sees him. Since everyone is getting ready for the art show, Ford stares at them and glares.

The night of the show, Ty and Krysta are getting ready for the show. Ty puts on his suit with his hair pulled back in a ponytail and is waiting for Krysta by the front door.

"Krysta, babe. We're going to be late," Ty slightly yells.

"Sorry, I'm coming," Krysta slightly yells back.

Krysta comes running out of the bedroom, trying to put on her shoes, wearing a Hervé Léger white-black-color-blocked bandage dress with black high-heel shoes and her hair braided to the side. Ty gently smiles as he softly laughs. Krysta slightly laughs with him as she walks over to him.

"You look beautiful," Ty says.

"You clean up really well too," Krysta replies.

They both leave the penthouse and head downstairs to ride down to the show in the limo. They pull up to the art building; Ty comes out and all he can see is flashing lights. He slightly laughs as he puts his hand out. Krysta gently takes his hand and Ty helps her out of the limo; she puts her hand up, slightly covering her eyes. Ty and Krysta both put their arm around each other as they walk into the building, but right before they could walk in, a reporter stops him.

"Mr. Smith., may I ask you a question?"

Ty looks at the reporter, then he looks at Krysta; she just smiles at him. Ty turns to the reporter.

"Hi, June Hayes. Mr. Smith, how do you feel about tonight's art show?"

"Nervous but also excited," Ty replies.

"And who is this beautiful young lady with you?"

"This is my date, but more important, this is my girlfriend," Ty replies.

Ty and Krysta look at each other, then they give each other a kiss and smile at each other. They walk into the building and see how the show looks. Krysta's face lights up with excitement; Ty looks at her and smiles. They walk around and look at all the art. As they walk around, they come across Ford. They stare at each other. Krysta holds onto Ty's arm a little tighter. Ty and Ford stare at each other, as if they are challenging each other, but Ty is just looking while Ford is glaring. But then they hear Lynne call out to them, causing them both to look over to her and walk over. Ty starts talking to Lynne's husband while Krysta and Lynne talk and laugh; Ford stares at them, then he slowly walks the other way.

As the night goes on, Ty comes across the photographer who is talking to Ty about going with him to do another photo shoot. Ty agrees to go with him but Ty tells him that Krysta has to come; that makes the photographer happier. But Ty also ask if they don't tell her just yet, causing the photographer to laugh. Krysta comes over to them and Ty gives her a kiss on the head. The night is filled with joy and amazement, for reporters are talking to all the artist, people are interested and buying the paintings. Ty is happy that all his paintings are being sold. Krysta looks at him and sees the look on his face. Ty looks at her.

"I like seeing you this happy." Krysta smiles.

Ty smiles at Krysta, then they give each other a kiss; they look back to see what other paintings are being sold. The night slowly comes to an end; Ty and Krysta slowly start to leave, but then just before, the boss calls out to Ty, causing them both to stop and look his way. Krysta tells him to go while she goes to say bye to Lynne. Ty and the boss are talking about the photographer wanting Ty to go with him to do a shoot. The boss talks about Ty trying to get the photographer to join the company. Ty gently laughs as he rolls his eyes, also telling him that he's not going to push, just going to see how the shoot goes first. Meanwhile after Krysta says bye to Lynne and her husband, she turns to go over to Ty. But she is stopped and gets a glaring look on her face, for she is stopped by Ford.

"You know, you are the first woman that I have met that is not interested in me." Ford smiles.

"Well, I feel sorry for those other women," Krysta replies.

Ford takes a step to her; Krysta slightly moves her arm back as if she's getting ready to swing. But then, Ty appears, gently wrapping his arms around Krysta's waist, stopping her from trying to swing. She wraps her arm around him. They look at each other.

"You okay?" Ty softly asks.

"Now I am," Krysta replies with a gentle smile.

They give each other a couple of kisses, then they look over at Ford.

"Ford, sorry, I didn't see you," Ty says.

Ford looks at him as if he's trying not to glare at him.

"Did you need something?" Ty asks.

Ford shakes his head, then Ty nods as he and Krysta turn to leave. Ford watches them leave, slowly starting to breathe heavy with anger. Ty and Krysta get into the limo and drive away; as they are in the limo, Ty tells Krysta that she has to get ready to pack her bags, for they are leaving for the shoot. She smiles with joy and gives him a kiss.

The next morning, Ty and Krysta are in the Bahamas, helping the photographer working on the shoot. Ty got Krysta to model with the others. Ty tells the girls where to stand while the photographer takes the pictures. But they also change places when the other has an idea. As the girls laugh and talk to each other, Ty and the photographer take pictures and talk. The photographer looks at Ty.

"She looks like a keeper."

Ty looks at him with his arms crossed, grinning; he looks back at Krysta and the photographer looks at him with a little confusion.

"You want to keep this one."

Ty looks back at him.

"Does she know?" photographer asks.

Ty looks at him as if he's going to laugh as he shakes his head.

"Not even an idea," Ty says.

"When?" asks photographer.

"I don't know yet," Ty replies.

The photographer nods his head, then he looks back at Krysta. As they both stare at the girls, Ty sees that they are in a good spot to take pictures.

They are in the Bahamas for almost two weeks, taking all different pictures. Taking in the morning, in the afternoon, and at night. Ty makes Krysta be a part of the shoot, Krysta pouting, but Ty making her laugh. The other models are happy that she is still modeling with them. Then one night, it's raining. Ty comes up with an idea that he and the photographer think is good. They have the girls stand out in the rain, around plant life. They have night lighting, all the girls, having them wear swimsuits. Some have covers and others don't, though they do have them change, wearing different kinds over swimsuits.

Chapter 13

*M*onths have gone by and everyone is getting ready for the holidays. For Christmas and New Year! The company is setting up for an event before the long holiday vacation. As Krysta is talking to Lynne, Ty is on the phone with his mother, trying to get her off the phone. Krysta walks over to him.

"Okay, Ma. Yes, we are going to be there for Christmas and New Year. I have to go." Ty looks at Krysta. "She's busy, Ma. We're getting ready for an event. We'll see you in a few days, I have to go, bye."

Ty hangs up the phone, then he looks back at Krysta who is trying not to laugh, causing him to slowly start laughing. They both start walking back over to everyone to continue to work on the event. As everyone is working, Ford is staring at Krysta from above; he stares at her for a while, but then he walks away.

The event comes and goes and the company is closed for the holidays. Ty and Krysta are on the family jet, heading to LA. They both slowly get off the plane, and there, they see Ty's mother and father waiting for them. Kate waves to them with complete joy and slowly starts running over to them. Krysta comes down the stairs and runs over to her with her arms opened; they hug happily. Ty walks over to his father; they shake hands and hug.

"Krysta, I've missed you *so* much. We have a lot to talk about," Kate says with joy.

Krysta smiles as she and Kate walk over to the limo, talking about what has been going on since they last saw each other. Ty and Nick slowly follow them.

"Guess I don't get to say hello to her right now," Nick says.

Ty and Nick start laughing. Everyone gets into the limo and heads to the house. As they arrive at the house, they see Lucas coming out of the house. Everyone gets out of the car, the butlers come out of the house and takes Ty and Krysta's bags to their rooms as the maids finish cleaning up. Lucas walks over to Krysta and gives her a hug and shakes Ty's hand, Ty looking at him as if he's going to laugh.

"I am shocked, Lucas. You're here to meet us or are you on your way to a date?" Ty asks.

Lucas just stares at him.

"You don't know me."

Lucas then leaves. Ty then walks into the house and sees Krysta talking to Kate and Nick. He walks over to them and sits down next Krysta, talking with everyone.

Then night comes; everyone is still talking and laughing, sitting in the living room, eating takeout. Ty and Krysta are sitting on the floor while Kate and Nick are sitting on the sofa. As they finish up, Ty asks Nick to go with him to the kitchen, for he has a question to ask him. He nods his head, and they clean up the living room and walk into the kitchen, leaving Krysta and Kate to continue talking.

"So what does my son have to ask me?" Nick asks.

"Dad, as weird as this question may be, I have to ask," Ty replies.

"So ask," Nick replies.

"What do you think about Krysta, truly?" Ty asks.

Nick looks at him with slight confusion, but then, he gets a look on his face as if he's thinking. He looks back at him and gently smiles.

"Well, she's beautiful inside and outside. She's easy to talk to, but you already know what you like about Krysta," Nick says. "So what's really on your mind?"

Ty slightly laughs as he takes deep breath. He slowly starts to tell Nick what's going on with him. As he tells him, Nick gets a shocked look on his face.

"*What*!"

"Dad, shhh, please do not tell Mom. She will kind of say it before I can. And I'd like it to be special. That's why I'm asking for your help," Ty says.

Nick's shocked face turns to a happy calm smile.

"I think I can do that."

Meanwhile Kate and Krysta are trying to guess what Ty and Nick are talking about.

"So what do you think they are talking about?" Krysta asks.

"One of us," Kate replies, slightly laughing.

"Think they'll tell us?" Krysta asks.

"No, but I know how to get my husband to talk," Kate replies.

They look at each other, smiling, and Kate winks at Krysta; they both start laughing. Ty and Nick slowly walk back into the living room. Ty sits back down with Krysta. Nick sits down with Kate staring at him as if she wants to know what's going on. Nick smiles at her but doesn't say anything; he looks back at Ty and Krysta who is giving Ty a small kiss on the cheek, causing Ty to look at her and reply with a kiss to the forehead. They then gently touch foreheads and look into each other's eyes, gently smiling at each other.

More hours pass by and the hour is getting late. Everyone is finishing their drinks, laughing hard. After finishing their drinks, they all get ready to head to bed. As they walk to the stairs, still talking and laughing, they hear the door opening. They all see Lucas slowly walking into the house; he sees them all staring at him.

"What?" Lucas asks.

"You're home," Ty says.

"Mind it, bro, mind it," Lucas replies.

"Okay, see you in the morning," Ty replies, trying not to laugh.

"Good night, Lucas," Krysta says.

"Night, Krysta," Lucas replies.

Ty and Krysta walk up stands to bed. Lucas walks over to Kate and Nick who are both staring at him as if they are waiting to see if he's going to say anything. But Lucas just looks around; Nick and Kate shake their heads then slowly walk upstairs.

"Good night, Lucas," Nick and Kate say.

"Night," Lucas replies.

Meanwhile Krysta is in Ty's room, sitting on his bed, watching Ty get ready for bed.

"I should head to my room soon," Krysta says.

Ty slightly turns his head to her, looking at her with a grin, a lift of his eyebrow and slight confusion. He completely turns around and walks over to her; he leans down to her, putting his hands on the bed, causing him to look Krysta face-to-face.

"And why would you be going to another room?" Ty softly asks.

Krysta looks at him as if she's trying not to laugh.

"Because that's where they put my stuff."

Ty gently smiles at her as he slowly shakes his head then looks back at her.

"Krysta," Ty says.

"Yes?" Krysta smiles.

"Your stuff is in the corner," Ty whispers.

Krysta slowly turns her head and sees her things in the corner, next to Ty's. She looks back at him and tries not to laugh. They give each other a small kiss, look at each other, then they kiss each other slowly. Ty slowly leans forward, causing Krysta to lean back but also wrap her arms around Ty's neck as he wraps his right arms around her. Holding her close to him until Krysta completely lies on the bed. But then, Lucas comes into the room without knocking.

"Hey, Ty, I need to talk to you—and I should have knocked," Lucas says.

Ty turns his head to Lucas who is just staring at Ty and Krysta. Krysta slowly moves her arms from Ty's neck. Ty looks back at Krysta.

"I'll be right back," Ty says.

He gives Krysta a kiss, then he stands up and walks over to Lucas but doesn't stop. He grabs Lucas by the arm and pulls him out of his room and gently closes the door. Ty turns Lucas around, causing Lucas to look at him.

"This better be good for not knocking," Ty says.

"Yeah, um… I kind of need your advice," Lucas replies.

"With what, Lucas? At this hour?" Ty asks.

"I met this girl," Lucas starts to explain.

"You meet a lot of girls," Ty says.

"Yeah, but this one is different," Lucas replies.

"You said the same thing about the other two," Ty says.

"But I meant it," Lucas said.

"You said that too," Ty replies.

"Come on, help me. How do I know that a girl likes me and not the…money I make," Lucas asks.

"Well, have you tried not taking her to an expensive restaurant? Have her pay a bill?" Ty says.

Lucas looks down slightly.

"Lucas, have you ever talked to a girl?"

"Yeah, of course I have," Lucas replies.

"I don't mean pillow talk, Lucas," Ty replies. "When's the next time you're meeting this girl?"

"Tomorrow. Why?" Lucas replies.

"Have you ever walked with a girl?" Ty asks.

"A walk?" Lucas asks.

"Yes, Lucas. You walk, you talk, you get to know them," Ty replies. "And don't start with I have money."

"How did Krysta—" Lucas is cut off.

"Krysta didn't know till we came for the holidays last year," Ty says. "She and I got to know each other."

"So the key is to talk," Lucas asks.

"How is it you don't know that?" Ty asks.

But before Lucas can answer, Ty puts his hand up then puts his finger to his lips.

"Go to bed, Lucas, it's almost four thirty in the morning. Bed," Ty says.

Ty walks away back into his room and gently closes the door. Lucas nods his head and walks to his room, thinking about what Ty said. Meanwhile Ty turns from the door and is about to continue walking in his room but pauses. For Krysta is still sitting on his bed but she's wearing one of his button-up shirts. Even though she's covered, she doesn't have the shirt buttoned. She smiles at Ty who lifts one of his eyebrows as he grins.

"Nice choice, great color on you," Ty says.

Krysta stands up and walks over to Ty who just watches her walk over to him slowly, looking at her up and down. She comes close to him and gently holds onto his T-shirt.

"You think light blue is my color?" Krysta gently whispers.

"I don't know, let's find out," Ty softly replies.

Ty then pulls Krysta into a kiss; she quickly replies to his kiss and their kisses quickly become deeper. Ty then picks her up, she wraps her arms and legs around him as he walks over to the bed. He gently leans down on the bed, both of them still kissing each other.

The next day, late noon, Lucas comes downstairs and sees Ty in the kitchen. He walks over to him; Ty looks at him, trying not to laugh. Lucas stares at him, and Ty just stares at him, waiting for him to say something.

"What, Lucas?" Ty asks.

"Okay, I need to ask you, where is a good place to take a girl?" Lucas asks.

"How should I know? Depends on the girl," Ty replies.

"Okay, so you have to help. Today, come with me to find a few places—" Lucas is cut off.

"Can't," Ty says.

"Why?" Lucas asks.

"I have plans with Krysta. The moment Ma gets her hands on her, I will never see her," Ty replies.

"Right, so what are you guys doing?" Lucas asks.

"Nothing really. We're going to the beach and have some late lunch. It's called a picnic," Ty replies.

Krysta comes downstairs with everything she and Ty needs for their time at the beach. She puts everything by the door then goes into the kitchen. She gives Lucas a small quick kiss on the cheek.

"Hi, Lucas."

"Hey, Krysta," Lucas replies.

Krysta goes over to Ty and they give each other a kiss, then she sees what Ty packed. She looks at him, then she takes the basket and walks to the front door. Ty then looks at Lucas who is pouting at him.

"Ask her what she wants to do," Ty says.

Ty then walks away and meets Krysta at the front door; they leave in one of the extra cars with Ty driving. They head to the beach, laughing. As they pull up to the beach, Krysta sees that there is no one around.

"Did you stop people from coming to the beach or something?" Krysta asks.

Ty looks at her, trying not to laugh.

"Everyone is probably at the festival," Ty replies.

"Oh, was there a festival last year?" Krysta asks.

"Yes, but I never brought a girl home before. So my mother was just…yeah," Ty replies.

"Okay, that just means I still get you all to myself," Krysta says.

Then she gets out of the car and runs down to the beach. Ty slowly gets out of the car and watches her. He walks to the front of the car and leans back against it with his arms crossed, smiling at her. Krysta turns her head to him and calls him to go down to her. Ty slowly walks down, but then, as he gets closer to her, he starts running. Krysta laughs and tries to run from him but he catches her and wraps his arms around her. Then he gently picks her up and runs into the water; Krysta screams in a laughing way. They both run up and down the beach, trying to get each other into the water, laughing happily.

Later they are sitting on a blanket, talking and laughing as they flirt with each other. Feeding each other the food that they have brought. Ty gently puts his hand on Krysta's face; she looks at him with desire yet confusion. They slowly move closer to each other, about to kiss till—"*Ty!*"

Ty slowly moves his hand from Krysta's cheek and puts it to his face, trying to cover it. But then he slowly looks over to who called his name—only to see that it's Lucas! Who has a girl with him and, from what it looks like, supplies for a picnic. Ty slowly shakes his head, and Lucas comes walking over to him. Ty and Krysta slowly stand up and Ty crosses his arms.

"Lucas, what are you doing here?" Ty asks.

"It's a beach," Lucas replies.

"You don't go to the beach, you sit at a pool," Ty replies.

Lucas slightly looks around.

"I would like you two to meet my friend, Janet. The one I told you about."

Janet is 5'3" tall, light-brown skin, short brown hair, and brown eyes. Nice slim body. She looks at Ty and Krysta, smiles as she and Krysta shakes hands. Ty gently shakes her hand then looks back at Lucas.

"It's really nice to meet both of you. I've heard so much of you," Janet says.

"Will you excuse me and my brother here…just for a moment," Ty says.

Then Ty quickly grabs Lucas's arm and pulls him away from the girls. They both watch the guys walk away, then they look back at each other and gently start laughing. Meanwhile Ty pulls Lucas back up to the cars.

"You brought her here knowing I was here. Why?" Ty asks.

"I get you're mad, but I need help and I can't get that if I just call you. One, you won't answer if you're with Krysta, and two, I thought this might be easier," Lucas replies.

"Lucas, just be yourself. Stop trying to be me to impress this girl," Ty replies.

"But I just—" Lucas is cut off.

"Fine, stay. Just don't bug me," Ty says.

He walks back down to the girls and Lucas follows. Ty comes over to Krysta; Krysta looks at him as they put their arms around each other.

"Why don't we go for a walk? Give them a chance to set up," Ty says.

"Okay," Krysta replies.

They both walk away and Lucas watches them, then he looks at Janet; he smiles at her nervously. Then he looks back over to Ty and Krysta. They both are walking near the water's edge, holding hands, talking about Lucas showing up. Krysta is trying not to laugh as Ty complains, but then, he hears her give off a small chuckle.

"How is this funny?" Ty asks.

Krysta looks at him.

"This is just the first time I heard you complain about something."

Ty starts laughing as he stares at Krysta, trying not to laugh more. They look over at Lucas and Janet who are still setting up. Krysta looks at Ty, then she tells him, "Let's go farther down the beach."

Ty looks at her and they continue walking, but as they continue walking, Ty stops, causing Krysta to look at him. For Lucas is running over to them, they both turn and look at him.

"What is it, Lucas?" Ty asks.

Lucas is slightly out of breath.

"I need to ask you something."

Ty stares at him for a minute, Krysta trying not to laugh.

"What?" Ty ask.

"So what is it that I should do now?" asks Lucas.

"With what?" Ty asks.

"The date…what do I do now?" Lucas asks.

Krysta turns her head slightly behind Ty's shoulder, trying to hide for laughing, for Ty is looking at Lucas as if he's twitching. Krysta then looks at Lucas.

"Lucas."

Lucas looks at her.

"Try just a walk or sit with her and talk," Krysta softly says.

Ty and Krysta turn around and continue walking, leaving Lucas to come up with an idea for his date.

Ty and Krysta return to the site with all their things, and there is Lucas, sitting, slightly talking but also looks like he's talking too much. Ty shakes his head; he looks at Krysta and they both have that same look. They walk over to Lucas and Janet, both of them look at them; they sit down. No one says anything, but then Krysta looks at Janet and talks about her bracelets, slowly breaking the silence. Ty slowly jumps into the conversation, making Janet and Krysta laugh,

"Look what you did. Now she's going to want something like those," Ty says.

As the three of them talk and laugh, Ty looks at Lucas, seeing that he doesn't know how to be part of the conversation. Ty looks slowly, leans over to Krysta and softly whispers in her ear; she looks at him and slightly nods. She looks at everyone, she gets up and walks over to Janet and whispers in her ear. Janet looks at her then back at the guys; she looks back at Krysta and slowly stands up. They both tell the guys they'll be right back. As they walk up to the cars; they both watch them walk away. Then they start walking.

"How's it going?" Lucas asks.

"Did you two have a talk yet or were you just blabbing?" Ty asks.

Lucas looks at him, not sure what he was doing, but then covers their faces, for the girls come back with water guns. Ty and Lucas both get up, slowly backing away, laughing as the girls are squirting them. Ty and Lucas look at each other, then they look over to the girls; they then start running to the girls. Krysta runs but Janet gets caught, Lucas and Janet start laughing. Ty wraps his arms around Krysta and spins her to him. He gently kisses her and she kisses him back. They look over to Lucas and Janet who are looking at each other laughing. Ty and Krysta walk over to them slowly.

"Really? A water gun?" Ty asks.

"You said wake things up a bit. That's all I could think of at the time," Krysta replies.

Ty slowly shakes his head, then he looks back over to Lucas and Janet. They come up to them and they all start laughing. But then Ty looks at Lucas and winks; Lucas slightly nods his head, then they both look at the girls who looks at them, then each other, with confusion. Then Ty and Lucas turn and gently put the girls over their shoulders and they run into the water. They scream as if they are laughing.

Everyone is laughing the day away till the sun goes down. They all are now sitting around a fire that Lucas and Ty made. Lucas and Janet are sitting next to each other. Krysta is sitting between Ty's legs, leaning back against his chest. Ty has his arms around her, keeping the blanket on her. They are talking till Janet looks at the time, then she looks at everyone. She tells them that there is still time for them to go to the festival. They all look at each other then back at her. Lucas sees that she really wants to go but Ty and Krysta are not into going. Ty looks at Lucas as if he's telling him to take her alone and get to know her.

"Yeah, we should go," Lucas says.

"Aren't you two going to come too?" Janet asks.

Ty and Krysta look at each other, then at Lucas, trying not to laugh. Lucas looks at Janet.

"Well, I think that they just want to go home and relax. They have been out longer than we have," Lucas says.

Janet looks at him, then she looks at Ty and Krysta.

"But would be really fun with you guys there."

Lucas sees her face, looking as if she's going to change her mind of going, causing him to quickly walk over to Ty.

"Talk," Lucas says.

Lucas gently pulls Ty away from the girls; Ty stares at him for a minute with a plain stare, Lucas breathing in a slight panic

"Ty—" Lucas is cut off.

"I know we're brothers and all but I was convertible. Keep taking me away from my convertible zone, we're going to have a problem," Ty says.

Lucas is looking at him with a puppy face, asking him to help him. Ty rolls his eyes and takes a deep breath, then he looks over to the girls talking. They walk back over to them; Ty kneels down next to Krysta. She looks at him.

"We'll go for a little while," Ty says.

Janet smiles with joy, then she looks at Lucas; they all slowly get up and pack their things. Ty and Lucas put out the fire then follow the girls to the cars. As they are walking, Ty looks at Lucas.

"I'm not staying. I have things to do, one hour. That's all you get."

"But what if Krysta wants to stay longer?" Lucas asks.

"Don't you even think about it. Leave her out of your date scheme," Ty replies.

Chapter 14

$\mathcal{E}$veryone is at the festival, having a good time; they all play the games and go on some of the rides. As they are walking, Krysta gently takes Ty's arm and points at one of the rides. Ty looks and sees that she's pointing at the wheel. Ty looks at her.

"Really?"

"Thought maybe you want a minute," Krysta replies.

Ty looks over to Lucas and Janet who are still walking ahead of them. Ty then gently pulls Krysta over to the wheel. Krysta slightly laughs; they get on the ride and the ride slowly starts moving. As they slowly reach the top, Krysta looks out and sees the lights of the festival and her eyes glow with beauty. Ty starts are her, slightly leaning his head onto his hand that's in a slight fist. Krysta slowly looks at him, smiling at him with confusion.

"What?"

Ty slightly shakes his head.

"Sometimes I wish I could see what you see."

Krysta moves over to Ty and they slowly move closer to each other; they gently kiss, then they look at each other. They touch foreheads and look out to the festival lights. But then, as they are going back down, they see Lucas and Janet waiting for them. Krysta tries not to laugh as she looks at Ty's plain face.

"I want to leave," Ty says.

"Stop, he needs your help. This might be his first real date," Krysta says.

Ty slightly looks at her, he takes a slight deep breath.

"It is."

Krysta starts laughing gently as Ty looks back down at Lucas and Janet. They get off the ride and walk over to them. Lucas walks over to Ty and gently pulls him over to him, gently whispering.

"You two went on the wheel and didn't bring us—me."

Ty stares at him for a minute.

"I needed a minute with my girlfriend. Since my brother came in on our date."

Lucas stares at him and Ty slowly shakes his head, then he walks over to Krysta, slowly wraps his arm around her. Ty then gently says to Krysta that it's about time for them to go home. She nods her head, then they say bye to Janet and Lucas. Janet thinks that it's about time to go but Krysta tells her that Lucas has one more thing they have to do before they leave. Janet looks and Lucas smiles as if he has no idea what she's talking about. Ty grins then he and Krysta slowly start to leave but Lucas runs after them.

"What do I do now? I have no idea what I'm doing," Lucas says in slight panic.

"Lucas, just talk to her. It can surprise you," Ty replies.

Ty and Krysta walk away, leaving Lucas to think of something to say to Janet. Lucas walks over to Janet; he takes a deep breath.

Meanwhile as Ty and Krysta are driving, Krysta is laughing so much that she's holding her stomach.

"It's not funny, can you stop laughing?" Ty says.

"Come on, you can't tell me that he didn't make you laugh. He was like a little kid going on his first date with the brother," Krysta replies.

"One, that sounded so wrong. Second, No, no, no, and no," Ty replies.

They come to a red light. Krysta smiles at him.

"Are you mad because you didn't get to romance me?"

Ty slightly looks at her. She slightly chuckles, then the light turns green and they continue driving. They pull up to the house and see that not all the lights are on.

"Must be out," Ty says.

They both get out of the car and walk into the house. They look around and see that no one is home.

"Well, I'm going to get everything out of the car," Ty says.

Krysta nods her head, then Ty goes to get everything. Krysta looks around, then she gets a look on her face as if she has an idea. Ty comes back into the house and sees that Krysta is gone. He closes the door and walks into the kitchen, cleans everything up, then slowly walks upstairs and into his room. As he closes the door and sees that the bathroom door is slightly open with a light coming out of it, he walks over to the bathroom and gently opens the door and sees Krysta in the tub. She turns her head, gently smiles at him, and he replies with a grin. He slowly walks over to her and kneels down. They give a small kiss.

"You should get in, get rid of that seawater smell," Krysta says.

Ty stands up and slowly starts to remove his clothes; Krysta slowly moves as Ty gets into the tub. He gently pulls Krysta to him and she leans back; they both wrap their arms about each other, they take a relaxing deep breath.

Later that night, Lucas comes home and runs upstairs; he goes right into Ty's room where Ty and Krysta are fast asleep, wrapped in each other's arms. Krysta's back is against Ty's chest as he has his arms around her and her arms around his. Lucas burst right into the room.

"*Ty*," Lucas yells.

They both slightly jump up and look at Lucas; Krysta turns and gently slams her face back into the pillow. Ty looks at him half-asleep yet anger in his eyes as he looks over at the clock and sees that it's almost four o'clock in the morning.

"I have to tell you everything. You are so right, just talking is amazing. I have a lunch date with Janet tomorrow and it's all thanks to you," Lucas says with excitement.

Ty slowly gets out of bed and walks over to Lucas, grabs him by the arm, and starts pulling him to the door. But Lucas just keeps talking about his date with Janet; Ty opens the door and gently pushes Lucas out. Lucas looks at him as Ty stares at him with that same half-asleep look.

"It is four o'clock in the morning. Go to bed, Lucas," Ty replies.

Lucas looks around then starts talking, still with excitement. Ty slowly shakes his head, then he gently slams the door and locks it.

"*Ty*," Lucas yells.

"Go to bed, Lucas," Ty slightly yells back.

Lucas is about to say something else, but Ty yells to him again to go to bed. Lucas nods his head and goes to his room. Ty gently gets back into bed and Krysta moves closer to him, putting her head onto his chest. As they wrap their arms around each other, they both quickly fall back asleep.

The next morning, everyone is downstairs, eating breakfast. Lucas comes downstairs with joy. Ty puts his head down, covering his face with his hand as he shakes his head, causing Nick and Kate to look at him. Lucas sees everyone and starts talking about his time with Janet. Nick and Kate are excited to see Lucas happy to talk about a girl. Lucas just talks and talks about Janet, then he sees what time it is and has to go meet up with her. Lucas quickly runs back upstairs to get ready. Ty looks over to Nick.

"Are you still helping me today?" Ty asks.

"Yeah, what time did you want to go?" Nick asks.

"Whenever you're ready," Ty replies.

"Where are you two going?" asks Kate.

They both look at her, then Ty looks at Nick.

"Father-and-son bonding," Nick replies.

As he stands up and walks away, Ty and Krysta slightly laugh, for Kate stands up and follows him, trying to get him to tell her where they both are going. Ty looks at Krysta; they both slowly get up then go to get ready for the day.

Krysta is sitting on the edge of the bed, putting her shoes on, then she looks up at Ty who is putting on his shirt. She stares at him as he buttons his shirt, then he sees her stares at him through the mirror. He turns to her.

"You okay?" Ty gently says.

Krysta nods her head.

"Yeah, just a little sleepy."

"Yeah, I'm sorry about Lucas. He's always been like that since we were kids. Every time something good happens to him, he comes bursting into my room to tell me about it," Ty replies.

"So what are your plans for today?" Krysta asks.

"Nothing really, just need my dad's help with something," Ty replies

"I hope you two have fun," Krysta says.

"Not going to be gone too long, have that Christmas party tonight," Ty replies.

"Yeah, I think your mom is going to take me shopping for a new dress again. She really doesn't need to do all that," Krysta replies.

"That's just her," Ty says. "I'll see you tonight."

They both give each other a kiss, then Ty meets his dad downstairs. Krysta slowly comes down and walks into the kitchen to Kate. Kate smiles at her and walks over to her with a joyful smile on her face. Krysta smiles at her as if she's going to laugh.

"Okay, my darling. What can we put you in tonight?" Kate smiles.

"Surprise me," Krysta replies.

Both Kate and Krysta leave the house to go dress shopping. Meanwhile Ty and Nick are walking into a jewelry store!

Later that night, Ty and Nick return to the house; they walk inside and see that Kate and Krysta are already home. Ty looks at Nick and they both look at the small bag that Ty is holding, both grinning.

"Dad, thank you for coming with me," Ty says.

"What is that? My son is happy? He asks me for help for a girl that makes him so happy, thought I'd never see. You don't need to thank me. It is an honor to do this with my son," Nick replies.

Ty grins at him, then they both give each other a hug. Kate comes to the railing, looking down at them.

"What are you doing?"

They both look up at her, watch her walk away from the railing.

"The party starts in two hours, let's go get ready. Hurry up," Kate gently yells down at them.

Ty and Nick look at each other, slightly laughing under their breath; then they both slowly walk upstairs. Ty walks into his room and hears the shower running; he walks over to the bathroom and slowly opens the door. He stands in the doorway, staring at the shower. Krysta comes out of the shower. She slightly jumps as she comes out, with a slight laugh, seeing Ty standing in the doorway with his arms crossed, looking at her up and down.

"What?" Krysta gently smiles.

Ty doesn't say anything; he just stares at her. She slowly comes out of the shower and walks over to get a towel. Ty just watches her. She wraps the towel around her. She turns to walk into the bedroom but stops, for Ty is standing right in front of her, causing her not to be able to go into the bedroom. They look into each other's eyes, Ty steps closer to her. He puts one arm around her waist and gently pulls her closer to him; she gently puts her hands on his chest. Ty slowly puts her other hand on her face; they move their faces closer to each other. They slowly give a kiss, then their eyes meet.

"I'm back," Ty gently says.

"Welcome back," Krysta gently replies.

They give each other another kiss, their kisses slowly become more heated and passionate. Krysta slowly moves her hands from Ty's chest to around his neck as Ty slowly moves his hand from Krysta's face to wrapping around her waist. After they completely wrap their arms around each other, Krysta's towel falls from her body but they didn't realize after about five minutes.

"Ty, Krysta, are you almost ready?" Kate slightly yells from the hall.

Ty and Krysta quickly stop kissing; they look at each other. They see that Krysta's towel fell. Ty quickly goes to the bathroom doorway while Krysta rewraps the towel.

"Yeah, Ma, almost," Ty replies.

Ty turns his head and looks over at Krysta who is walking over to him; they slightly smile at each other. Krysta walks out of the bathroom and Ty watches her, then he slowly closes the door to take a shower. Krysta then gets ready with the new dress that Kate got her. It's a long red off-the-shoulder banded sleeve side-slit cocktail dress.

She puts on her silver earrings; she also puts her hair slightly up and slightly to the side. Then Kate knocks on the door, asking Krysta if she needs help with her makeup. Krysta opens the door and goes with Kate for her to help her with the makeup.

Meanwhile Ty comes out of the bathroom with a towel around his waist and sees that Krysta is not there. He sees that she's hasn't seen the bag on the bed, for it's still slightly covered by his vest. He walks over to the bag and puts it in his nightstand drawer. Then he starts to get dressed. After about ten minutes, Ty comes outs of his room and starts walking downstairs. He's wearing a black dress suit with a red shirt, his hair is half-up and half-down. He walks over to Nick who is wearing a white dress suit but with a black shirt. Ty shakes his head and looks at him as if he's going to laugh. Nick looks at him, nods his head, looking at him as if he's impressed with what he's wearing. Then they both turn and see Kate and Krysta slowly coming down the starts. Ty stares at Krysta as if he's seeing her for the first time. Nick looks at him then back up at their ladies walking to them. Krysta walks over to Ty

"I wish I had words," Ty says gently.

Krysta smiles softly as she slightly bites her bottom lip.

Ty puts his arm out and Krysta gently wraps her arm around his; they both walk outside to their limo. Kate and Nick watch them. Kate looks at Nick who slowly looks at her with a look, knowing that she's going to say something.

"What were you two doing today? You both were gone all day long," Kate asks.

Nick kisses her on the cheek.

"We're going to be late."

Kate looks at him, knowing that he's hiding something, causing her to smile but also wanting to know. She goes with Nick to the limo and both limos drive to the party.

*****

The week goes by and it's the day before New Year's Eve. Ty is getting nervous and Nick is trying to keep him calm.

"Relax, Tyler. You haven't even talked to her yet," Nick says.

"Easy for you to say, she can see that something is wrong," Ty replies.

Nick gets up and walks over to Ty and helps him to relax.

"Do you know what you're going to do?" Nick asks.

Ty looks at him, grins, as he slowly nods his head.

"Yeah."

"Then stop worrying. You have your answer," Nick says.

Ty nods his head, then he tells Nick that if Krysta asks, that he'll be back. Nick nods his head as he watches Ty leave.

The hour gets late and Ty is yet to return to the house. Kate is a little worried, Lucas is talking Krysta's ear off about his time with Janet. But then, Ty comes into the house; Kate walks over to him, asking him where he has been but Ty just grins at her, then he looks for Krysta. Ty walks into the living room and there he sees Lucas and Krysta.

"Lucas, what are you doing to my girl?" Ty says.

They both look at him; Krysta smiles as she gets up and walks over to him. They give each other a kiss, then they look at Lucas who is now talking on his phone; they both slightly laugh, then they look back at each other.

"I have something I want to show you," Ty says.

Krysta looks at him with confusion yet a small smile; she nods her head, then they both leave. Kate looks at them, trying to understands why Ty is leaving when he just got back. She looks at Nick who is reading a book then back out to the front door.

Meanwhile Ty is driving with Krysta looking at him confused yet curious as to where they are going. As they continue driving, Krysta starts to recognize where they are. Ty takes Krysta to the place that it all began; he takes her to the hilltop that looks over the water, where the water and sky look as if they are touching. She smiles with joy as Ty parks the car. Krysta walks almost to the edge with amazement once again. Ty watches as Krysta stares at the sunset reflected in the water, all the colors. Ty then grabs something from the back seat of the car, then he walks over to Krysta. She looks at him, then they both sit on the grass. Ty gives Krysta his sketchbook. She looks at him with confusion yet a small smile.

"I want you to look at this. Till the last page," Ty gently says.

Krysta slowly opens his sketchbook and her face slowly changes as if she's going to cry but also happy.

"This is how it all started for us," Ty gently says.

Ty gave Krysta his personal sketchbook with all his sketches and it's filled with her! With the very first sketch that he did of her. She slowly looks through every one of Ty's sketches, smiling at every one of them. Then she comes to the last page but there is nothing there; she looks at Ty with confusion. Ty slowly stands up then helps Krysta stand; they walk over to the edge of the hill. Ty asks Krysta to look out and tell him what she sees. Krysta smiles then looks out to the open sky. Ty is standing behind her, waiting to hear what she has to say, but she shakes her head, not understanding what Ty is asking. She turns back to him but he's not eye-level, she slowly looks down. Ty is kneeling down behind her, softly looking up at her, with Krysta looking at him as if she's about to lose her breath. Her eyes slowly water as she sees Ty slowly pull out a small box from his back pocket. Ty slowly opens the small box and Krysta puts her hands gently to her mouth. For in the small box is a silver-colored crystal flower wedding-engagement ring.

"Krysta, I love you and know that you have been through a lot. But I want you to know that I'm not going anywhere. I promise that I will never hurt you, I'll be with you and only you. You are my best friend, the best part of my life and has ever come into my life. I wish that I could give you words that will help you know that I want to be with you forever," Ty says softly.

The water falls from Krysta's eyes as she slowly moves her hands from her lips. Ty sees that she's smiling; she slowly starts to nod her head.

"Yes…yes!"

"Yes?" Ty confirms.

As he slowly stands up, he takes Krysta's hand and slowly puts the ring on her finger. She looks at her hand, then she looks at Ty.

"You know, you had me at I love you," Krysta says.

174

They both look at each other with joyful smiles; they give each other a kiss and wrap their arms around each another. They touch foreheads, then Ty picks her up and spins her around with joy and laughter. They give each other another kiss and touch foreheads again.

"I love you," Krysta says.

"Back at you," Ty says.

Chapter 15

*L*ater that night, Ty and Krysta return to the house but not into the house. Ty and Krysta are quickly walking into the backyard, passionately kissing each other. With every other step, they pull each other closer.

"Um… Ty. The house is the other way," Krysta says, panting. "Why are we—"

"I want you all to myself," Ty replies, panting.

Ty pulls Krysta back into another kiss; she quickly replies as she wraps her arms around his neck. Ty gently picks Krysta up by her thighs and continues walking. He brings her to the pool house, gently banging into the doors, still kissing each other. Ty opens the doors; after a few steps, Ty slowly leans down, gently putting Krysta on the bed. Softly laying on top of her with one arm laying over her head and his other hand slowly sliding down her thigh. Krysta has one hand in his hair and her other hand on his chest, slowly moving down to his side. Sharing kisses with each other, feeling like fire, as they start to remove each other clothes. Ty slightly leans up, both staring into the eyes with heated desire. Ty slowly removes his undershirt; Krysta gently puts her hand on his abs. Ty leans down to her, she pulls him into their kiss. They look into the eyes, Ty slowly stands up and gently pulls Krysta off the bed. She stands, Ty turns her around and softly kisses her neck. She puts her hand on his head, slightly at the back of his neck, gently with his hands on her sides.

Then he slowly moves his hands to her back and leisurely unzips her dress. Steadily starts to pull down her dress. As it slides to the floor, she turns to Ty. They stare, both slowly panting, till they gently pull each other back into their kisses. Both slowly lean back down onto the bed as they slowly start to remove their underclothes. They make love to each other all night long as if it was their first time!

The next morning, Kate comes running into the living room where Nick is reading the newspaper. He looks up at her calmly.

"He's not in his room and she's not there either," Kate says.

"What?" Nick replies.

"Ty and Krysta, I can't find them anywhere. And his car is here. Where are they?" Kate asks.

"I don't know…but let it go. He's a grown man," Nick replies calmly.

Then he continues to read the newspaper. As he takes a sip of his coffee, Kate looks at him, then she rolls her eyes and continues looking for Ty and Krysta. Lucas comes downstairs and sees that Kate is all over the house in a small panic. He stares at her, almost about to laugh, then he walks into the living room and sits next to Nick.

"What's going on with Ma?" Lucas asks.

Nick takes a sip of his coffee with a calm grin on his face.

"She can't find Ty and Krysta."

Lucas nods his head, then he makes himself a cup of coffee and puts on the TV. they both listen to Kate walk all over the house, looking for Ty and Krysta. Meanwhile in the pool house, Krysta is slightly lying on Ty, both still kissing each other. They look at each other; Krysta slightly bites her bottom lip as they look at each other.

"Why do you keep smiling at me?" Ty softly says.

"You know that name goes pretty well," Krysta says.

Ty grins at her yet looks at her with a little confusion.

"What?"

"Krysta Smith."

Ty's grin turns to a soft smile as Krysta joyfully smiles at him. Ty leans up to her and kisses her and gently pulls her back down to him. He slowly rolls over, causing him to be slightly on top of Krysta but still kissing each other. Krysta slightly wraps her arms around Ty's neck as he gently wraps his arms around her waist. But then Kate comes storming into the pool house and stares at them. They stop kissing and quickly look over at her.

"*Ma,*" Ty slightly yells.

As he covers Krysta's body more with sheets, Kate stares at them. "*You've been in here all this time!*" Kate yells.

They both stare at her, then they look at each other, then they take a slight deep breath. Kate walks over to them quickly; they both stare at her, trying not to laugh. Kate stares at them with confusion yet a little anger.

"Why are you two in the pool house?" Kate asks.

Ty takes another deep breath then looks down at Krysta who slowly turns her head to him. Kate looks around and sees their clothes on the floor. Then she looks back at them; she stares for a minute.

"Somethings up…you two have done this in the house before. What's different?" Kate asks.

Ty and Krysta looks at each other, still trying not to laugh.

"Mom, can we get dressed first?" Ty says.

Kate looks at them, then she slowly leaves the pool house. Ty leans back on the bed and Krysta starts laughing. She turns to Ty and gently touches the side of his face; he looks at her as he runs his right-hand fingers through his hair.

"We have to tell her," Krysta softly says.

"I hope you know what that means," Ty replies.

Krysta gives him a kiss and he slowly replies; they look at each other, then Ty slowly gets out of bed. He puts his pants on then slowly walks out of the pool house. He sees his mother sitting by the pool. He walks over to her and she looks up at him. He slowly sits down next to her. She looks at him with concern.

"What happened! Something happened. You have been acting strange lately. Who died?" Kate asks in slight panic.

Ty looks at her as if he's going to laugh.

"Mom, nothing happened. No one died."

Kate nods her head.

"Then what's going on?"

"Can you take a breath for me. Cause you are going to get really, really excited," Ty replies.

Kate looks at him with confusion, Ty stands up and takes a breath but also gently grins at her.

"Mom., Krysta and I are…" Ty pauses, "I proposed to Krysta last night. And she said yes."

Kate stares at him, then her eyes slowly start to widen with joyful shock as she slowly starts to stand up. She screams with excitement as she hugs Ty. Ty gently laugh with her, then Kate runs into the pool house. Krysta is out of bed, wearing Ty's red shirt from last night; she looks over at Kate who runs over to her and hugs her with tears of joy in her eyes. Krysta hugs her back with joy with Ty standing in the doorway, smiling at them. Kate turns and looks at Ty; she tells him to come over. Ty slowly walks over to them and she hugs both of them. Kate then looks at both of them with happy tears.

"This is what you and your father were up to," Kate says.

Ty nods his head and she hugs them both again.

Kate runs into the house over to Nick. He looks at her and sees that she has happy tears. Lucas looks at her with confusion; Nick gets up and gently pulls her in for a hug. She hugs him back, putting her face on his chest.

"Why didn't you tell me?" Kate asks.

Nick doesn't say anything. He just gently laughs, Lucas looking at both of them with confusion. He gets up and asks them what he is missing. Nick and Kate look over to him and smile; they look at each other then back at Lucas.

Meanwhile back in the pool house, Ty is putting his clothes on while Krysta is putting on a bathrobe. Ty walks up behind her and slowly wraps his arms around her. Krysta smiles as she leans her head back and wraps her arms around his. Ty softly kisses her shoulder; they look at each other and they give each other a kiss. They look at each other, then Krysta turns to Ty and slowly wraps her arms around his neck. They slowly move closer to each other, but then, Lucas comes bursting into the pool house. They both look at him; Krysta slowly moves her hands down to Ty's chest as Lucas walks over to them. He stops right next to them, then he looks and sees the ring on Krysta's finger. He stares at her finger with shock, then he looks at both of them then screams with joy. Ty slightly covers his ear and Krysta tries not to laugh too much. Lucas gently grabs Krysta's hand and stares at her ring, then he looks over to Ty. Then he looks up at Ty who is slightly grinning at him. Lucas softly grins at Krysta, then he quickly pulls them both into the house. Kate and Nick are in the kitchen, making some more coffee. Lucas turns to them with a plain face. They all stare at each other for a minute till Lucas breaks the silence.

"Why didn't you tell us anything?" Lucas asks.

Ty stares at him with a calm, relaxed trying-not-to-laugh face.

"You have a big mouth."

Lucas's jaw drops. Krysta turns her head slightly, hiding her face in Ty's arm, hiding that she's laughing.

"I do not," Lucas replies.

"Yeah, you do. You would have given hints. And you wouldn't stop grinning, plus if she asked you what's wrong with you, you would have told her," Ty explains.

"What about me?" Kate asks.

Everyone looks at Kate who is slightly pouting. Ty and Nick look at each other then back at Kate.

"You're no better," Nick and Ty replies.

Kate's jaw drops with an even more pouting face, causing everyone to start laughing.

*****

Time goes by and everyone is enjoying Christmas, and at the New Year's Eve party, everyone is staring at them, Krysta's ring, and congratulating them. Everyone is asking Ty how he proposed and how Krysta felt in that moment. As Krysta talks about it, her eyes water but her smile is a sun, full of joy. Ty and Krysta look at each other, then forgetting everyone is there, they give each other a kiss; they touch foreheads. Some ask them to tell them again about how the proposal happened. Ty looks at them then over at Krysta who is talking to some of the other girls staring at her ring. Ty slowly moves away from everyone and over to Krysta; he gently wraps his arms around her. She looks at him and sees that he looks as if he's hiding.

"Dance with me." Ty looks at everyone. "Excuse me, ladies, mind if I steal my fiancée for a dance?"

Ty then gently pulls Krysta away and walks over to the dance floor. The girls look at each other and softly laugh. Ty and Krysta start dancing to soft classic music, softly smiling at each other. Everyone is saying how cute they are, then they hear the countdown; everyone walks outside as they count down.

"Happy New Year!"

Fireworks blow into the night sky; everyone yells with joy as they watch the fireworks. Ty and Krysta stand next to each other with their heads leaning on each other, watching the fireworks. Ty and Krysta look at one another then they give a kiss

"Happy New Year," Ty says.

"Happy New Year," Krysta replies.

They look back at the fireworks and Krysta has peace in her eyes, as if everything that she has been through is gone.

The next morning, Ty wakes up to the hint of sun coming through the window; he turns and sees Krysta peacefully sleeping next to him. He grins, then he slowly leans over to her and gives her a kiss on the cheek, gently lying back down next to her as he wraps his arms around her. After about ten minutes, Nick comes into Ty's room and sees that they are still sleeping; he walks over to Ty. Ty slowly turns his head to Nick and he sees that Ty is not sleeping.

"I thought you were sleeping," Nick says.

Ty slightly shakes his head.

"No, she's just sleeping peacefully, I didn't want to wake her," Ty softly replies.

"Can we talk?" Nick asks.

Ty nods his head; he slowly gets out of bed. He puts the covers back over Krysta, then he walks to the door with Nick. They walk downstairs and outside to the poolside.

"So, Dad, what's on your mind?" Ty says.

Nick looks at him.

"How is she…with everything?"

"What do you mean?" Ty asks.

"With everything back in New York. Is she okay? With everything she's been through with him around," Nick continues.

"Oh, well, she clocked him. If that helps," Ty replies with a grin.

Nick looks at him with shock, then he slowly starts laughing. Ty starts laughing even more with Nick. Ty slowly starts to tell him everything that happened in New York with Krysta, Ford, and himself. Nick listens, and as Ty talks about everything, he sees that even though he has a grin on his face that he's also concerned. Nick puts his hand on Ty's shoulder

"Son, I want you to listen to me when I tell you. There's nothing to be worried about. This girl is happy because of you and you are happy because of her. And remember that we are here for you, okay?" Nick says.

Ty nods his head and smiles, then they both walk back into the house. They see Kate making some coffee. Nick walks over to her and gives her a kiss on the cheek; as Ty walks by, he gives a kiss as well. Then he goes upstairs to see if Krysta is awake. He walks into his room slowly; there he sees that she's awake. But it looks as if she has just woken, for she is still sitting in the bed and slightly yawning. He completely walks into the room. She looks up at him, still with a tired look on her face. He crawls on the bed, up to her, and gives her a kiss; she gently replies with a small smile.

"Hey, beautiful," Ty says.

"Hey back," Krysta replies.

"How long did you plan on sleeping?" Ty asks.

Krysta slightly laughs. Ty stares at her for a second.

"You okay?" Ty asks.

"I don't know. I guess I'm tired. I slept really well and my body just wants to go right back to it," Krysta replies. "But it's wrong. We're supposed to be here for the holidays."

"Krysta, stop. If you are tired, sleep. No one is going to say anything. Okay, if you want to sleep, sleep. I'll come bug you later," Ty replies.

They slightly laugh under their breaths. They give each other another kiss. Ty gets Krysta to lie back down. He gently caresses her hair as they stare at each other; Ty then sees Krysta slowly starting to fall back asleep. He grins at her as her eyes fall completely. He gives her a kiss on her head, then he slowly gets off the bed and goes back downstairs. Everyone looks at him and they don't see Krysta.

"Hey, where's Krysta?" Lucas asks.

"Sleeping, she said she's really tired," Ty replies.

"That's a good thing," Kate says.

Everyone looks over to her.

"Her body is finally forgetting," Kate continues.

Lucas looks at them with confusion.

"What does that mean?" Lucas asks.

Everyone looks at him then at each other, remembering that Lucas doesn't know what happened to Krysta. Ty takes a deep breath, then he turns over to Lucas.

"I can't tell you everything. All I can't tell you is that Krysta has been through a lot. For me to tell you more means Krysta is okay with that," Ty explains. "She'll have to tell you when she's ready. Same as she did with Mom and Dad."

Lucas just stares at them, even more confused.

Late in the night, Krysta wakes up to see Ty sleeping next to her and smiles, then she slowly gets up and goes downstairs for a glass of water. As she gets her water, she turns and slightly jumps, for Lucas is standing behind her.

"Lucas, you scared me," Krysta softly says.

"Sorry, can't sleep," Lucas replies.

"Are you okay?" Krysta asks.

"My brother said something to me today. That caused me to have a lot on my mind," Lucas replies.

Krysta looks at him with confusion; Lucas looks at her, calm yet serious.

"What happened to you that makes my brother not able to tell me?" Lucas asks.

Krysta stares at him for a minute with guilt; she takes a deep breath, then she slowly starts to tell Lucas everything that happened to her before and when she met Ty. As she explains everything, Lucas's face turns to shock and tears fall from Krysta eyes.

"Krysta," Lucas says.

Krysta's face shows hints of fear, then she looks back at Lucas. "Night, Lucas."

Krysta quickly puts her glass of water on the counter and runs upstairs.

"Krysta." Lucas runs after her.

She quickly goes into the bedroom and closes the door, causing Lucas to stop. Krysta is standing back against the door. Breathing heavy and shaking, she looks over to Ty who is still fast asleep. She quickly walks over to the bed and lies down next to him, wrapping her arms around him. Ty slightly wakes up and wraps his arms around her, falling back asleep. Krysta just holds him, trying to calm herself. Lucas stares at the door, then he slowly backs away and walks down the hall to his room, feeling guilty after remembering Krysta's face. The fear in her eyes, the pain on her face.

The next morning, Kate and Nick come downstairs and see Lucas sitting in the living room, holding a cup of coffee with a guilty look on his face. They both walk over to him to see what's wrong. He looks up at them then slowly tells them what happened. They look at him with concerned shock then at each other. Meanwhile in Ty's room, Ty is slowly waking up. Till he sees Krysta sitting on the bed, in a ball, shaking. Causing him to quickly lean up and gently put his hand on her back.

"Krysta, what's wrong?" Ty gently asks.

Krysta look over at him slowly.

"Tell me."

Krysta slowly starts to tell Ty what happened. Ty slightly glares with anger, then he takes a deep low breath, then he softly wipes the tears from her face. Krysta then tells him that she's going to take a shower. Ty watches her get out of bed and walk into the bathroom; he hears the water running. He looks at his bedroom door, takes a deep breath, then he gets up and walks to the door. Krysta is in the shower, trying to calm her breathing till she feels a gentle touch behind her. Causing her to turn and see that Ty is in the shower with her. He moves closer to her and wraps her arms around her and she wraps her arms around him. He gently kisses her head; Krysta's breathing calms as she rests her head on his chest. Ty then gently starts to wash her back. Krysta looks up at him and they give each other a kiss. They look at each other and give another kiss, their kisses slowly get a little heated.

After about an hour, Ty and Krysta goes downstairs and Ty tells Krysta to go to the car. As Krysta walks outside, Ty slightly storms into the living room, right over to Lucas. But Nick steps between them.

"Ty—" Lucas is cut off.

"I said when she is ready, she'll tell you! Not for you to go and ask her!" Ty yells.

"She told Mom and Dad," Lucas replies.

"You make it sound as if it was easy! She didn't tell them the day she got here! You had no right to guilt my fiancée into telling you what's going on," Ty replies.

Lucas stares at him for a minute.

"It wasn't my story to tell," Ty angrily says.

"Okay, you two," Nick asks.

"Taking Krysta out, be back whenever," Ty says.

Ty walks away without saying anything else, leaving everyone to watch him leave. They hear the car drive away. Kate looks at Lucas.

"You and your brother have a strong bond. And him not being able to tell you what going on is a lot to take. But when it comes to someone you love, you don't just go and tell their stories without them knowing."

"I know... I just—I love Krysta as family. I just want to know what happened," Lucas replies.

"We know that, and Ty does too. Seeing him like that is hard. Remember, he's the one who took care of her, helped her through all of that and more. Seeing her like that again put him back in that state where—" Nick explains.

"He has to protect her," Lucas continues.

"Give him time to cool off. It will be okay," Nick says.

Meanwhile driving around, Ty and Krysta are not saying anything. Ty comes to his spot and parks the car. He gets out and stands in front of the car, looking out to the sky. Krysta stares at him, then she slowly gets out of the car and walks over to him.

"I'm sorry," Krysta softly says.

Ty looks at her with confusion.

"For?"

"For overreacting with everything last night with Lucas. Causing you to get angry," Krysta replies.

"Krysta, I'm not angry with you. You haven't had to talk about what happened to you for a long time. With Lucas bringing that up again, I know that would be painful," Ty pauses. "I just don't like seeing you in that pain. And I just took it out on Lucas."

Krysta softly smiles, then she moves closer to Ty, wraps her arms around him as she rests her head on his shoulder. Ty wraps her arm around her and gently lays his head on her head, both looking out to the sky.

Later on, Ty and Krysta return to the house; Kate and Nick are out while Lucas is waiting for them. Ty sees Lucas sitting in the living room with a guilty look on his face. He walks over to him with Krysta walking behind him. Lucas looks up at them then gets out of the chair. They all stand face-to-face. Lucas looks at Krysta.

"Krysta, I'm so sorry," Lucas says.

"Lucas, stop. You don't have to say sorry. I overreacted," Krysta says.

"No, you didn't. Going through something like that is not something you can easily get over. And for me to bring it up when you are not ready to talk about it," Lucas replies.

"It's fine. I thought I was completely over it. But I guess some of it still bothers me," Krysta replies.

She walks over to Lucas and gives him a hug and a kiss on the cheek. She looks back at Ty and then slowly walks upstairs, leaving them to talk. Ty looks at Lucas with a small grin

"Ty, I—" Lucas is cut off.

"I'm sorry," Ty says.

Lucas looks at him with shock.

"She became so close to me in a short time. When she told me her story, the fear I saw in her eyes. I never want to see that again.

When she said that she told you her story... I saw that fear again. And it just made me angry," Ty continues.

Lucas nods his head.

"I can't say I completely understand what you are feeling since I don't have someone like that in my life. But I get wanting to keep them safe, so I'm sorry for making her feel that fear again."

Ty walks over to Lucas and puts his hand on his shoulder, smiling, then he walks over to the stairs, leaving Lucas. Lucas stares at him, then he quickly walks over to him before he goes up. Ty looks at him with confusion.

"So when's the big day? Are you being safe? Remember you want to have a fun honeymoon," Lucas says.

Ty gets a shocked look on his face yet a little twitch in his eyes. "*What*!"

Lucas is running up the stairs and Ty watches him, slowly shaking his head, still with that small twitch. Ty slowly walks up the stairs after he hears Lucas's door close. He walks into his room and sees Krysta lying on the bed, watching TV. She looks up at him, gently smiling; she asked him if everything okay with him and Lucas. Ty walks over to her, telling her what happened between them. She is smiling and is happy to hear that they are okay. Ty walks into the bathroom; Krysta hears the water running, then she looks back at the TV. After about ten minutes, Ty comes out of the bathroom, he changes into his sleepwear. He gets on the bed and sits down next to Krysta who is still watching the TV. Ty looks at her.

"Are you sure you're okay?" Ty asks.

Krysta looks at him, then she completely turns her body as she leans up, smiling at Ty.

"Yes."

Ty grins at her; she moves closer to him and gives him a kiss, then they look at each other. Ty gently pulls her into another kiss that slowly starts to turn into heat.

The next morning, Ty and Krysta are packing their things to get ready to head back to New York. Kate is pouting with Nick trying to get her to stop, for she is trying to come up with ways to get Ty and Krysta to stay longer. But he gets her every time she tries something.

Lucas is talking to Ty in the kitchen while Krysta is now trying to help Nick with Kate.

"See you soon?" Lucas asks.

"Yeah, we might be having a show out here in LA," Ty replies,

"That's nice. I can see your work up close than on TV or in the news," Lucas replies.

Ty gently laughs, then they both hear Kate outside; they look at each other, then they both walk to the front door. They look at their mother with shock, then slowly at each other, trying not to laugh. For Kate is trying to break the limo that will be taking Ty and Krysta to the airport. Ty shakes his head; Lucas is using the door to stand from laughing so hard. Ty walks down over to Nick. He looks at him.

"She misses you," Nick says.

"Yeah, I know. But I still have to go. I already have them asking for new things," Ty replies.

Nick nods his head, then he walks over to Krysta who is trying to stop Kate from taking the air out of the tires. Nick walks in front of Kate; he turns and looks at her, then he walks toward her and picks her up by putting her over his shoulder. Ty walks over to them. He looks at Kate and gives her a kiss on the cheek.

"I love you too, Mom. I will see you soon." Ty grins.

Krysta walks over to them, says bye to Nick, and also gives Kate a kiss on the cheek, then she walks over to Ty and they both get into the limo. Everyone waves bye to them as they slowly drive away, Kate smiling yet pouting at them drive away.

Chapter 16

Later that night, Ty and Krysta return home and see that Bobby has been home, for the house is a wreck. They look at each other then slowly walk into the house and into the bedroom. They put their bags down and Krysta goes over to the bed and flops. Ty looks at her with a grin. Then he walks to the other side of the bed and slowly lies down and takes a deep breath of relaxation. Krysta looks at him, then she slowly crawls over to him; he looks at her as she rests her head on his chest. They both slowly fall asleep.

The next morning, Krysta wakes up and sees that Ty is not in bed but she hears the water running in the bathroom. She slowly gets out of bed and walks to the bathroom. She walks over to the shower.

"Hey," Krysta softly says.

Ty opens the shower, sees Krysta at the sink.

"Hey, sleepy."

"What time did you get up?" Krysta asks.

"I woke up around about two hours ago, but I didn't get up till ten minutes ago," Ty replies.

Ty stares at Krysta gently combing her hair; she turns her head and looks at him with a small smile. He grins at her

"You going to join me?"

She gently smiles at him, then she slowly walks closer to the shower. They stare at each other. Krysta slowly starts to remove her clothes. Ty helps her in as he slowly closes the shower. As they are in the shower, Ty gently cleans Krysta's back, softly kissing her neck. She looks at him and wraps her arm around his neck; they kiss. Slowly getting more heated and passionate, Krysta turns around and they wrap their arms around each other. But then they hear the bedroom door burst open.

"Ty, you here!"

They both look toward the room, then they hear Bobby running into the bathroom.

"Ty?"

"Yeah, Bobby," Ty replies.

He looks at Krysta, slowly shaking his head. Krysta tries not to laugh.

"*Ty*—" Bobby is cut off.

"Bobby, do not come into this bathroom. I mean it," Ty says.

"Why?" Bobby asks with confusion.

He stares into the bathroom, then he sees clothes on the floor, with a blank look on his face, then slowly turns to shock.

"Ooh, my bad. Hi, Krysta," Bobby slightly yells.

They hear Bobby run out of the room. Krysta starts laughing, then she looks up at Ty who is still shaking his head. Krysta gives him a kiss. Ty returns it, then they look at each other.

"He missed you," Krysta softly says.

Ty gives Krysta a kiss, then he slowly gets out of the shower as he tells her that he'll be right back. Krysta slightly laughs, then she turns and slowly starts to wash her hair. Meanwhile Ty walks out of his room and looks at Bobby. Bobby looks at him and smiles. Ty has his towel around his neck and he puts some shorts on.

"Ty," Bobby says.

"Bobby, how many times have I told you to knock?" Ty replies.

Bobby walks over to him, then he slowly leans to the side to look at Ty's bedroom door. He looks back at Ty.

"Where's Krysta?"

Ty lifts one of his eyebrows as he looks at Bobby.

"What is it, Bobby?"

Bobby looks at him with a look of thinking, but then he gets a happy look on his face.

"Just happy that you are back, and you are back just in time."

"Why?" Ty asks.

"Oh, because there is a party tonight and you two have to come," Bobby replies.

Ty stares at him for a second, then he turns and goes back into his room, closing the door behind him.

"Okay, party," Bobby says.

Ty walks into the bathroom as he removes his shorts and hangs his towel back up. He looks at the shower and hears that Krysta is still in the shower. He slowly walks back into the shower and wraps his arms around her. She turns her head to him as she wraps her arms around him; they look at each other and give a kiss.

Later that night, Ty and Krysta go with Bobby to a party at a coworker's house. They see some of their friends there. They all talk and laugh the night away. Then as Krysta is talking to some of the other girls at the party, one of them sees the ring on her finger. Her eyes widen with shock, then she looks at Krysta who is laughing.

"Krysta."

Krysta looks at her.

"What is that?"

Krysta looks at her hand then back at the girls who all are looking at her hand with shock. She slowly starts to smile, then the girls look around for Ty. Ty is talking with Bobby and some of the other guys. One of the girls yell Ty's name. Everyone looks over to her as the music stops then slowly over to Ty as they part. Ty looks at her with shock yet confusion, slightly looking around, holding his beer. Then he sees Krysta who slowly puts her left hand up; he gently laughs, for now he knows why the girls yelled his name. Bobby looks at her then at Ty; he looks back and forth a few times till he truly has a look at Krysta's hand. He gets a shocked look on his face, then then he looks at Ty but he's walking over to Krysta. He looks over at them; Ty and Krysta give each other a kiss. Everyone surrounds them, wanting to hear about the proposal. Ty and Krysta look at each other, smiling, then Ty slowly starts to tell everyone how it happened. The night goes on and Bobby is still in shock about Ty and Krysta's engagement. Till Ty finally gets Bobby to relax and show how joyful he is for the both of them.

It's the morning and Ty and Krysta have to return to work.

"Krysta, if you do not get out of bed—"

"Don't you mean if we don't get out of bed," Krysta states, smiling.

Ty looks at her, grinning, they touch foreheads as they look in the eyes.

"Get up," Ty gently says.

He gets out of bed and walks into the bathroom. Krysta watches him, then she slowly gets up and goes to see what she's going to wear to work. But then, she stops when she hears the shower. She looks into the bathroom and walks to the door. She walks over to the shower and opens it Ty looks at her as she slowly removes her clothing.

"That would make us really late for work," Ty says.

"Then you don't want me to join you?" Krysta softly asks.

"I didn't say that," Ty replies.

And he pulls her into the shower, quickly wrapping their arms around each other as they kiss. Ty closes the shower with one hand and holds Krysta to him with the other. After an hour, Ty and Krysta are finishing in getting dressed for work. Krysta puts her earrings on as Ty is tying his shoes, then he walks over to her and gently kisses her head.

"Are you ready?" Ty asks.

"Yes," Krysta replies.

They both get their coats and head to work. They walk into the building and they pass by Lynne. They all say their hellos but Lynne doesn't see the ring. They both then head to their spaces, but as Ty is walking to his studio, he comes across the boss.

"Ty, you are late."

"Right, I have to get to my studio. I have a few ideas and I can't do that standing here. Talk to you later," Ty says.

Ty continues walking. He watches Ty walk by him with confusion but still walking. Ty goes into his studio and looks around. He walks over to all his sketch boards. Meanwhile Krysta is sitting at her desk, looking at some of the work. But as she's sitting there, someone walks up behind her. She slightly looks up with a slight glare.

"You so much as touch me," Krysta says, "Ford."

"Still wish you were on vacation?"

Krysta turns her head and looks up at Ford.

"I'm starting to."

Krysta turns her head back to her work but Ford just walks around sits on the chair. Krysta doesn't look at him but he just stares at her with a grin.

"You must have really enjoyed your vacation. You look great," Ford says.

Krysta doesn't reply. All she does is focus on her work, then she picks up a few papers. She stands up and walks out of her office and walks down the hall. Ford watches her, then he slowly stands up and walks out of her office. As Krysta is walking down the hall, she bumps into Amy; she looks at Krysta and glares. Krysta just slowly turns and continues walking, but as she turns, Amy gets a shocked look on her face. For she sees Krysta's left hand, but before she could say anything after coming out of the shock, Krysta is already gone. She glares even more, then she takes a deep angry breath. She runs down to the front of the building to Lynne who looks at her with confusion. Amy is breathing heavy.

"Need some water or maybe a lung?" Lynne says.

"I just want to know if it's true," Amy asks.

"If what's true?" Lynne asks.

"That Ty…proposed," Amy asks.

Lynne looks at her with happy shock, then she gets up and runs to the elevator, heading up levels. In Ty' studio, Ty's having everyone set up for the his next photo shoot that he wants to do. Krysta is also in the studio, talking to one of the other artist. Lynne comes running into the studio and looks at Ty who looks at her as if he's going to laugh. Then she sees Krysta and quickly walks over to her. Krysta looks at her with a small smile. Lynne gently yet quickly grabs her left hand. Her face turns to complete shock, for she sees the ring on her finger. She looks back at Ty then back at Krysta. To Ty, to Krysta, back and forth for a minute. Ty looks at Krysta and she smiles at him.

"*Oh my god, when!*" Lynne yells with excitement.

Everyone looks at Lynne then at Ty and Krysta who are looking at each other, slowly shaking their heads with small smiles.

Later on, everyone has Ty and Krysta in the main lobby, talking to them about their engagement. All the ladies looking at Krysta's ring, all the guys telling Ty he has a good one. Everyone also wanting to hear how it all happened and how Ty knew that Krysta is the right one. Ty looks at Krysta, she returns his gaze with a small smile.

"She became my best friend, the way she looks at me makes me feel at home," Ty answers.

"And you became mine." Krysta smiles.

Everyone listens to Ty and Krysta talk about how everything happened between them. But as they are talking and making everyone laugh, they don't realize that Ford is watching them from the second floor, leaning on the railing. Glaring at the two of them till his glare turns to shock. For walking by is Amy who is very angry. Ford looks at her.

"So how long have those two been engaged?"

Amy looks at him then down at Ty and Krysta.

"Ty and Krysta? I don't know."

Ford's faces slowly turns to shock mixed with anger as he slowly looks down at Ty and Krysta. He stares at her.

"What did you say her name was?"

Amy walks over to the railing and looks down at everyone in the lobby.

"Krysta, the one with her arm around Ty. You've been here this long, and you don't know her name."

Ford stares at her, still with that deep glare.

"How long have they been together?"

"I don't know. A little over a year, I guess? From what I heard, she used to work at a café somewhere around here. He asked her to be his model, sometime around late summer, early fall, I guess. Why?"

Amy looks at Ford and sees the way he's looking at Krysta. She shrugs her shoulders then walks away. As Ford stares at her, he looks close to the side of her face and sees that it truly is Krysta. His hands slowly turns into a fist as he sees Ty and Krysta give each other a kiss and smile at each other. Meanwhile downstairs, with everyone, the boss walks over to Ty and Krysta, telling them how happy he is for them. And that they all should celebrate their engagement.

The day goes by and Ford just watches Krysta go about her day as if he's nowhere around. Till night came and everyone is going home, Krysta is still at her desk, finishing up with some work. Ford slowly walks up behind her, just standing there, watching her with a deep glare in his eyes. She stands up as she puts the papers in her desk, slowly turns around, and sees Ford standing right behind her. She looks at him with a plain look on her face, then she rolls her eyes as she walks around him and out of the office. Ford watches her; he slowly walks to the doorway and watches Krysta walk down the hall. Krysta walks down to Ty's studio; she slowly walks inside and looks at Ty. Ty is looking at his photos, seeing which ones he likes the and the ones that will go with the next gallery. Krysta walks over to him but he doesn't see her; she smiles and gently wraps her arms around him, causing Ty to stop and look at her. He grins as he gently wraps his arms around her arms.

"Having a hard time deciding?" Krysta asks.

"Yeah, there's a few. But there's something missing," Ty replies.

"Well, what are you looking for?" Krysta asks, "Once you know, it comes to you with ease."

"Yeah, why don't we just call it a night? It's almost twelve," Ty says.

They wrap their arms around each other as they slowly walk out of Ty's studio and head to the elevator. With Ford watching their every move till the get into the elevator, he walks back into his office and goes onto his computer. He starts typing and looks at the screen. He slowly takes out his phone for directions. For Ford has looked up Ty's address and how to find it. Later that night, while Ty and Krysta are sleeping, Ford is watching their building from his car. Meanwhile Bobby is slowly going home after having a few drinks; he bangs into Ford's car. Ford quickly gets out of his car and walks over to Bobby. Bobby looks at him.

"My bad. I can fix that…well, I can get my friend Ty to fix it," Bobby says.

Ford looks at him.

"You know Ty?" Ford pauses. "What about Krysta?"

"Oh, yeah. That's his soon-to-be wife." Bobby smiles.

Ford pauses while staring at Bobby then gets a very small grin.

"Don't worry about the car. To make up for it, why don't we go for some drinks tomorrow night?" Ford says.

"I don't even know you. But I'm always down for a drink," Bobby replies.

Ford watches Bobby walk into the building, then he gets into his car, slowly drives away. Meanwhile Bobby walks into the penthouse and sees that everyone is sleeping. He gets some water then goes to his room.

The following night, Ty and Krysta are out with their coworkers, celebrating their engagement, dancing, laughing, drinking wine and champagne. What makes the night more relaxing is that Ford is not at the celebration. While Ty is talking to some of the other workers, Krysta is on the dance floor with her friends, Sam and Lynne. Ty looks over at them and sees Sam calling him over with her hand. He slightly laughs, then he puts his drink down and walks over to the dance floor. Sam and Lynne smile then slowly back away as Ty slowly wraps his arms Krysta. Krysta slightly turns her head to him and smiles. Ty takes her hand, gently pushes her as he spins her; he pulls her back to him. Holding each other close and start dancing as they smile at each other. Meanwhile Bobby is hanging out with Ford at a nearby bar, talking about relationships. Without Bobby knowing what happened, he doesn't understand that Ford is talking about Krysta. He talks about her eyes, lips, and body, but Bobby just listens with a grin as he drinks his beer. As time goes by, Bobby and Ford start walking to the penthouse.

After the celebration, Ty and Krysta are heading home; they're both in the elevator, going up to Ty's penthouse. As they are in the elevator, Krysta looks at Ty who is looking at his phone for messages. She moves closer to him as she tries not to laugh, then she gently takes his phone, causing him to look at her. They stare at each other.

"Pick," Krysta softly says.

Ty lifts one of his eyebrows as he slightly grins; he steps toward Krysta, quickly grabs his phone but also Krysta's hand, and pulls her completely to him. He kisses her and she kisses him right back as they wrap their arms around each other. Krysta then gently pushes Ty against the elevator wall while still kissing each other. They arrive at their floor and slowly come out of the elevator. They both slightly hit the door, still kissing each other while Ty tries to find his keys. He softly pulls away from Krysta.

"Hold that thought."

Krysta gently laughs as Ty pulls out his keys. He looks back at Krysta who pulls him back into kissing. Ty opens the door, holding Krysta to him, and closes it with his other hand as they quickly walk inside. They walk right over to Ty's bedroom door; Ty gently pins Krysta to the door. Ty moves his hand down to Krysta's thighs and picks her up, she wraps her arms around him. He then wraps one arm around her waist as he opens the door with his other hand. Walking inside and gently falling onto the bed, still kissing each other, they look at each other.

"Ty, the door," Krysta gently says.

Ty gives her a small kiss, then he goes and closes the door; he turns to Krysta who is leaning on the bed, smiling at him. Ty stares at her as he slowly starts to remove his shirt. He walks over to her and softly leans down to her. She slowly leans up to him, they kiss. They look at each other, then they kiss again, and it slowly starts to become more passionate. Ty moves forward onto the bed, causing Krysta to move backward on the bed. Ty then slowly starts to lean down, causing Krysta to lean back. Ty then slowly starts to remove Krysta's clothes as she wraps her arms around his neck. They look into each other's eyes, they kiss and make love. Meanwhile as they love each other, without them knowing, Ford is in the penthouse and he sees them! He's standing on the other side of the doorway, glaring at them till he sees the door close. After a few minutes, Bobby comes walking over to him and shows him a little of his work.

"Do you like any of these for your house?" Bobby asks.

Ford just stares, deeply glaring at Ty's bedroom door. Bobby looks at him with confusion then at Ty's door.

"Is there something about that door you don't like?" Bobby asks. Causing Ford to look at him.

"Apologies. My mind went somewhere else. Um, I just saw two people come in."

"Oh, yeah. That must have been Ty and Krysta," Bobby replies.

Ford nods his head, then he looks at Bobby's work and they slowly start talking about new things Ford is thinking about for his house.

Later in the night, Ford is gone and the penthouse is quiet. Ty wakes up; he slowly gets out of bed and out of the room. He goes into the kitchen and gets a bottle of water. He closes the door, but as he closes the door, he slightly jumps. For Bobby is standing next to him without saying a word. Ty stares at him for a second. Ty slightly looks around then back at Bobby, waiting for him to say something.

"Bobby?"

Bobby looks at him.

"Are you all right?" Ty asks.

"Yeah, I'm just thinking. I have a big job to do for this guy I met, but I'm just trying to think of how to put it all together. He was here, looking at some of my work," Bobby replies.

"Nice, good for you. Wait…you had some guy here that you just met? Why?" Ty asks.

"Relax, he's a big-time rich guy. He just wanted to see something out of normal taste," Bobby replies.

"Well, if you ever need any help, just let me know," Ty says.

"Well—" Bobby is cut off.

"But not know," Ty quickly says.

"Right," Bobby says.

Ty walks back into his bedroom, gently closing the door behind him. He softly puts the bottle of water on the nightstand and slowly gets back into bed. He gently wraps his arm around Krysta; she slightly moves back to him. Making her back lean back against his chest.

The next morning at work, everyone is working on the next gallery opening. Krysta comes down to Ty's studio and gives him some paperwork. As she walks over to him, Ty looks at her with a grin. But the grin is not his normal grin, causing Krysta to look at him with confusion but with a small smile. He walks over to her; Krysta watches him, trying not to laugh as he walks over to her, still with that same look.

"I need you," Ty says.

Krysta stares at him, then she looks around the studio, then she looks back at Ty.

"Oooh no."

"I know but—" Ty says.

"No, Ty," Krysta says.

Krysta tries to walk away, but Ty quickly walks in front of her.

"Honey, I know but remember the other day, when I said something was missing with my photos?"

"Yes," Krysta replies.

"That's what I need from you," Ty says.

Ty gently takes Krysta's hand and walks over to the backroom and asks her to change. As Krysta goes to change, Ty looks at the studio and tells everyone what to do for his idea. He tells the other ladies where to stand and how. After ten minutes, Krysta comes out from the back; Ty and everyone looks at her. Her hair completely out with curls, a long white dress. Ty walks over to her and guides her over to the others, for his idea are angels. All the ladies are wearing long white dresses but Krysta is the only one that is different. Her dress is a long white deluxe angel dress; they all have small wings but Krysta doesn't. Ty has the studio like the sky with clouds; they all sit around each other with Krysta at the top cloud. She has beautiful long angel wings, on the outer part of the wings are pure white and the inner wings have hints of silver. Ty starts to take pictures; he has all of them in different stances. They are lying, sitting, standing, and gently touching hands.

After a few hours, Ty tells everyone to take a break but he tells Krysta to stay. She looks at him, then she looks at everyone leaving for lunch. She looks back at him with a small pout; he gently smiles at her and walks over to her.

"One more," Ty softly says.

She takes a small deep breath with a smile, then she walks over to the setting. Ty stares at her for a minute. But then, he walks over to her and gently moves her to the side, starts to move things around. He looks at the floor and sets things as if she's near a small riverbank, with grass and a large beautiful weeping willow tree, puts Krysta back on the set. He goes to the back and rolls out a medium fan. He rolls it over to the set but not too close. Ty then softly runs to the door and closes it; he walks over to Krysta and has her sit on the grass. He then walks away over to the fan and turns it on low; as the fan blows, it gently causes pieces of Krysta's hair to slightly cross her face. Ty throws up fake white feathers, the wind from the fan blows them over to Krysta. She softly laughs as she puts her hand up to them and Ty starts to take pictures. Her face is gentle and peaceful; she looks at Ty and gently smiles. Ty takes a picture of her looking at him, then he zooms in on her eyes and takes a picture. He then slowly moves the camera from his eyes and stares back at Krysta with a soft grin. He puts his camera down and walks over to her and kneels down in front of her and they give each other a kiss. As they stare into each other's eyes, Ford is watching them, for he cracked the door. He stares at them with deep anger then closes the door and storms down the hall back to his office.

*****

A few days have passed, it is late in the office and the last day before the gala. Ford is getting angry and is making a move on Krysta. She is putting everything away as she is getting ready to go home. Ford stops her from leaving the office by walking in front of her but she rolls her eyes and walks around him. But before she could get even five steps away—"You are good, Krysta!"

Causing her to stop and slowly turn to him with a little fear on her face.

"What did you just say?"

Ford walks over to her and she glares at him but still with a little fear in her eyes.

"To think I was trying to get you…but I already had you," For says.

"You didn't have shit," Krysta replies.

"You've changed since I last truly saw you," Ford says.

"You never saw me. You just used me while you were out doing whatever you wanted," Krysta replies.

"You let him see you," Ford asks deeply.

"He saw me long before you did," Krysta replies.

"Well, that will come to an end," Ford says.

Krysta stares at him with confusion. She slightly looks around but no one is around. Looks back at Ford, holding her ground.

"No, it will not."

Krysta gets ready to turn and walk away but Ford stops her.

"I can end everything he has ever worked for with a snap of my fingers."

Krysta stops and looks him.

"End it," Ford says, "you come to me."

Ford turns and walks away from her. She watches as he leaves the building, thinks about Ty and what Ford could do. Her eyes water, thinking about every one moment she and Ty has had. The laughs, the talking, the moment with the eyes, the gentle touches. The confession to the first kiss to the first night. The water leaves her eyes, down her face, then she slowly walks down the hall to Ty's studio. She slightly looks inside and sees how Ty is looking at his drawings and his pictures; she smiles, thinking about every last office night. Finding him in that same deep thought as if he thinks something is missing when there's not. She takes a deep breath as she wipes her face then walks into the studio. She walks over to him; he looks at her and grins.

"Hey, almost done. Just trying to get these in the right order so they can have them for the show," Ty says.

Krysta nods her head but doesn't say anything, causing Ty to look at her and sees that she's not looking at him.

"Hey, are you—" Ty asks.

He turns from his work and looks at her but she still doesn't look at him. Ty takes a step toward her, then he gently takes his hand to her chin and gently causes her to look at him. He can see that something is wrong.

"What's wrong?" Ty softly asks.

Krysta puts her hand on his hand, holding it, remembering how gently his hands and touch are. How he always looks at her with those soft gentle eyes, just looking completely at her as if nothing else is there. She takes a step to him and gently but quickly pulls him into a deep and passionate kiss. Ty is in shock at first, but then he wraps his arms around her; as she wraps her arms, they kiss as if there is nothing else that matters. Nothing is in the room, on their minds, just the love they have for each other.

That night, as Ty is in the bathroom, Krysta quietly leaves the penthouse and goes to Ford's house. Ty comes out of the bathroom and sees that Krysta is not in the room; he gets dressed then comes out of the bedroom, looking for Krysta. He calls out her name but there is no reply. With a confused look on his face, he remembers what happened in the studio. Then Bobby walks into the house and looks over at Ty with a tired look on his face.

"Yo, what's up?" Bobby says.

"Hey," Ty replies, still in thought.

"Work is not going so good. That guy, Ford, once again didn't show up for work on his house," Bobby says.

Ty gets a shocked look on his face as he looks over at Bobby taking a bottle of water out of the fridge. Ty walks over to him quickly and turns Bobby to him.

"What did you just say?" Ty asks.

Bobby is looking at him with confusion, then he tells him about Ford being his new client. Ty stares at him with shock, then he remembers something that Ford said to him a few days back.

"You have a nice home. Needs some work."

Ty looks at Bobby.

"Bobby, has the guy ever been in the house?" Ty asks.

Bobby looks around, thinking for a minute.

"Yeah, I think."

"I don't need I think, Bobby. I need to know, has he ever been in this *house*!"

"Relax, you don't need to get a loud," Bobby says.

"Bobby!" Ty yells with irritation.

"Okay, that night you and your coworkers were celebrating your and Krysta's engagement," Bobby replies.

Ty thinks back, Ford's comment, his glaring, Krysta's face was the same when they first met.

"Shit," Ty says.

"Ty, what's wrong," Bobby asks, nervous.

Ty quickly grabs his phone and keys and runs out of the penthouse. Bobby looks at him with confusion, also thinking something's wrong. Meanwhile Ty is running to his truck while on the phone.

"Lynne, are you still at the office?" Ty asks.

"Yeah, why? I'm about to leave," Lynne replies.

"I need Ford's address!" Ty yells.

"Why?" Lynne asks.

"Just give it to me!" Ty yells.

"Okay, hold on," Lynne replies.

Ty starts up the truck and speeds out of the parking garage. Lynne gives Ty the address. But before she could ask what's going on, Ty hangs up the phone and speeds to the address.

Meanwhile Krysta arrives at Ford's house and looks at him with anger as she walks into the house but doesn't say anything. Ford closes the door and walks over to her; she turns to him, still looking at him with that same look on her face.

"What do you want, Ford?" Krysta asks.

"I want you…to give yourself to me," Ford replies.

Krysta stands tall.

"I'd rather burn in hell and be ripped to shreds."

Ford slaps her and she takes a step back; she slightly looks at Ford, then she backhand slaps him across the face. Ford almost fall to the floor; he looks at her.

"What's the matter, Ford? Didn't see that coming?" Krysta says.

She takes another step to him.

"I didn't come here to fix your fantasy. I came here to tell you to back off my fiancé."

Ford starts to breathe heavy, then he quickly gets up, not giving Krysta enough time to react. He grabs her and slams her into the wall, hard, that her head slightly starts to bleed. He holds her by her neck; she looks at him, having a hard time breathing.

"You will be mine whether you like it or not," Ford deeply whispers.

He throws Krysta to the floor. She slowly starts to breathe as she tries to get up but Ford strongly pins her to the floor. With one hand and with the other, he starts to rip her clothes; but then Ty comes busting through the door and sees them on the floor. He runs at Ford; he grabs Ford by the back of his shirt and punches him off of Krysta. Ford looks up at him as he spits out blood. Ty stares down at him, blocking him from getting to Krysta who is truly catching her breath.

"Let's see you try that with me," Ty says.

Ford stands up. He and Ty stare at each other, then Ford runs at Ty as if he's going to tackle him. But Ty stands his ground, grabs Ford by the shoulders, stopping him, knocking him to the ground. Ty then turns his hand into fists and uppercuts Ford in the stomach then punches Ford in the face. Ford falls the floor; he looks at Ty quickly gets up and tries to punch Ty. But Ty puts his hands up like he was boxing, watching Ford's every move. Every time Ford tries to throw a punch, Ty would dodge then land a punch. Till Ford has had enough, Ty punches Ford into a lampstand in the hallway. Ford looks at Ty then at the drawer; he quickly opens it when he sees Ty take a step toward him and pulls out a gun and shoots Ty. Krysta hears the gunshot and sees Ty fall to the floor. She quickly gets up from the floor as she sees Ford walk over to Ty and put the gun to his face. She runs right over to them and quickly grabs the lamp and hits Ford's arm with it. Causing him to drop the gun, then she hits with the lamp. Ford falls to the floor and Krysta runs over to Ty. She helps him up and runs down the hall and into a room. They come into Ford's office room; she closes the door and tries finding something to stop the bleeding. She kneels down beside him, holding a small blanket she found. Ty feels the pain from her keeping the pressure.

"The bullet went through," Ty says.

Krysta looks at him with deep worry.

"What are you doing here? How did you even know?"

Ty looks at her with a grin yet pained look on his face.

"Bobby said that Ford has been to the house. I started to put the pieces together, some of the things Ford said to me and the one thing that really made me think—the way you kissed me at the studio."

They both look at each other. When they hear footsteps, Krysta takes Ty's cell phone, causing him to look at her.

"Krysta," Ty softly says.

Krysta kisses him.

"Stay here."

Krysta slowly yet quickly gets up and goes out the other door. She hears Ford yelling her name. She takes a deep breath. She takes Ty's phone and starts to dial Ford's number. Ford looks at the house phone then answers.

"What's the matter, Ford?" Krysta asks.

"You little bitch, you're not going to get away from me," Ford yells.

"Oh, Ford, Ford can't take a girl not falling at your feet," Krysta says.

"After I beat your ass like I did before, I will force you to be mine and make that dying boy of yours watch," Ford yells.

"You're going to have to find me first, you panzy-ass man whore!" Krysta yells.

Krysta hangs up the phone and hears Ford yell in anger. She slowly comes out of the room; she sees Ford's shadow, slowly calms her breathing, then as Ford comes around the corner—"Hey."

Ford turns his head and Krysta punches. Ford covers his face as he takes a couple of steps back. He slowly moves his hands and looks at her, feeling the blood slowly run down his nose. Krysta glares at him.

"Let's go."

He takes a step toward her

"You want to fight me?"

Krysta slaps him with her right hand then left hand. She takes a step back and holds her ground. Staring at him with an angry glare, Ford looks at her.

"You can fight me, Krysta, but you can't win against me. All I have to do is grab you," Ford says.

Ford runs over to Krysta and grabs her by the neck and slams her against the wall. Krysta is holding his hands from gripping her neck tighter.

"You think you're something special because you have some man give you a spread. Don't kid yourself," Ford says.

Krysta looks at him, glaring, then she cracks a small grin.

"Yeah, well, guess what my man taught me?" Krysta replies.

Krysta remembers a time Ty was giving her a boxing lesson.

Ty and Krysta are in his old boxing gym in their workout clothes.

"I thought all you know is boxing?" Krysta asks.

"No, I know a few things. Now say someone has you by the throat, looking right at you. They think they have you…then…"

Krysta takes her right hand, middle-finger knuckle, and punches him right in the arm! Causing Ford to loosen his grip, Krysta slaps his arms away. Then she balls up her fists and punches Ford in the stomach, then the face. Ford puts his hand on his face, then he screams and runs at Krysta. He tackles her, pushes her into a stand in the hall, causing everything to fall and break. Krysta's face shows the pain but then glare at him and knees him in the stomach. Then she pushes him away with her leg. They both fall to the floor, slightly breathing heavy and glaring at each other.

"I loved you," Ford says.

"You didn't love me, it was just the idea. And I let it because I thought that's what love is. Till I met him and I knew everything was wrong," Krysta replies, "I know what love is. And you don't."

Krysta slowly stands up.

"You're weak, Ford."

Ford gets more angry; he stands up and once again, he runs at her. Putting her hands up, she moves out of the way and punches Ford on the side of his face. Before he could fall from loss of balance, Krysta punches him in the stomach. But her punches are different, for she's using her knuckles to punch. As Krysta punches Ford, he swings his hands back. Hitting Krysta in the face, they both fall again. The right of Krysta's lip starts to bleed and the left side of her head. Ford's face has a few small cuts and his noise is still bleeding. They both stand up slowly, Ford walks over to her.

"How does this work for you? You can't hurt me," Ford asks.

Krysta slaps him with her right then left hand.

"Sure about that?" Krysta replies.

"Hell yeah," Ford says.

Ford grabs her by the back of her head tight, gripping her hair.

"Whether you like it or not, Krysta, you are going to be mine. Even If I have to force you, time and time again," Ford says angrily.

Krysta elbows Ford in the face then quickly in the stomach; Ford lets her go and she runs. Ford quickly runs after her, she runs into the living room. Ford runs right into her, causing them both to fall into the coffee table. Krysta slowly starts to crawl away but Ford grabs her ankle. Krysta looks at him then kicks him in the face, right off of her. As she stands up, Ford gets up and grabs her arm, making her turn to him and slapping her across the face. But Krysta backhand slaps him across the face, then with her right hand, punches. Ford takes a couple steps back.

"What's the matter, Ford, is that all you *got*! Can't do no more than that! I'm ready now, Ford, come on, come on!" Krysta yells.

Krysta walks over to Ford, grabs him by the back of his head, punches him to the floor. She looks at him and her eyes water as she starts to remember everything he did to her. Every hit she makes is a memory of all the hits, the words, the treatment. She does one final kick, causing Ford to fall to the floor on top of the broken glass. She sees that he's not moving; she runs to see Ty.

Krysta runs into the office room and sees Ty with a weak look on his face. She slowly walks over to him, seeing that he's still bleeding. She kneels down next to him and gently puts her hand on the side of his face. Ty, very slowly, puts his hand on the side of her face.

"Are you okay?" Ty softly asks.

Krysta gently smiles, but before she could answer, they hear a click. They both quickly turn their heads and see, standing in the doorway, is Ford, holding a gun at them. Ford, breathing heavy, his clothes are slightly ripped and his face is bleeding.

"So this is where you were hiding. Good, now you can watch me take her as mine," Ford says. "But first, you have too much life in you."

Ford points the gun more at Ty. Krysta looks at him but sees that he has a weak yet cocky grin.

"Too late," Ty says.

Ford and Krysta look at him with confusion till they hear the front door burst open. Police come storming into the house. They all look at Ford and yell at him to freeze and put his gun down. Ford looks at them then back at Ty who slowly lifts his hand, showing that Ty had the police listen in on his and Krysta's call. Ford glares at him; he drops the gun and puts his hands up in the air. Some of the police surround Ford, arresting him, while some others go to Krysta and Ty and call the medics. Ty and Krysta touch foreheads as they gently hold each other with tired smiles.

"I love you," Krysta whispers.

"I love you," Ty whispers.

Bonus Chapter

Five years have passed since everything happened with Ford who is now in prison and his family disowned him. His father and mother could not understand, how could their son could treat one of their beloved friends' daughter that way? They apologized to Krysta time and time again, but she didn't blame them. They also apologized to Ty and his family; they also didn't blame them. What was even more shocking to Ford is that Ty is the second son of Nick Smith who has more power than Ford or his family does. Ford was sentenced to thirty to forty years in prison due to assault, attempted rape, and attempted murder.

As for Ty and Krysta, Ford sees them every day on the TV. For as they are beloved and happily married. Krysta became one of the five top models, Ty became a high and wanted-everywhere photographer. He's still an artist; his art is talked about all over. Ty and Krysta are now living in LA in a big beautiful house. With their wonderful twin boys after being married for three years who Kate and Nick just can't get enough of. Every day, they are at Ty and Krysta's, loving them and spoiling them. And Lucas is finally getting married to Janet. In everything that they have been through, Ty and Krysta found something in each other that they never knew that they were looking for. They found the love in art.

About the Author

Rayna Johnson is a girl raised in New Bedford, Massachusetts, by a single parent with her older brother and little sister. She didn't start writing until junior high. They started out as twelve pages, then twelve turned to thirty-two. Then thirty-two turned into two hundred to three hundred pages. How many words, she doesn't know. She writes as if she's seeing a movie or a TV series. And in truth, that is what started all this. An idea from a movie and a TV show that she watched. She was bored in her social studies class, had a blank notebook, and just went from there.

To Nana

Love Always

Regyna

CPSIA information can be obtained
at www.ICGtesting.com
Printed in the USA
JSHW042020130920
7839JS00001B/37